THE LEGACY OF EVE

NATASHA BOYDELL

First published in 2022 by Bloodhound Books.

www.bloodhoundbooks.com

Print ISBN 978-1-5040-7258-8

ALSO BY NATASHA BOYDELL

This Missing Husband

The Woman Next Door

PROLOGUE

Eve's salty tears ran down her face and mingled with her sweat. What had she done to deserve this? She was a prisoner, trapped in an unendurable agony inflicted upon her by her own body. Her mother used to say that the pain of labour was the curse of Eve; punishment for the sins of the first woman. Eve had never understood why, despite this belief, her mother had chosen to call her daughter by the same name, as though sealing her fate from the very beginning.

It does explain a lot, I suppose, she thought now, *because I definitely would have eaten that apple.*

She shifted position in a vain attempt to find relief. But nothing worked; there was no escape. Eventually she gave up and lay on her back, staring hopelessly up at the ceiling which, through the blur of her tears, looked like it was going to fall in on her. She hoped it would. Seconds later she was writhing around, desperate once again to ease the pain.

She had never experienced anything like it, hour upon hour of torture. In the beginning, it had ebbed and flowed but now it was persistent and brutal. How long had she been subjected to this nightmare for? She had lost track of time, her senses thrown off-kilter by the windowless, artificially lit room that she feared she may never escape from again.

She was afraid and she was angry. Angry at everyone she had ever known and at anyone who so much as looked at her. She was oddly contrite, too, because it had made her see her own mother in a different light. *If I'd known that she went through this because of me, perhaps I would have been nicer to her, made more of an effort to be a good, kind daughter. But it's too late to go back now.*

'Eve?'

She flinched as Mike's warm hand touched her back. She didn't want him anywhere near her. She couldn't even look at him; she hated him with every bone in her traitorous body. It was his fault that she was here; he had made her go through this despite the grave doubts that she had expressed from the start. He had showered her with false promises that everything was going to be okay. He had lied; it was not okay. She didn't know what she'd ever seen in him now. She should have trusted her instincts and run, but instead she had let herself be drawn in.

A fresh wave of pain hit her, this one even worse than before, and she let out a wail so visceral that for a second she thought there was a wounded animal in the room, until she realised it was coming from her own mouth. Somewhere in the distance she heard a woman's voice, quietly at first and then louder. She ignored it. A hand appeared on her shoulder, gently but firmly pushing her down on to the bed and she pulled and scratched at it, desperate to get it off her.

'Eve, love,' Mike said, alarmed. 'The midwife needs to examine you. You have to stay still.'

The contraction passed and she flopped on to the bed, defeated. He tried to mop her brow with a cold flannel, but she batted him away, like he was an annoying fly she wanted to swat.

She looked up to see a midwife at the end of the bed, smiling at her. 'It's time,' she said.

Eve stared at the woman, confused. She was sure that she'd seen her before, but a lifetime ago. How could that be? Then she remembered it was the same midwife who had greeted her when she first got to the hospital. The woman had stayed awhile, busying herself while chatting about the many babies she had delivered, and then she had finished her shift and clocked off with a cheery wave. How long had she been gone? How was she back already? What had she been doing while Eve was stuck in this purgatory, trapped between her old life and her new one? Something normal and pleasant? Perhaps she'd gone home to a loving partner and they'd shared a bottle of wine and a home-cooked meal. Maybe she'd gone out with friends for dinner or to see a film. Or even just an early night, curled up in bed with a good book before drifting off into a peaceful sleep and waking up fresh-faced, ready to deliver some more children.

Eve was not fresh-faced, she was rancid. Sticky sweat had dried to her body and long strands of her dark hair were cemented to her forehead. She wanted to shave it off. She wanted to punch everyone. She wanted to kill the man who stood next to her. She wanted to die.

'When I tell you to push, I need you to push down like we talked about, okay, Eve?'

Eve nodded, barely listening. She didn't want to push. She hadn't even wanted this baby. They had barely known each other when she got pregnant and by the time she realised that she'd made a mistake, it was too late. She looked at him now, her eyes burning. He smiled back at her, calmly observing her with the same deep-brown eyes that had lured her in months ago and fooled her into believing that her life was about to get better.

'Okay, Eve, push now, come on, push!'

She closed her eyes and pushed half-heartedly.

'Push, Eve.'

'I am!' she screamed. It was all she had left to give, so it was all the midwife was getting.

A minute later the midwife urged her again. 'Push now, Eve, push.'

This time she barely even tried. She wanted to give up, to curl up into a ball and disappear.

'Eve!' The midwife sounded urgent now. 'I really need you to push. Come on!'

'Eve,' Mike begged, from beside her. 'Come on, Eve, you can do this.'

But she couldn't do it and she didn't want to do it.

Another wave of pain. Another round of people shouting at her. *Screw them all.* But then an urge came over her, which was so strong that she could no longer deny it. Even if her mind was conflicted, her body was not, and it had decided that it was time to get this baby out. She closed her eyes and pushed with everything she had. She pushed, and screamed, and pushed.

The pain stopped. The world came back into focus. She heard a cry and the midwife showed her the baby, holding it up to her like it was some sort of sacrificial offering.

'A girl,' she said.

Eve's arms stretched out towards the baby, suddenly desperate for her. The tears on her cheeks were no longer of agony but of joy. How quickly things could change, the pain and fear of the last twenty-four hours already forgotten, amnesia kicking in straightaway. She almost laughed with the euphoria of it all. This was heaven, not hell; she no longer hated everyone, she loved them. The midwife bundled the baby off to examine her and Eve watched carefully, concerned, seeking reassurance that everything was okay. Mike placed his hand in hers and squeezed it gently and this time she didn't flinch from his touch. She squeezed him back.

And then she was there, her very own daughter, placed gently into her arms. Eve looked down at her baby's beautiful little red, scrunched-up face and couldn't believe how much she loved her already. She held out a finger and the baby grabbed it, gripping on to it tightly.

'Hello Annie,' she said, 'I'm your mum.'

Annie gazed back at her with eyes that already seemed too wise for her tender age. Minutes passed but it felt like seconds. All Eve wanted was to hold her daughter for the rest of her life.

'Can I hold her?' Mike asked.

She did not want to let Annie go. But she was starting to feel fuzzy, the effects of a long and laborious birth catching up with her. Her vision was becoming blurry again, and she was tired, dog-tired. Her arms were starting to sag, too, and she nodded at Mike, giving permission for him to reach down and take Annie from her. She watched them for a while, enjoying the tender moment between father and daughter, and when Mike turned and beamed at her she tried to smile back but she no longer had the energy to move her mouth.

She was dizzy. *I'm just exhausted from the ordeal,* she thought. *But at least I finally understand now why women go through this. It's the best feeling in the world.* For she was certain now that, despite everything, having this baby was the right decision after all. Everything she had been through, the good and the bad, had been worth it for this moment. The past was forgiven, only the future mattered.

The midwife was calling for someone. Another person appeared, and then another. A doctor was looking at her and his lips were moving but she couldn't understand what he was saying; his words were jumbled up. The midwife was frowning. It didn't make any sense, what were they looking so worried about? Annie was fine, she was perfect. Even as the room started spinning, Eve could see her, lying peacefully in her father's arms. Then she realised that it wasn't the baby they were worried about, it was her.

'What's wrong?' she tried to ask but the words wouldn't come out.

Someone was shouting. 'Eve, stay with us! Eve!'

But the urge to sleep was becoming irresistible, it was pulling her down, tempting her. *Just a little nap, then I'll feel so much better. Annie and I have our whole lives to spend together.*

'Eve, can you hear me?'

Just a little rest and I'll be raring to go. And Mike and I will talk, properly talk.

She was fading now. It was time. But she wasn't afraid, she was happy, happier than she had ever been in her life. She looked at Annie one last time.

Then she drifted away.

CHAPTER ONE

PRESENT DAY

Annie yanked the unyielding front door shut, pretending that she hadn't seen the peeling flakes of wood and paint that scattered to the floor like dandruff, and turned to the couple beside her.

'What do you think?' she asked, with a little too much enthusiasm.

'It's in quite a state,' the man replied, wrinkling his nose in distaste. His wife was already shuffling down the garden path, as though she couldn't get away from the property fast enough. Once she had reached the safe sanctuary of the public pavement, Annie saw her reach into her handbag for some antibacterial gel and apply it liberally to her hands.

Given that the house had been marketed as 'in need of modernisation' this should not have come as a surprise to the potential buyers, but Annie had been in the property business long enough to know that the customer was always right, even when they weren't. She nodded effusively, trying to look suitably impressed by the man's most profound and astute observation.

'Mmm, yes, you're quite right,' she said. 'But I'm sure you'll agree that it's priced accordingly and it's extremely rare for houses to come up for sale on this street. It's a very popular area with families because of its proximity to good local schools.' She looked pointedly at the baby bump protruding out from under the woman's maternity dress.

But even as she said it, she knew she was wasting her time. They weren't going to buy this house, just like they weren't going to buy the three others she'd shown them. Time-wasters was what her boss Lil called these types of customers; people who refused to deviate from the unrealistic picture they'd painted of the home they felt entitled to own. But Annie liked to think of them as optimistic in their belief that they would find the property they wanted at the price they could afford, if only they played the game strategically, like it was Monopoly rather than real life. She couldn't help but feel sorry for them when the realisation dawned that they couldn't even afford a battered old garage on Old Kent Road these days, let alone a hotel on Mayfair. After that, they went one of four ways: accept their fate and compromise, stay put, move out of London, or ring the bank of Mum and Dad. Looking at this couple, she guessed it would be option four.

She glanced at her watch. Her boyfriend Gabe was picking her up in half an hour and she needed to get a move on if she wanted to be ready in time. She still had to walk back to the office and do some admin before she could finish for the day. There was no point in trying the hard sell on this couple, who looked like they were starting to suffer from a lack of oxygen from having been outside the boundary of London's North Circular Road for too long. They were clearly itching to get back to the safety of the inner circle, where they could still call themselves trendy city dwellers rather than predictable suburbanites.

'Well, do call me if you'd like a second viewing,' she said, shaking them both firmly by the hand and waving as they climbed into their eggshell-coloured convertible Mini Cooper and sped off without so much as a backwards glance. She imagined them returning home to their pristine, split-level flat and scrolling through properties for sale on their phones, desperately searching for the one they'd missed, the one that ticked all their boxes. The one that didn't exist.

With a final, wistful glance at the house, which she would give her right arm – and her left if push came to shove – to be able to buy, Annie turned and began to head back towards the high street, just a few minutes' walk away. She passed a young woman who she'd sold a flat to the previous year and they exchanged brief pleasantries, and then she strolled past her favourite café and waved at the owner inside. She smiled. The suburb of Palmers Green may not make the top ten trendy areas list, but it was a vibrant, friendly community and there was nowhere else that she'd rather live.

Today, the pavements were filled with families heading to or from the park near the station. The funfair was in town and even over the noise of the traffic Annie could hear the distinct bass boom of dance music in the distance. She passed a little girl in a buggy, being pushed by her mother. The girl was clutching on to a candyfloss stick, her mouth sticky with pink sugar, and she stared at Annie, glassy-eyed. Annie gave her a wink and continued walking. It was the perfect day for a trip to the fair, a glorious late spring afternoon after weeks of relentless rain. The trees were blossoming, and the flowers were starting to bloom in front gardens, signalling new beginnings. This year it felt even more symbolic.

As the sun warmed her bare arms, Annie sighed with the satisfaction of having finished viewings for the day. Although she loved her job and was accustomed to working on Saturdays, she still got excited when she could join everyone else in official weekend mode. She tried to shake off the disappointment that always niggled at her after an unsuccessful day. It happened sometimes, no matter how hard you tried, and anyway, there was plenty to be happy about. The thought made her pick up the pace and she turned on to the high street, where the calming tranquillity of the residential streets was instantly replaced by the hustle and bustle of life. All around her people wandered in and out of shops or sat at tables on the pavement, sipping coffee. The Greek and Turkish restaurants had flung their doors open and the smell of food cooking on charcoal wafted out, making Annie's mouth water.

She reached the office, pausing as she always did, to look at the display of properties outside. She knew them so well that she had made a game out of it; and whenever she was struggling to sleep at night, she would go through each property in order, listing the address and price in her mind, always nodding off before she reached the end.

The little brass bell hanging above the door tinkled as she let herself into Lillian Gold Estate Agents. Lillian, known to everyone as Lil, glanced up from her desk and peered at Annie from over her reading glasses. Her hair was piled up on top of her head in an untidy knot, which looked extremely glamorous on Lil. When Annie had tried to replicate it once, she'd looked as though she had a bird's nest sitting on her head. Gabe had asked her if she was storing eggs for some magpies, and she hadn't attempted it since.

'How did it go?' Lil asked.

Annie pulled a face which told her boss everything she needed to know.

Lil shrugged. 'Never mind. That last house you showed will be under offer by the end of next week, you mark my words. In fact, I've just booked in a viewing for Tuesday morning. Lovely couple, the ones we sold that garden flat to over in Barnes Close three years ago.'

'Oh, I remember them. They were so friendly. They had a little sausage dog, didn't they?'

'That's right. They've got two children now too, so they need to upsize.'

'Blimey, they've been busy. Well, anyway, that *has* cheered me up.'

Lil nodded. 'Good. Are you all done for the day now?'

'Just got a couple of things to finish, then I'm off.'

'Right you are.'

Lil pushed her glasses back up the bridge of her nose and continued reading some paperwork. Annie sat down and switched on her computer so that she could quickly type up her notes, ready for Monday morning's meeting. There were only three of them in the team, since two colleagues had left and hadn't been replaced, and they had worked together for so long that their meetings often felt like a family gathering rather than a work commitment. But Annie still liked to be prepared. She was just finishing up when she heard a car horn outside and she looked up to see Gabe parked in a loading bay, waving frantically at her from the driver's seat and gesturing towards an incoming traffic warden. She grabbed her bag and dashed outside.

'Hey,' she said to Gabe as she climbed into the passenger seat and gave him a kiss.

'Hey yourself.'

Gabe pulled the car into the line of traffic slowly crawling down the high street. In front of them an enraged motorist was tooting his horn at a delivery driver who had decided to stop in the middle of the road to unload. The man in the car gesticulated and shouted at the van driver, who gave him two fingers in return. Annie wound down her window and rested her arm on the door frame, watching the scene unfold with mild curiosity.

'How was work?' Gabe asked, turning down the radio.

'Rubbish,' Annie replied. 'It was like trying to sell beach houses to an Eskimo today. And what's worse is that I can't even drown my sorrows in a glass or ten of wine.'

Gabe looked apologetic. 'Sorry babe.'

'Don't worry, it's worth it,' she said, putting a hand over her stomach with a smile. She glanced at Gabe, who was grinning too. They were giddy, like a pair of overexcited children, and even now that she'd had time for it to sink in, she still couldn't believe it. Not after they had all but given up hope.

They had tried, unsuccessfully, for a baby for nearly two years. After the first year they'd had some tests, which hadn't raised any red flags, and they had been sent on their way again. The doctor had told them that it was too soon to go down the IVF route and that because everything was in working order, they should just keep trying for a little longer. So that's what they had done, with increasing desperation. Before they started, Annie had no idea that baby-making could be so all consuming and heartbreaking. It became an emotional rollercoaster of anticipation and disappointment on a continuous monthly loop. Even their sex life started to feel more like an exercise in painting by numbers because it was planned with such military precision.

Eventually it took over their life, until it became impossible to think about anything else. They forced themselves to remain stoic and cheerful as friends announced pregnancies and new arrivals in quick succession, telling themselves how lucky they were to have such a free, unencumbered lifestyle when everyone else was burdened by lack of sleep and stinky nappies. But the truth was that they were both becoming disheartened and as time went on, the first seeds of resentment started to grow – towards their friends, the unfairness of life in general, their reproductive systems, and finally each other. Eventually they agreed, with no small degree of relief on both sides, to press pause on baby-making and just enjoy life for a while.

They booked a spur-of-the-moment holiday and spent two weeks relaxing and enjoying the company of their fellow childless travellers. When they returned home, they made a conscious effort to enjoy their freedom, eating out whenever they felt like it, visiting places they hadn't explored before, or queuing for last-minute discounted tickets to theatre shows or comedy nights in town. Annie ditched the folic acid in favour of French wine. Ovulation sticks were ceremoniously tossed into the wastepaper basket. Gabe firmly instructed his mother to stop banging on about when she was going to become a grandparent. They even bought tickets to Glastonbury, much to the envy of their friends who moaned that they hadn't had a single evening away from their dearly beloved offspring in months, let alone a weekend. Life, they both agreed, was sweet. And so, of course, that was the moment when it finally happened.

Annie didn't even realise anything was amiss until she got a notification on her phone from a period tracker app she'd installed ages ago, when they were in the depths of Project Conceive. She still inputted her dates into it each month out of habit and the alert flashed up on her screen while she was at work, trying to negotiate a deal. `Your period is three days late. Did you forget to enter it?`

No, I bloody well didn't, she had thought, looking at the notification with wide eyes. She had just about managed to muddle through her call and afterwards she had stared at her phone, warning herself not to get overexcited because it was definitely a false alarm, while simultaneously considering what colour to paint the nursery. The rest of the afternoon dragged on, each minute feeling more like an hour. All she could think about was getting to a chemist and buying some pregnancy tests. Her thoughts swung between excitement and realism. *I'm not pregnant. But what if I am! But I'm not. But what if I am!* She was so preoccupied that she even booked in a viewing of a house they had already sold and had to call back, embarrassed, to cancel.

At home-time she couldn't get out of the door fast enough. She detoured to the shops and bought a two-pack of tests, thrusting the box deeply into the pocket of her yellow raincoat, and made her way up the hill towards the flat she shared with Gabe. As soon as she arrived, she stuck her head around the kitchen door and said hello to her boyfriend, who was making dinner, and then snuck off to the bathroom before he could ask any questions. She didn't want to tell him until there was actually something to tell him; he'd had enough disappointment already.

Over the years, she had peed on a stick so many times that she could probably do it in her sleep. But she was so accustomed to seeing one solitary line staring back at her that she wasn't quite sure what to do with herself when the second one appeared after a couple of minutes. She gave it the full ten minutes, in case it changed its mind, and then carried the test out of the bathroom, holding it in the palm of her hand like it was a rare and delicate flower. Gabe, who was frying vegetables and humming along to a song on the radio, glanced at it absent-mindedly when she thrust it under his nose and then turned his attention back to the frying pan, until his brain caught up with his eyes and he did a double take.

'What the...?' he asked, looking at it in shock.

'It's positive.' She grinned back manically, like a Cheshire cat on amphetamines.

'Are you serious?' Gabe asked, brow furrowed, still not sure if he'd got the wrong end of the stick. But there was nothing wrong about this stick.

'Seriously serious.'

Gabe dropped the wooden spoon he was holding and picked her up instead, spinning her around in a circle, which was quite an achievement in their tiny kitchen. They laughed at each other, blissfully tangled up in the shared joy of experiencing the moment they'd been dreaming of for so long. For a short while the world stood still, just for them. Then Annie's work phone rang, bringing them back to reality with a thud. Gabe picked up his spoon and carried on cooking the slightly charred vegetables and Annie answered the call. But she couldn't wipe the beam from her face, and she thought her glorious bubble of bliss would never burst.

It did, an hour later. The adrenaline wore off and Annie's joy was replaced with the realisation that this was only the first of many hurdles to overcome and that it could still go wrong at any moment. She'd done enough googling to know how many women had early miscarriages and even if they got to the twelve-week scan, there were still a million-and-one things that could go wrong after that. It didn't bear thinking about.

'At least we can get pregnant,' she told Gabe. 'That's the main thing, right?'

'Yes, absolutely,' Gabe had agreed, nodding vigorously. 'That's what matters.'

Neither of them meant it though. This miracle baby had to be okay. It just had to.

They decided to keep the news to themselves, too scared to breathe a word to anyone in case they jinxed it. But as the weeks went by and Annie experienced all the classic symptoms of pregnancy, they began to relax, bit by bit. With each wave of nausea or crushing fatigue, Annie felt more like a mother-to-be. Gabe, who had hovered around her at first like an overattentive waiter, was back to his usual, laid-back self and life returned to a new kind of normal.

Being duplicitous had been a challenge, however, especially at work when Annie constantly wanted to fall asleep with her head on the desk or vomit into the wastepaper basket. She'd hunkered down for a few weeks, making excuses not to go out for dinner with friends because she knew she wouldn't be able to hide her secret. There was no way the 'I'm on antibiotics' line would work when she turned down a glass of wine. She'd always been a terrible fibber, even as a small child. Her dad, Mike, used to joke that he could read her like a book. He only had to look at her, he said, and she would immediately confess to any wrongdoing without further ado.

But now she was ten weeks pregnant and with her first antenatal appointment booked in for the following week, she and Gabe were feeling confident enough to break the news to their families. When her dad had invited them over for a barbecue they had agreed that it was as good a time as any. Annie had been so excited about it all week but now, with only a forty-five-minute car journey between her and the long-awaited big reveal, she could feel her insides churning.

'How are you feeling?' Gabe asked, placing his hand over hers.

'Shitting bricks,' she admitted.

'Why? He's going to be made up.'

Gabe was right. Annie's father had always been discreet enough not to probe into their baby-making plans, but Annie knew he desperately wanted to become a grandfather, and as she was an only child all his hopes were pinned on her. The pressure of that made her fret even more.

'You don't think it's too soon? Perhaps we should wait until after we've had the scan?'

'We've been over this already. We're just telling your dad,

we're not placing an advert in *The Sunday Times*. It'll be fine, okay?'

She nodded and gazed out of the window. The traffic had finally thinned out and they picked up speed as they travelled north up the main road towards Hertford, the town they had moved to from Northampton when Annie was a few months old and where Mike still lived with his girlfriend, Val. Although these days they no longer lived in the family home that Annie had adored, but in a new build with all the mod cons just on the fringes of town. Val had insisted that Mike sell the cottage, with its leaky roof and persistent damp problems, for something more sensible.

Even though she hadn't lived there in years, Annie had still been livid when their beloved old house went on the market, and she still missed it terribly now. But Val made her father happy and if anyone deserved some happiness in life it was him. So, while she had quietly seethed as Mike cleared out years of memories from the cottage and moved into the Lego house, as Annie called it, she had gritted her teeth and watched from the sidelines as Val took control of her father's life and he gladly let her.

Before Val, Annie had never known her dad to have a girlfriend. Her mum, Eve, had died giving birth to her and Mike had raised her as a single parent. He had not been lacking in offers or attention; over the years women had swarmed around him like moths to a flame, offering sympathy, support and sometimes sex when they discovered he was a widow, but he had rejected them all. He was happy on his own, he said, and that suited Annie just fine because she had her father's undivided attention and no competition. For nearly two decades they lived in an exclusive party for two. With no other family left in their lives, Mike was Annie's everything; her father, mother and best friend rolled into one.

She was the Robin to his Batman; the dream team, as he used to call them.

As a child, Annie had never thought to question the set-up but once she grew up, she finally understood that Mike had sacrificed his own needs to put Annie first. He hadn't wanted anything to distract him from his responsibility to raise, love and protect his daughter as best he could because he was all that she had. It wasn't until Annie left home at eighteen that he began to think about his own needs again. Within a year Val appeared, a divorcee with pearl earrings and floral dresses, and embedded herself firmly into Mike's life. They had met, in all places, at the funeral of an old colleague of Mike's and had bonded over sherry and sausage rolls. When Annie was feeling particularly uncharitable, she liked to refer to Val as the Grim Reaper.

Over the years, though, Annie and Val had reached an unspoken agreement. They would never be close, but they rubbed along together well enough. Val had never shown any desire to be a substitute mother and that was just how Annie liked it. By the time Val and Mike got together Annie was old enough to stand on her own two feet and it was actually a relief to know that her father would not be on his own. Val took care of him, which no one had done properly for years, and Annie was pleased. Thanks to Val's home cooking, he had thickened out considerably but anyone could see that he was content, especially now that Annie had found her place in the world, with a career she enjoyed and a 'proper' boyfriend. Mike hadn't said a word when she had brought home a succession of weird and wonderful suitors over the years, none of whom had lasted long. But when she had first introduced him to Gabe, she had sensed his approval immediately. Even Val, with her pursed lips, had been won over by Gabe's charms, particularly when he informed her that her potato salad was the best thing he'd ever tasted.

As they pulled up outside the yellow-brick house, Annie wondered how Val would feel about having a baby or toddler around, stealing Mike's attention, making a mess, and breaking things. She glanced nervously at the freshly painted black door and turned to Gabe.

'Ready?' she asked.

He nodded. 'Let's do it.'

They got out of the car and let themselves in through the unlocked garden gate, walking down the side of the house towards the pristine square of lawn at the back, bordered on one side by a garden path and the other by neat, meticulously pruned rows of roses and hyacinths. Mike was already out on the patio, fanning the barbecue, and he looked up when he heard their footsteps. He was wearing one of Val's frilly floral aprons, which looked more like a napkin over his ever-expanding stomach and Annie suppressed a giggle as she reached over to give him a hug.

'Hi love,' he said, hugging her back. He smelled of charcoal and fabric conditioner. He turned and called through the open back door, 'Val, the kids are here!'

Val emerged, carrying a salad in each hand, which she carefully placed on the outdoor table before rubbing her hands on her apron and stepping forward to air-kiss Annie and Gabe.

'How are you?' she asked, moving away before they had a chance to respond. Annie and Gabe caught each other's eye in shared amusement.

'Drinks!' Mike declared. 'Beer for you, Gabe? Annie?'

'Lemonade please,' she replied.

'Right you are,' Mike said, heading inside to get the refreshments.

'How's life in the big smoke?' Val asked as she straightened out the linen tablecloth. She wrinkled her nose at the very mention of London. A country girl born and bred; the market town of Hertford was as cosmopolitan as Val got. She loathed the capital, declaring it too expensive, dirty, and overcrowded for her liking, thank you very much. She had only been to Annie and Gabe's flat once in the eight years that they'd lived together. Val genuinely thought there was an oversized rat waiting to pounce on passers-by at every street corner and a criminal with an eye mask and swag bag just across the road on the other side.

'Fine thanks, Val,' Annie replied, sitting down at the table and popping an olive into her mouth.

'Did you know they're building a wonderful new housing estate just outside of Hertford? It's the same company that built this development. Three bedrooms. *Very* affordable,' Val said.

Annie resisted rolling her eyes. 'Thanks Val, but we're happy where we are.'

'But London is so overpriced. And your flat is miniscule.'

'It's tiny but perfectly formed,' Gabe said, sitting down next to Annie and giving her a wink.

'Well, I suppose it is just the two of you,' Val said, and Annie could feel the older woman's eyes boring into her, waiting to see if she would be contradicted. Val's ears had clearly pricked up the second that Annie asked for lemonade rather than her usual gin and slim. Refusing to take the bait, Annie smiled sweetly at Val and put another olive into her mouth. From the corner of her eye, she could see Gabe fidgeting with the tablecloth like a guilty schoolboy under Val's scrutiny. While she didn't take a great deal of interest in the finer details of Annie's life, Val certainly cared about the main events: weddings and babies.

Thankfully Mike reappeared a few seconds later and Annie relaxed. There was no way that she was going to let Val find out about the baby before her father did.

'So, what's new with you guys?' Mike asked, after he'd

distributed the drinks and returned to his post at the helm of the barbecue, placing burgers over the hot coals.

Annie looked at Gabe and he nodded. She took a deep breath. 'Well, funny you should ask that, Dad, because we do actually have some news.'

'Oh, yes?'

'I'm, well, we're, erm, pregnant.'

Mike's head swivelled towards her, his mouth open. The burger that he'd been holding between a pair of tongs fell on to the patio with a splat. 'Oh Annie!' he said, rushing forward. He threw his arms around her and gripped on to her so tightly that she thought he might crack her like a walnut.

'Easy, Dad,' she said with a laugh, and he quickly let go.

'Did I hurt you?'

'No, you're all right, Dad, don't worry about that.'

Now that they were face to face, she could see how misty-eyed he was.

'You're going to be a mother,' he said, looking at her with such emotion that she thought he might burst.

'And you're going to be a grandfather,' she retorted.

'Blimey.'

'I know.'

In the background she could see Val hovering, waiting for the cue that she was allowed to intrude on this intimate family moment. Annie, her heart filled with joy, turned and smiled at her and Val hurried forward and embraced her in a fog of flowery perfume.

'What joyful news,' she said.

'Thanks Val.'

'You really ought to think about one of those new builds.'

Mike strode over to Gabe, shaking his hand vigorously and slapping him on the back. He was grinning from ear to ear, beaming at everyone. He was going to make the most wonderful grandfather. Even Val would probably be knitting hats and booties by the end of the evening, her way of showing that she cared. And Gabe's parents would be just as delighted when they heard the news. How lucky they were, Annie thought, to be surrounded by so many people. She'd had a happy childhood, with a father who loved her. It had been more than enough for her. But this baby was going to be luckier still. It would have a proper family. It would have grandparents who loved it so much that they would probably compete over how much time they got to spend with it. And, most importantly, it would have a mother.

It hit her like a truck and Annie, light-headed, sat back down on the garden chair, clutching on to the armrests. Gabe and Mike were discussing fatherhood over by the barbecue and Val had gone back inside to fetch the condiments, so no one noticed Annie sitting alone, pale-faced, trying to catch her breath, her head spinning and her heart pounding. For weeks this secret that she and Gabe had been keeping from the world hadn't felt real, as though they were characters in a TV programme rather than living their own lives. But now that the news was out in the open, it was like someone had ripped off a protective plaster and exposed her. Her life, as she had always known it, was about to change forever. She was no longer Annie Branning, free spirit and slightly dippy estate agent; she was Annie Branning, mother-to-be. Soon there would be someone in her life who depended on her for everything. Love. Happiness. Survival.

It was what she and Gabe had wanted and now they had it. But was she ready for it? And, more importantly, would she be good enough? She glanced at her father, who was laughing and clinking beer glasses with Gabe. And then at Gabe, who was looking every inch the proud father-to-be. Finally, she looked down at her stomach, imagining a tiny little poppy seed inside, which was growing every day, transforming into a baby. *Her* baby. Hysteria rose inside her and she snorted, putting a hand over her mouth. Her father and Gabe stopped talking and looked at her curiously. And then she was laughing and crying at the same time; nerves, shock, disbelief and excitement all rolled into one. The men exchanged glances, not sure what to make of her.

'Get used to it,' Val said, as she put some ketchup and mayonnaise down on the table. 'That's pregnant women for you. Mad as a box of frogs, the lot of them.'

CHAPTER TWO

'Lil, I need to come into work late tomorrow,' Annie said, peering at her boss from over the top of her computer. 'I've got a hospital appointment.'

'Everything okay?' Lil asked, glancing up.

'Oh yes, all fine, just routine,' Annie replied, looking down quickly before Lil could read anything into her expression. Her boss was as shrewd as a fox and never missed a trick. But she only had to keep the secret for another couple of weeks and then, all being well, she could finally spill the beans. It didn't stop her feeling guilty though, especially when it came to Lil.

Lil didn't have children of her own, but she treated Annie and her colleague Brian like they were her adopted kids. It was a successful employee retention strategy because they'd both worked for her for more than ten years and wouldn't dream of moving elsewhere, even when larger companies came sniffing around, promising BMWs and eye-watering bonuses. The compact little office on the high street was like a second home to them both. Their team had grown and contracted again over the years, depending on the state of the property market and whether the business was doing well, but the three of them had been a constant; celebrating together, commiserating together and complaining together.

Lil had taught Annie everything she knew about being an estate agent and Brian, who had worked there even longer than Annie, always joked that he was a lifer and would work there until he retired or dropped dead, whichever came sooner. Annie didn't know the full story, but she knew enough to understand that Lil had helped him out in some way in the past. He had told her once that if it wasn't for Lil, he'd be in a gutter somewhere but then he'd clammed up and changed the subject, and she hadn't wanted to probe.

Annie had been in her mid-twenties when she met Lil. She was living in Hertford and feeling lost at sea, uncertain what she wanted to do with her life or her career. She'd tried a few jobs but none of them had stuck and she had ended up working in a café down the road from the house she shared with friends. She had no interest in either coffee or catering but it was convenient and so three years and no pay rises later, she was still there. One morning she had been nursing a particularly bad hangover and was propping up the counter, feeling sorry for herself, when Lil wafted in, looking effortlessly glamorous, and asked for a cappuccino to go.

'Can I get you anything to eat with that?' Annie had asked, ringing up her order.

'No thanks, just the coffee.'

'It's just that we have these amazing cinnamon buns in today, freshly baked, and they're quite famous in these parts. In fact, they've been voted the best buns in the county, according to the locally renowned and well-respected food blogger Hearty Hertford.'

'Is that so?' Lil had replied, looking at Annie curiously.

'Yes,' Annie continued, getting into the swing of it now, eager for a distraction from her nasty hangover. 'People queue around the block to get one of these little gems and you've ended up right here, at the front of the queue, just as they've emerged from the oven. They'll all be gone within the hour. This is a once-in-a-lifetime opportunity, madam.'

By now Lil was looking highly amused. 'Go on then, I'll take two to go.'

'Perfect,' Annie said, reaching for one of the cardboard takeaway boxes under the counter and carefully placing the buns in it. 'Are you from around here?' she asked conversationally.

'No,' Lil replied. 'I'm just visiting a friend who lives nearby.'

'Well, enjoy yourself,' Annie said, passing her the coffee and buns.

'You have natural sales talent,' Lil remarked as she handed over a ten-pound note.

'Thanks,' Annie replied, fishing in the till for some change and wondering if she could get away with scoffing a sausage roll before she served the next customer.

'I'm serious. You're wasted here. Ever thought about being an estate agent?'

Not once in Annie's entire life had she ever thought about being an estate agent. She smiled politely and said, 'No, not really, but it sounds like a fascinating job.'

The woman looked at her thoughtfully and then fished around in her bag, pulling out a business card which she handed over to Annie.

Annie took it and read the neat gold writing embossed on it: Lillian Gold, Proprietor, Lillian Gold Estate Agents.

'I'm Lil,' the woman explained. 'I'm based in north London and I'm looking for a junior, someone I can train up within the business. If you're interested, give me a call.'

Annie thanked her and slid the card into her back pocket. Her stomach rumbled and she looked around surreptitiously before bending down under the counter and devouring a sausage roll in seconds. Then she grabbed her phone, messaged her new boyfriend to see if he wanted to meet up after work, served a young family who had just walked in looking for coffees and babycinos and completely forgot about Lillian Gold and her fancy business card.

It was two weeks later that she remembered again. She had run out of clothes and was doing some much-needed laundry in the kitchen. As she turned her jeans inside out, the business card fell to the ground and she picked it up and reread it, considering it for a minute or two before chucking it into the recycling bin. The woman had been nice enough, but she was happy here, in Hertford, and she had no intention of moving to London. And anyway, she didn't want to be an estate agent. She thought about the ones she saw in town, who cruised around in their suits and fancy cars, looking slick, ears glued to mobile phones as they negotiated deals and tried to meet their ridiculous sales targets. No, that wasn't her world at all. She turned the washing machine on and went off to attempt to make an acceptable outfit from her remaining clothes.

But for the rest of the day, she couldn't stop thinking about Lil and the job offer. She was fed up of working in the café for minimum wage. She'd had enough of living in a single room in a big, messy houseshare and dreamed of having her own place. And she strongly suspected that she was being ghosted by her latest boyfriend, who worked in the shop next door to the café and seemed to duck down under the counter every time she walked past. That afternoon she popped round to her dad's for a cup of tea and mooted the idea to him.

'An estate agent?' he had said, incredulous, as he handed Annie a mug and a packet of biscuits.

'Yeah.'

'And this woman is a stranger? She just walked into the café and offered you a job?'

'Not a job, Dad, an interview,' Annie corrected him. 'She said I had natural sales talent.'

'And it's in London, you say?'

'Yep.'

Mike looked thoughtful and Annie held her breath. Her dad's opinion was more important to her than anything and if he said the idea was half-brained, that would be the end of the matter.

'There's no harm in going to her office for a chat, love. You've got nothing to lose.'

With relief, Annie realised that was what she had wanted him to say. 'Thanks Dad.'

As soon as she got home, she had fished out the card from the recycling bin and called Lil.

'Ah, yes, Annie from the coffee shop, I'd given up on you,' Lil said, when she answered.

'Yeah, sorry about that, Lillian, I wanted to take a couple of weeks to really think it through carefully,' Annie lied. 'But I'd love to have a chat if you're still interested.'

Two weeks later, Annie gave notice on both her job and her room and a few weeks after that, she moved into a studio apartment in Palmers Green and started her new job. It all happened so quickly that she barely even had time to consider whether she was making a monumental mistake by accepting a job that she didn't know if she wanted from a woman she'd sold cinnamon buns to. But nothing ventured nothing gained, as her dad had said when she'd told him she was moving, and even now there wasn't a week that went by when she wasn't thankful that she'd taken the risk.

True to her word, Lil had trained her up, teaching her not just how to do the job but how to love it too. While other friends had adventured to the heart of metropolitan cities, beautiful beaches or foreign countries, she'd found happiness in the most unlikely of places. This small north London suburb had become the centre of her world, the place where she had found her career, her people, and the love of her life.

Annie had met Gabe a couple of years after she moved to Palmers Green. She and Brian were on their own in the office, gossiping when they should have been making follow-up calls, when he came in looking for a flat to rent. He had sat down at Brian's desk, but as he flicked through property brochures, he kept glancing over at Annie. He was rugged-looking, with dark-brown hair and stubble, and he was older than her usual type, but there was something about him that drew Annie to him. They made eye contact a couple of times and she was so self-conscious that she hid behind her computer screen until he left, with a backwards glance towards her desk. As soon as he was gone, Brian turned around and observed her, eyebrows raised.

'Someone wants to get in your pants,' he said.

'Oh leave it out, Bri, he's a customer,' she replied.

'He's *my* customer,' Brian corrected. 'Which means you can get nasty with him as much as you like, my dear.'

She threw a pen at him, hitting him in the chest. 'Stop it.'

'I will not stop it. He's hot and you need some action. When was the last time you shagged anyone?'

Annie thought hard. 'Before I moved here,' she admitted reluctantly.

'So, you need to sample the local delights. And he is dee-light-ful.'

Annie rolled her eyes and got on with her work, thinking no more of it. But a few days later, Brian came into the office after a day of viewings, looking as pleased as punch with himself. He glanced at Lil, who was on the phone, before sidling up to

Annie's desk, depositing a piece of paper with a name and phone number on it and looking at her pointedly.

'What's that?' she asked.

'Hot man's phone number,' he whispered.

'Brian!' Annie was horrified.

'Oh calm down, it's not a big deal. While I was showing him around a flat, I just happened to mention that you were single and ready to mingle, and he just happened to mention that he wouldn't be averse to you having his number.'

'I feel sick.'

'Stop being such a drama queen,' Brian hissed back and then started to move away as he noticed that Lil was looking at them suspiciously. 'Just call him, for the love of God.'

That evening, after pacing around her flat in circles for thirty minutes, she sent him a text message and he replied immediately. She was so surprised by the speed of his response, having been accustomed to more elusive men, that she immediately declared him to be a serial killer and vowed not to reply. Ten minutes later, curiosity got the better of her. After a few messages back and forth, he hadn't asked to meet her in a deserted alleyway or sent her photos of his intimate body parts, so she threw caution to the wind and agreed to meet him for a quick coffee. The coffee turned into a walk in the park, which turned into dinner, which turned into drinks, which turned into Annie moving into his flat three months later.

Gabe had just come out of a long-term relationship which had eventually fizzled out when, according to him, they both realised that they were still together out of habit rather than love. It hadn't been ideal that they'd worked this out two weeks before their wedding day, but at least the feeling had been mutual, avoiding too much heartache. Although Annie wasn't entirely sure that Gabe's mother had forgiven him yet, especially as she had already bought her mother-of-the-groom outfit, which included an eye-wateringly expensive fascinator from Harrods.

Gabe had moved out and rented a flat while he and his ex sold the house they co-owned and divided the assets between them.

It was all exceedingly civilised, but Annie had still been hesitant when she realised that he had only been single for a matter of weeks. After just one date with him she already knew that she wanted to be more than a rebound and she was worried that she was heading for another fall. Yet there was something about him that she couldn't put her finger on, but which made her feel in the pit of her stomach that men didn't come better than this one.

The second time they met she had told him, with forced conviction, 'I think it's too early for you to start dating women again.'

'You think I should date men?'

'Ha bloody ha,' she said, trying to remain serious. 'You're fresh out of a relationship. It's too soon. Perhaps we should put the brakes on for now?'

But Gabe had shaken his head. 'Meeting you has only reinforced how wrong things were between me and my ex. I've wasted years of my life being with someone I wasn't really in love with. I'm not making the same mistake again. And you, Annie, are no mistake.'

'I'm not sure,' she said, with less conviction this time.

'Well, I am.' He looked into her eyes and her belly did a flip-flop.

I tried, she thought gleefully, and with that she shrugged off her fears and allowed herself to dive head first into the relationship, despite Brian's protestations that he was only meant to be a cheeky one-night stand and she had, as usual, put far more effort in than was necessary. But it had been a risk worth taking because they were just as in love as ever and she couldn't, and didn't want to, ever imagine a world without Gabe. She knew that marriage was never going to be on the cards for them because it still gave Gabe the heebie-jeebies after his last experience of getting engaged, but they had always agreed that they wanted to have a family together.

Sometimes Annie still couldn't believe it was finally happening. By this time tomorrow she would have had her first appointment at the hospital and would officially be a maternity patient or whatever it was that they called expectant mums. It was a booking-in appointment, her letter from the NHS had said. The letter was boring but she had read it over and over again, securing it with a magnet on the fridge so that she could look at it each morning when she opened the door to get milk. She had already googled everything there was to know about the appointment. The midwife would ask her a bunch of questions, do some tests, and send her on her way. The big appointment, the one that really mattered, was the scan in a couple of weeks; another gruelling fortnight to wait before they knew for sure whether the pregnancy was viable. But each appointment, each step forward, took their dream closer to reality.

And until then, as hard as it was, she just had to get on with life and that included buying and selling houses. Annie sighed. This hospital appointment couldn't come soon enough.

CHAPTER THREE

Annie fanned her sweaty face with a piece of paper. The midwife, who had introduced herself as Louise when she came to get her from the waiting room, looked at her apologetically. 'It gets very hot up here, I'm afraid,' she said.

Annie nodded. She was starting to wilt in the airless room. It felt like the appointment would never end and the midwife had been running late which meant that she'd been kept waiting for nearly an hour. She was hangry and fantasising about getting the hell out of there and hauling her arse to McDonald's for a burger and milkshake. Instead, she mopped her brow with the back of her hand and tried to ignore the river of sweat which had formed in her cleavage.

'We're nearly there,' Louise said as she typed notes on her computer.

'Oh, take your time, I'm fine,' Annie fibbed.

Louise finally stopped typing and turned to look at her again. 'Are there any health issues in your family, Annie?'

'Nothing significant on my dad's side that I know of. He does have high cholesterol but that's because his girlfriend overfeeds him. His parents died a long time ago, before I was born, but it was a car accident; it wasn't health related.'

'Okay,' Louise said, typing again.

'But the main event, if you want to call it that, is that my mum died giving birth to me.'

'I'm so sorry to hear that,' Louise said. 'May I ask what happened?'

'She lost a ton of blood and they couldn't save her in time.' Annie laughed, trying to lighten the mood. 'I'm very pleased that modern medicine has moved on since the eighties.'

Louise nodded. 'Yes, it has. But what happened to your mum must be playing on your mind now that you're pregnant yourself. How are you feeling?'

The question took Annie by surprise. 'I'm feeling grand,' she said.

'Good.' Louise smiled. 'But it's important that you tell me if that changes, okay? Now, do you have any more information about what happened to your mum?'

'Not really, no. Why, is it important?'

'Some studies have found that genetic factors may be relevant to the risk of a post-partum haemorrhage. It would be helpful for us to know more if that's possible.'

Annie began to sweat even more. 'I had no idea,' she said. 'I always thought it was just a terrible, freak accident. That's what my dad's always told me. I didn't really think about it in relation to me giving birth. I mean, how many babies have been delivered safely since then? Millions?'

'Many millions. And in all likelihood, it *was* a tragic accident, just like your dad said. Out of interest, was there ever any investigation into it? Any suspicion of negligence?'

'Not that I know of.' Annie was nauseous now. She put a hand over her mouth.

'Try not to worry, Annie. As you said, medicine has moved

on a lot in the last thirty-five years. Childbirth is incredibly safe in this country, and from what you've told me there are no other risk factors. But perhaps speak to your dad and see if he can give us some more information.'

'Okay,' Annie agreed.

Louise continued typing into her computer and Annie looked away and sniffed loudly. The midwife stopped typing again and glanced at her. 'Are you okay?'

'I'm fine,' she said, laughing self-consciously as she quickly wiped a tear from her cheek. 'I don't know why I'm crying. It's silly. I'm just feeling a bit nervous, I think. We've wanted this baby for such a long time and now I'm worried that something bad might happen.'

'That's completely understandable. It's common to feel anxious or overwhelmed during pregnancy and your situation is particularly difficult. Do you experience anxiety regularly?'

'No,' Annie said, shaking her head vigorously. 'No. Honestly, I'm not anxious at all, I'm fine.'

'Okay. What about your mum's parents? Your grandparents.'

'I've never met them,' Annie admitted. 'My mum had lost touch with them by the time she met my dad. I think they had some big argument and they never spoke again. Gosh, you must think my family is totally weird. I never really gave it much thought until now.'

Louise laughed. 'Believe me, Annie, in this job I've heard everything.'

Ten minutes later, the appointment finally ended and Annie couldn't wait to escape the airless room. She sent Gabe a text message to tell him all went well, and then walked briskly through the maze of corridors until she found her way to the main entrance. The fresh air soothed her nerves and she stood with her eyes closed for a moment before heading towards the car park. As she walked, she fished her phone out of her bag and called her dad.

'Hi, it's me,' she said, when he picked up.

'Hi love, everything okay?'

'Yes, it's fine. I just had my first hospital appointment.'

'How did it go?'

'It went okay but she asked a lot of questions about Mum. What happened to her and so on.'

'Why? Does she think it's relevant?'

'It might be,' Annie replied, trying to keep her voice steady. The last thing she wanted to do was stress out her dad. It occurred to her that he might be more anxious than he was letting on about her being pregnant, and she was kicking herself for not connecting the dots before now.

'All I know,' he said, 'is that she had a major haemorrhage soon after you were born and lost a lot of blood very quickly. They did everything they could to save her.'

'But did they say what caused it?'

'No. It was just described to me as a complication of childbirth. Maybe I should have probed them further but at the time I wasn't thinking straight.'

'Don't worry, Dad, it's not your fault. But it would be good to find out a bit more if we can. Apparently it can sometimes be genetic. Do you have any record of it anywhere?'

He was silent for a while. 'I don't remember having anything in writing and if I did, I doubt I still have it. But I can contact our old GP in Northampton and see if they have any records.'

'Thanks, I appreciate it.'

'Listen, Annie, don't let this concern you. What happened to Mum was a tragic accident but that's all. You're in safe hands with those doctors and midwives, okay? I want you to enjoy your pregnancy. It's such a special time for you and Gabe. Nothing bad is going to happen.'

'I know. Thanks Dad.'

She hung up and continued walking. There was no time for a McDonald's now, but she had to eat so she quickly detoured to the hospital café and picked up a sandwich and a packet of crisps. Sitting in her car she devoured them both and then polished off a bag of chocolate buttons she had stashed in the glove compartment for good measure, now that she was eating for two and all. Much revived by the sugar hit, she started the engine, pulled out of the car park and made her way back towards Palmers Green.

As she drove, she replayed her conversation with Louise over again in her head. She had been fixated on getting pregnant for so long that she hadn't given much thought to what happened after that. Now it was all she could think about. Was there some sort of genetic predisposition which meant that she was destined for the same fate as her mum and, if so, would they be able to save her?

Visions appeared in her mind of her dying in hospital, of Gabe having to raise the baby alone, of her dad crying and saying that history was repeating itself. She shook them off. She was being absurd; influenced by a heady combination of pregnancy hormones and too much binge-watching *EastEnders*. Yet the whole experience had made her think about her mum and what she went through.

Annie had wondered many times how different her life would be if her mum had survived. Over the years she had experienced sadness, grief, anger, guilt, resentment. But it was a complex thing, to miss someone you didn't even know. It was the actuality of having a mother rather than the individual that she craved. Like when she was asked to draw a picture of her family at preschool and she realised, for the first time, how different her own family was to the other children. Or at school sports days and plays, when she saw her friends eagerly scanning the crowds for their mums and smiling with relief when they spotted them. Annie's dad had always done his best to make every event, but occasionally it didn't quite feel the same. Or when, at thirteen, she had started her period and her dad had tried to help her but she had slammed the door in his face and fallen on to her bed crying, frightened and angry. She had emerged red-eyed an hour later, to find a little package waiting for her outside her door – sanitary products, some chocolate, a magazine – and she had rolled her eyes with embarrassment while, simultaneously, a small smile played on her lips because she understood that she was not alone after all.

Then there had been stretches of time when she barely thought about her mum. Her life with her dad was the only one she had ever known, and it had been a good one. He had celebrated her first steps and listened with joy to her first word, 'dada'. He had wiped her snotty tears and put plasters on her bloodied knees. He had taken her to birthday parties and play dates, and chatted with all the mums, the token dad in the room. He had let her paint his fingernails and toenails pink and put lipstick on him. He had picked her up from house parties late at night and cheered her up when she fell out with a friend, or a careless boy broke her heart. He had been there for every important moment in her life and while she had taken much of it for granted at the time, now she realised that as dads went, he was one of the good ones.

When she had realised that she was pregnant, her first thought was how thrilled her dad was going to be when he found out. It had been a wonderful moment, telling him the happy news and seeing his reaction. His words came back to her: 'Enjoy your pregnancy, it's such a special time.' What about her mum, had she enjoyed her pregnancy? Had she been head first in a toilet with crippling morning sickness, or had she breezed through the nine months? Had she been nervous about giving birth or had the thought that it might be dangerous not even crossed her mind? Had she been excited about having a baby? Annie's parents had been young when they got together and her mum fell pregnant after a whirlwind romance, but her dad had always made the story sound romantic; two star-crossed lovers who fell madly in love and were over the moon when they were blessed with a child. Some blessing she had been in the end though.

The sound of her phone ringing cut through her thoughts, and she answered it on loudspeaker.

'Hey babe, it's me,' Gabe said. 'You okay?'

'Yeah, just a bit drained,' she replied. 'What's up?'

'Mum's just called. She and Dad are coming to visit this weekend.'

Annie groaned inwardly. Gabe's parents, Diana and Bruce, lived in Bristol and enjoyed coming to London every couple of months so that they could combine seeing their son with visiting art galleries and dining at new restaurants in town.

Annie had never felt comfortable in Diana's presence. She was always perfectly polite, but she had a veneer of reserve that Annie had never managed to infiltrate. Diana obviously didn't think Annie was good enough for her beloved Gabriel. He was her firstborn and, Annie suspected, her favourite. It didn't help that Diana had adored Gabe's ex-fiancée and still talked about her shamelessly, even in front of Annie, as though she was the beacon of perfection that Annie should aspire to.

When Annie had done some low-key stalking of Gabe's ex on social media to see what all the fuss was about, it had made her feel even worse. The woman was a cardiothoracic surgeon who went to spin classes every day, for goodness' sake. Who did that? Annie could never compete with Gabe's ex and had eventually given up trying to win over Diana. The tension had been exacerbated by the fact that they weren't getting married, which meant that Diana still had no excuse to wear the fascinator. But perhaps the baby might finally be the thing that brought them closer because the one thing that Diana wanted more than anything else in the world was a grandchild.

In the interests of fairness to both parties, Gabe had called his mum and told her about the baby as soon as they got back from the big reveal at Annie's dad's house. No doubt Diana was coming down to interrogate her and make sure that she was doing everything right.

'It's a bit short notice. Where are they going to stay?' she asked Gabe. They had a sofa bed in the living room at the flat and had offered to give up their own bed many times, but Gabe's parents always declined. Diana liked her luxuries.

'Mum's booked a room at the hotel they stayed at last time. They're driving down on Friday afternoon and they've invited us out for dinner. They've already made plans for Saturday.'

'Okay, maybe we can take them to the Italian restaurant they enjoyed last time? I'll book a table later. Anyway, I've got to go, I'm nearly at the office.'

She rang off and found a space to park. Despite already being late for work, she detoured to her local café and ordered a cappuccino to go, sipping it rebelliously while imagining Diana tutting at her for consuming caffeine. When she got to the office, Brian was the only one there.

'All right, slacker, where've you been?' he asked.

'Mind your own beeswax,' she replied. 'Where's the boss lady?'

'Doing a viewing of that big house we took on last week. The one owned by the Spurs player. Hey, do you and Gabe fancy coming over for dinner on Friday night? Ian's cooking.'

Ian was Brian's boyfriend and one of the most incredible

cooks Annie had ever known. He worked as an architect by day, and by night he made culinary masterpieces. She had told him more than once that he should apply for *MasterChef* but he always said that he couldn't think of anything more terrifying than showing his meat and two veg to John Torode.

'I'd love to, Bri, but we've got Diana and Bruce visiting from Bristol this weekend. They sprung it on us at the last minute.'

'Ah well, never mind, next time.'

'Believe me, I'd much rather spend my Friday evening with you and Ian.'

'Well, I would invite them to come but I swear last time I met them, Bruce tried it on with me.'

'Don't be so ridiculous,' Annie scoffed.

'I'm *joking*, Annie.' Brian paused. 'Or am I?'

Brian ducked as Annie threw her cushion at him. But he'd done the job. She was laughing again, any lingering thoughts of her daunting hospital appointment forgotten for the time being.

'So, tell me, Annabelle, are you taking all of your antenatal supplements? Monitoring your caffeine intake?' Diana leaned over the dining table and studied Annie intently.

Annie's full name was not, and never had been, Annabelle, but that's what Diana had called her when they first met, and she had been too terrified to correct her. It had become a running joke now and Gabe found it hilarious, which made it hard for Annie to keep a straight face.

'Yes, Diana,' she replied solemnly.

'Of course, in my day we all drank red wine and smoked cigarettes but things are very different these days, aren't they? Now we know a lot more about how much harm they can do.'

Annie had never smoked in her life but suddenly she would

have killed for a cigarette. 'Yes, that's quite right,' she said, looking at Gabe for moral support. He winked back.

'And you know which food and drink to avoid? I've been reading all about it on the interweb and I found a terribly helpful article about it. Shall I send it to you?'

'Thank you, Diana but don't worry. I've done all the necessary research.' Annie sipped on her tap water pointedly.

'Good.' Diana sat back, satisfied. She and Bruce had three children who were all in their late thirties and forties and none of them had procreated. She had, on several occasions, made it clear what she thought about leaving it too late to have babies. Gabe's sister had a successful career as a lawyer and his brother's job as a wildlife photographer took him around the world. Both were happy and neither were itching to settle down. Annie knew that Diana was proud of her children and their successes but what she really coveted was a grandchild. And now she had it, Annie realised with a sinking feeling, there was no way they'd be able to keep her away.

Diana fixed her gaze on Gabe next. 'Dad and I have been talking. Clearly you're going to have to move house before the baby comes. We want to help financially.'

Annie glanced at Gabe. They hadn't really talked about the long-term logistics yet because it had felt too premature, and they didn't want to run before they could walk.

'We're not ready to have that conversation yet, Mum,' Gabe replied diplomatically. 'But thanks for your offer. It's noted and appreciated.'

'You'll need at least three bedrooms,' Diana continued, as if she hadn't heard him. 'So that there's a decent room for me to stay in when the baby comes. I can hardly reside in a hotel for months on end, can I?'

Annie was alarmed. *Months on end? What the frickin' hell?* She turned to look at Gabe again, but he was nodding thoughtfully, as if his mother was talking sense. 'You're right, we'll bear that in mind,' he said. She wanted to kick him under the table.

'I know you've always refused our help in the past, Gabriel, but things are different now. You can't be stubborn about it anymore. It's not just you to think about.'

Gabe nodded, almost contritely, and Annie marvelled at the power of a mother over a son, even one in his forties. 'I know, Mum,' he said.

'And will you go back to work after the baby comes, Annabelle?'

'Yes, I plan to,' Annie said, 'but I haven't really worked it all out yet.'

Fearing that Diana was going to criticise working women next, Annie tried to think of a way to change the subject. Next to her, Bruce was tucking into his pasta, oblivious to the conversation. She supposed that four decades of being married to Diana would do that to a person.

'Bruce,' she said suddenly, and he looked at her, startled. 'How's the golf?' It was the one subject she knew he could talk about endlessly, and he took the bait and started complaining about the shocking service at his new country club. Annie relaxed again, pleased to be out of the spotlight, but the conversation they'd had with Diana played on her mind.

After dinner, Diana and Bruce got a taxi back to their hotel and Annie and Gabe started walking back towards the flat. It was a beautiful evening and they ambled slowly past the shops until the road became residential and the crowds thinned out. They passed a church, its intricate stained-glass window illuminated in the darkness, giving off a warm glow. A young couple sat on the low brick wall outside, kissing and giggling. Annie snuggled up to Gabe.

'That was nice,' she said.

'Mmmm.'

'But, oh my God, how funny was it when your mum suggested that she might come and stay with us for, like, *months*?' she said, waiting for Gabe to laugh along with her. But he didn't.

'It might not be a bad idea, An,' he said.

She stopped and looked at him. 'Are you serious?'

'A newborn baby is hard work. And with your own mum not being around, you're not going to have the support that other new mothers have. You might be grateful for Mum's offer.'

'I'll have you, won't I?'

'Of course, but I'll have to go back to work after my paternity leave and you'll be on your own for most of the week. I'm just thinking of you.'

'Can you seriously imagine us sharing our home with *your mother* for months on end though, Gabe? I mean, that's what would tip me over the edge, not the baby.'

'Well, months might be a bit extreme but perhaps a few weeks at least. Just think about it. We don't have to decide anything right now, we've got plenty of time to consider our options.'

'To be fair, there's no way we can afford a three-bed place anyway.'

'We might be able to,' Gabe said, hesitantly. 'With my share of the money from the house I owned with my ex and some help from Mum and Dad, I reckon we'd have enough for a decent deposit on a house. I've heard there are some lovely ones being built just outside of Hertford.'

She poked his arm. 'You're not getting me out of Palmers Green, Gabe Adams. This is our home and this is where we are going to raise our baby. Capiche?'

Gabe squeezed her back. 'I don't give a monkey's where I live, as long as it's with you.'

'And your mother, clearly.'

'All right, Annabelle, let it go. It might not happen anyway.'

'But would you accept money from them? You've always refused in the past.'

'Maybe. Mum's right, it's not about me anymore, we've got a little one to think of now. They have to take priority over my pride and let's face it, our flat is too small.'

'True. Anyway, let's not talk about it now, we've got plenty of time to sort all that out. Months and months before the baby comes; it feels like another lifetime.'

'It'll be here before you know it, An. And we need to be prepared.'

CHAPTER FOUR

'And that's the baby's head.'

The sonographer pointed to a blob on the screen and Annie squinted as she tried to make it out. 'Oh yes, I can see it,' she said. She was lying, she couldn't see it at all, but she didn't want to look like the idiot who couldn't even make out her own baby's head.

She looked at Gabe who was holding her hand. 'Can you see it?' she asked him.

'Yeah,' he said. 'Yeah, I can.'

She turned back to the sonographer. 'Is everything okay?'

She nodded. 'Everything looks fine.'

Relief coursed through her body. They had been waiting in anticipation for this moment for weeks, the date etched into their minds, and now it was finally here and the news was good. One more hurdle overcome. From this moment on they could share their joy with their wider circle and begin to properly enjoy the pregnancy. In a few weeks, her bump would start showing and she would look pregnant too. It was all finally happening for them. She wanted to whip out her phone and start calling and texting people immediately, but instead she turned her attention back to the screen. She was grinning from ear to ear, waiting for the sonographer to finish.

Afterwards, they left the ward, holding on to their copies of the scan.

'He or she looks just like you,' Gabe joked.

'No, those eyes are definitely yours,' Annie retorted.

Outside the hospital they stood side by side, their fingers moving rapidly across their phones as they messaged their parents to tell them that everything had gone well. When they were done, they made their way back to the car. Annie had the day off and had arranged to visit her friend Caz, who was on maternity leave with her second child, but Gabe had to go into the office in central London. It was a little strange to be slotting right back into normal life after such a momentous moment, but life went on. She dropped Gabe at the nearest train station, gave him a kiss goodbye, and then made her way towards Finchley, where Caz lived.

Annie and Caz had been best friends since the age of four. Thanks to a nasty dose of chickenpox, Annie had started primary school later than all the other children. It was just a week, but those few days she missed out on could have been years. When she walked into the classroom, holding the teacher's hand and looking shyly down at her shoes, all the other children had stared at her like she was an exhibit. She was 'the new girl' and she felt out of place and terrified.

At break time, she had stood alone in a corner, desperate to play but too scared to join in.

Then a tall, determined-looking girl with bruised shins and long brown hair in pigtail plaits had marched up and stood squarely in front of her, her hands on her hips. 'Come here,' she said. It was an order, not an invitation, but Annie gladly obliged. The girl, who she later learned was Caz, took her over to a rowdy gaggle of children who were about to start a game. 'The new girl's playing too,' she declared. From that moment on, she was officially in the fold and after a few days no one even remembered that she'd started school late.

As children, Caz and Annie were inseparable. They were yin and yang; Caz was confident and fearless while Annie was shy and reserved, but they slotted together like two peas in a pod. Annie loved going to Caz's house with her warm, cuddly mum who always gave Annie a hug and a fuss, and her three brothers who Caz moaned about but Annie adored. As the only child of a single parent, it was like another world to Annie, and she fell in love with it.

But equally Caz enjoyed going to Annie's house, the blissful tranquillity of being able to play uninterrupted, without smelly boys trashing their game or making fun of them.

Caz loved going on adventures with Annie and Mike, paddling in the river or searching for creepy crawlies in the mud and eating sandwiches in the woods. They spent most weekends alternating between each other's houses, their activities evolving as they did; play dates, sleepovers, midnight feasts, parties.

As teenagers, they did each other's make-up and shared clothes, even though Caz was a good few inches taller than Annie. When a notorious bully started teasing Annie for being the head teacher's daughter, Caz set her older brothers on him, and he never came near Annie again. They even started going out with boys from the same group of friends so that they could double date. They were like sisters but without the constant bickering. At eighteen, they both moved away from home to study and Annie cried for days, convinced that she'd never get over the heartache of being parted from her best friend. But they quickly adapted to not being in each other's pockets. They had their own paths to follow, which took them in different directions for a time, before uniting them again in London. These days they both led busy, and often separate, lives but they always made the effort to meet up at least once a month.

Annie pulled up outside Caz's house, checked that the baby scan photo was tucked safely inside her bag, and made her way up the path. Caz opened the door before she'd even rung the bell.

'It's so good to see you,' she said. She leaned towards Annie as if going in for a hug and then thrust baby Harry into her arms as quick as a ninja. Annie looked down at the baby, wondering how she had ended up holding him, while Caz smiled contentedly and turned towards the kitchen. 'Coffee?'

'Yes please,' Annie replied, eying Harry. She'd held friends' babies before but now that she was pregnant, she was more aware of it and wondered if she was doing it right. Harry started fussing and she jiggled him about nervously, hoping he wouldn't cry. 'Where's Noah?'

'Preschool,' Caz said. 'Thank God. It's like a warzone when they're both at home.'

'How's it all going?' Annie asked, following her into the kitchen.

'It's fine, it's much easier the second time around,' Caz said. 'You know what you're doing a bit more and even when you don't, you don't really care.'

'Are you getting any sleep?'

'Sleep? Are you crazy, woman? I don't sleep.'

Annie gulped. She loved her sleep and she needed it too, as Gabe would attest to the following morning if she'd had a bad night. 'How long have you got left of maternity leave?'

'Another four months,' Caz replied. 'Then I'm back in business, baby.'

Annie drifted into the living room and slowly sat down on the sofa, glancing down at Harry. His head was resting on her shoulder and he was dribbling on her dress. She had no idea if he was in the right position. Was his face too close to her armpit? Could he breathe? Death by body odour wouldn't be pleasant for the poor chap. Caz walked in, put two cups of coffee on the table, sank down into an armchair with a satisfied sigh and helped herself to a chocolate biscuit. The cat, sensing a rare opportunity, immediately jumped into her lap and curled up, gazing smugly at the baby. Caz stroked it absent-mindedly and observed Annie.

'What's new with you then?'

'Well, funny you should ask,' Annie said, leaning down and trying to reach into her bag on the floor without dropping Harry into it. She fished out the scan photo and handed it to Caz.

'Woah!' Caz said, snatching it from Annie and staring at it. She stood up and hurled herself at Annie, sending the poor cat flying. They hugged tightly, trying not to squash Harry, and when Caz eventually pulled back, she was wiping away a little tear. She was one of the few people who knew about Annie and Gabe's baby-making battles.

'This is epic news, Annie. I'm made up for you. I can't believe you kept it quiet though!'

'I know, sorry Caz. Call me superstitious.'

'Don't worry, I get it. How are you feeling?'

'Relieved,' Annie admitted. 'Happy. Nauseous, but that's a good thing, right?'

'Oh yeah,' Caz said. 'When I was preggo with Noah I chundered into a wastepaper basket in the middle of a meeting with the Home Secretary.'

Annie laughed with delight. Caz was a civil servant, and her work stories were legendary.

'Everything okay though?' Caz asked. 'With the baby?'

'Yep fine, everything's as it should be. My first appointment was a bit weird though.'

'How so?'

'The midwife asked loads of questions about Mum. How she died, what caused it. Apparently, it can be genetic.'

Caz frowned. 'I didn't know that. Does it put you at greater risk?'

'She doesn't know. She wants me to find out more about what happened. I spoke to Dad and he's going to try to locate her medical records for me.'

'Well, your dad will get to the bottom of it. Still, I never thought about it before, Annie, but what happened to your mum must be playing on your mind now that you're pregnant.'

'It wasn't at first,' Annie admitted. 'It is now. I ended up bursting into tears at the appointment. The midwife must have thought I was mad.'

'Don't worry about that, love, they've seen it all. When I gave birth to Harry and the midwife told me that it was another boy, I wailed like a banshee while the poor woman stitched me back up.'

'Poor Harry. Always knowing you wanted him to be a Harriet.'

'The stupid thing is, I didn't even want a girl that much. I was just knackered and hormonal. My point is that pregnancy does weird things to us, so don't worry about a few stray tears.'

'Thanks,' Annie said, reassured by her friend's words. Ever since the appointment she'd been feeling on edge, like she was waiting for something bad to happen, and she couldn't shake it off.

'But seriously, Annie, I'm here if you want to talk to me, okay?'

'I know, thanks. Anyway, are you ready for our big night out on Friday?'

They were going out for dinner and drinks in town with a couple of their old friends from secondary school and it was the first time they'd all got together in months.

'Oh yes,' Caz said. 'I've pumped enough breast milk to last for days. This girl is going out on the tiles, baby, and I'm not coming home until morning. Or, failing that, 10.30pm at least.'

'Well, I'm knackered ninety-nine per cent of the time, so it won't be a late one for me but I'm looking forward to a catch-up with the girls. It's been ages.'

'How's Val the old gal? Is she still stuffing your dad with food like a turkey?'

'Yep, and now me too.'

'And what about Gabe's folks? Was Diana pleased that you're finally producing heirs?'

'Yes, but get this. She said she wanted to move in for *several months* when the baby comes and Gabe didn't even think it was a bad idea.'

Caz snorted. 'If the stress of a new baby doesn't tip you over the edge, she will.'

'That's almost exactly what I said to Gabe.'

'Where would she sleep anyway? In bed with you and Gabe?'

'Thanks for that image, Caz, I'll be having nightmares about it imminently.'

'Any time.'

'Well, here's the other thing. Gabe reckons we should buy a house. Like proper grown-ups.'

'Can you afford it?'

'Apparently so, with Diana and Bruce's help.'

'So do it. You work in the right industry for it anyway. Can't you get one on the cheap?'

'It doesn't really work like that, Caz. They don't sell houses at trade price to estate agents.'

'Well, either way, if Diana and Bruce have the cash to splash, don't be proud about it. Take it and buy yourself a nice house. Believe me, you'll need an extra room to hide in when the baby comes.'

Looking at all the baby and toddler paraphernalia scattered around her friend's house, Annie had to admit that she was probably right. She had no idea how she would even fit half of it into her and Gabe's tiny flat.

When she got home later that day, she switched on her laptop and pulled up the details of the house she'd fallen in love with a few weeks ago. Just as Lil had predicted, they'd soon had an offer on it which the owner had accepted, but it had fallen through when the buyers failed to secure a mortgage and it was about to come back on the market again. She knew it wouldn't be available for long. With some TLC, it could be beautiful.

Could they afford it though? She closed her eyes and imagined the house belonging to her, fingering the keys on completion day – except this time she was the one collecting them rather than handing them over. She thought of her and Gabe, repainting the walls, decorating the room that was destined to become a nursery or weeding the overgrown back garden. It was all very grown up. Did she want that? Yes, she realised, she did. It came as a surprise as she'd always been content living in the flat with Gabe, insisting that they didn't need more space, that it would only be more rooms to clean and tidy. But everything was different now.

She had looked at the photos for a little longer and then, on the spur of the moment, grabbed her trainers and keys and walked round to have a look at it. It was exactly how she remembered. The front garden was full of rubbish and the paint was peeling off the door and walls, but she saw right through that to the house that it could be. A man passed her on the pavement, a baby in a carrier strapped on to his chest, and a little dog on a lead walking alongside him. He looked up at the house.

'You here to view it?' he asked.

'No. Yes. Sort of,' she said, and shrugged apologetically at her own indecisiveness.

'Well, I hope someone buys it soon: it really needs some love. We live four doors down, so we might see you around.' He waved and continued walking towards his own house. She stood and looked at the house for a little while longer before turning round and walking back home.

The next day at work, she still couldn't stop thinking about it. She swivelled in her chair to look at Lil, who was nose-deep in the accounts at her desk.

'Lil?' she asked, tentatively.

'Mmm?' Lil replied, not looking up.

'That house on Brighton Road. The fixer-upper. Do we have any viewings booked in yet?'

'Three on Saturday I believe,' Lil replied. 'Why?'

'If I wanted to put an offer in, would that be kosher?'

Lil's head sprang up in surprise. '*You* want to buy the house?'

'I'm not sure, maybe?'

Lil stood up and walked over to her desk. 'Okay, well we'd have to declare it to the vendor. Transparency is key here. And I would handle all correspondence with him, you'd have to distance yourself from it entirely. But there's nothing to stop you from putting in an offer.'

'Okay, cheers, Lil.' Annie went back to her emails, but she could sense Lil hovering at her desk. She looked up at her boss, who was watching her curiously.

'I didn't know that you were considering buying,' she said.

'It's a new thing, we have to do all our sums first, but we're thinking about it.' Annie tried to sound non-committal. They were going out for their monthly team dinner soon and Annie was planning a grand, ceremonial announcement about the baby. But Lil's eyes were still boring into her, and she felt her resolve weakening.

'And you need a three-bed terraced near a good primary school, do you?'

'Yuh-huh,' Annie said, cringing.

'Okaaaaay,' Lil replied. 'Anything else you want to share, Annie?'

Annie held up her hands in surrender. 'Fine, you got me, Lil, I'm pregnant.'

Lil clapped her hands together with delight. 'How wonderful, Annie! Congratulations to you and Gabe. That's such tremendous news.'

'What's tremendous news?' Brian asked, as he barged through the door and caught the end of their conversation.

Annie gave up all hopes of her surprise reveal over dinner. 'I'm with child,' she told him.

'Oh Annie.' Brian hurled himself at her, embracing her in a bear hug and getting all emotional.

'What's wrong, Bri? Don't panic, it's not yours.'

'I'm just so thrilled for you, Annie. I'm going to be an uncle,' Brian said, hugging her again.

'Uncle Brian, yeah I like the sound of it,' Annie told him with a giggle, caught up in Brian's excitement. It wasn't the big reveal she'd planned but it was still turning out to be a wonderful moment.

'Well, I would get some champagne but it's not very fitting, is it?' Lil said. 'So, cake will have to do instead.' She picked up her keys and headed for the door. 'Back in ten.'

While Lil was gone, Brian made them both a cup of tea and

perched on her desk. 'I'm going to miss my drinking buddy though,' he said.

'Yeah, sorry about that, Bri.'

'Uncle Brian may not be very good at babysitting either. I'm not sure that I *do* babies.'

'Don't worry, no expectations there, mate.'

He looked concerned. 'You will come back to work, won't you? After you've had the baby?'

'Wild horses wouldn't keep me away. I'll be back before you know it.'

'Thank Christ for that.'

Lil returned a few minutes later with a supermarket celebration cake and they tucked into their slices, clinking their mugs of tea together. Then the phone rang and someone else came into the office to enquire about selling their flat and they had to get back to work, but a warm glow lingered over Annie for the rest of the day. When she got home from work, she relayed her conversation with Lil about the house to Gabe. She had shown him the photos and floor plan the previous evening to test the water, interested to see how he would react. They hadn't discussed Diana's offer of a loan yet, and even if they did take her up on it, she wasn't sure if Gabe had a fixer-upper in mind. But he had seemed enthusiastic, and his reaction had spurred her on.

'So Lil says it's okay to put in an offer, as long as we do it all by the book,' she told him. 'But can we even afford it?'

Gabe reached for his laptop and opened a spreadsheet.

'Blimey, Gabe, what's that?'

'Our finances.'

Annie stared at it, impressed and a little intimidated. She'd never seen this super-organised, on-top-of-things side to Gabe before. He was usually the person who realised he'd forgotten his wallet just as he got to the checkout in a supermarket.

'So, how much moolah have we – and by we, I mean you – got then?'

Gabe showed her the figures and her eyes widened in amazement.

'I didn't realise that I was dating a sugar daddy.'

He pointed to a number on the spreadsheet. 'This, combined with a cash injection from Mum and Dad, should be enough for the deposit. Our salaries can cover the mortgage payments.'

'How are you feeling about taking money from your parents?'

'Well I'm practically a middle-aged man, so it's not ideal, is it? I've always taken pride in being able to stand on my own two feet. But, as Mum said, it's not about me anymore. If we want to live in London and buy a house, we're going to need their help.'

'I think you're right,' Annie agreed.

'Let's not be hasty though, Annie,' Gabe said. 'This is just one house. We need to look at many more properties, speak to my parents and make an appointment with a mortgage advisor before we even think about putting an offer in on anything. Okay?'

'Received, over and out,' Annie replied. But she was already picturing the love seat she'd seen on Instagram positioned in the bay window of what would be the living room. In her mind's eye she was sitting in it, gazing out of the window at the cherry blossom tree outside while her baby slept peacefully in her arms. *What colour cushions?* she wondered. *Pink, definitely pink.*

CHAPTER FIVE

'To sweet reunions!' Caz declared, holding up her Prosecco. Everyone raised their glass in unison. Annie, who was nursing a lemonade, tried to look enthusiastic. They'd only been out for a couple of hours and Caz was already three sheets to the wind. She was on a mission tonight. On the other end of the debauchery scale, Annie was already dreaming of her bed.

Her nausea had finally passed but she was still feeling permanently tired and was in bed by nine o'clock most evenings. Even though she'd had a lovely time catching up with her old school friends over dinner, she was more than ready to call it a night and retire to her flat, where Gabe was waiting for her. The others, however, had different ideas.

'I'm going to order some shots,' Sally declared, standing up and making her way to the bar.

The others cheered her on while Annie groaned. It was going to be a long night and she wondered how soon she could sneak off without offending them. Annie, Caz, Sally and Laura had become friends as teenagers, when they were united over their shared love of Daniel Brent, the school heart-throb. Many blissful hours had been spent discussing him in intricate detail at sleepovers and following him around the school corridors like devoted puppies. They never did get their man. But they did get a friendship that had endured over the years. Even so, with the many different responsibilities of life, they hardly ever got together as a group anymore. Sally had three young children, lived in a small village in Sussex and volunteered as a school governor. Laura was a successful barrister and had a toy boy lover and a flat in Highgate. Their lives had become as different as they were, but whenever they got together, it still felt like old times.

'Sorry you can't join us, Annie,' Sally said when she returned with a tray of shots, not looking remotely sorry. After three pregnancies, she'd done her time.

'Ah you're all right, it's quite fun watching you three get blotto to be honest,' she replied.

'I haven't had a night out in over six months,' Sally admitted. 'Although I'm not looking forward to taking the kids swimming tomorrow morning after this.'

'Can't Marcus do that?' Caz asked. Marcus was Sally's famously elusive husband. They all knew he existed because they'd briefly witnessed him in the flesh on Sally's wedding day, but he'd failed to appear at any other social engagements before or since.

Sally looked scornful. 'Marcus is apparently allergic to swimming pools. And school runs. And children's birthday parties. Anyway, he plays golf on Saturdays.'

'That's bullshit,' Laura declared furiously. 'They're his kids too. There's no excuse for that kind of behaviour in this day and age. Parenting is both your responsibility.'

'Tell that to Marcus.'

'*You* tell that to Marcus.'

'It's hard though. I mean, I don't work. So, I don't feel like I have a leg to stand on.'

'Well, you do. Marcus is taking the piss, pure and simple. And you're letting him get away with it.'

'That's easy for you to say, Laura. You don't have kids. You're not even married, what do you know about being a mother and wife anyway?'

'More than you, it sounds like.'

The two women scowled at each other from across the table and Annie exchanged glances with Caz. They'd discussed Marcus and his lack of responsibility between themselves, but they'd never said anything to Sally about it. Maybe they should have done but she could be defensive and they hadn't wanted to pry into her private life if she didn't want to talk about it. On this occasion, however, the shots had clearly made Laura a bit too loose lipped.

'I'm going for a wee,' Caz announced loudly, breaking the awkward silence.

Annie grabbed her bag. 'I'll come with you.'

They scuttled away, relieved to escape the tension at the table. Left to their own devices for a while, hopefully Sally and Laura would clear the air. Either that or one would have decked the other by the time they returned. In the loos, Annie and Caz crammed themselves into one cubicle, just like they'd done on nights out many moons ago. Caz sat down on the toilet and looked up at Annie with an inebriated grin.

'I'm so made up for you, An. About the baby. I really am.'

'Cheers mate.'

'I'm worried about you too though.'

'Why?'

'All that stuff with your mum. You're being so brave about it, but it must be hard.'

'I'm fine, honestly.'

'I love you, Annie, you know that, right?'

'Of course I do, you big lush.'

'I just want you to know that I'm here for you, okay?'

'What's brought on this sudden rush of emotion? Other than tequila?'

Caz stood up, zipped up her jeans, and shuffled aside for Annie to take her place. 'I've just been thinking about you a lot recently. The prospect of childbirth is terrifying enough as it is, without having what happened to your mum hanging over you.'

'Don't worry about me.' Annie put her hand on her heart and said mock-solemnly, 'I put my faith in the miracle of medicine.'

'Joke around all you want, Annie, but at some point it's going to hit you like a shit-ton of bricks and I just want you to know that I'm here for you. And not just for the pregnancy but for after the baby's born too. It's really hard being a new mum.'

'You seem to be doing a pretty good job of it.'

'What you see on the outside isn't the same as what's happening behind closed doors. You don't see the tears, the exhaustion, the guilt. All I'm saying is that it's going to be harder than you think it is. And there are going to be days when you really wished your mum was there with you.'

'Well, this is a fun conversation, isn't it?'

'I'm not trying to bring you down, Annie, I just worry.'

'Well don't. Anyway, I've got Gabe, haven't I?'

Caz nodded. 'Gabe's a good one. He'll be a wonderful dad. Not like Marcus the knob.'

'Keep your voice down,' Annie whispered, horrified in case Sally was outside, listening.

'Well, he is a knob though, isn't he?' Caz said, making no effort to be quiet. 'And I love Sally, you know I do, but she needs to put her foot down more. She lets him walk all over her.'

Annie was inclined to agree but the reality was that she had no idea what it was like to be a mother, and how this might impact her relationship with Gabe. Would she be a control freak like Sally or more laissez-faire like Caz? Would Gabe be a hands-on dad, like she imagined him to be, or would he soon be disappearing off to play golf at every opportunity to avoid changing a nappy? It seemed unlikely; Gabe hated golf. As Annie stood up from the toilet, Caz threw herself at her without warning, hugging her tightly and nearly sending her toppling back down on to the loo again. 'I love you,' she said again.

'Come on,' Annie said, laughing. 'Let's get back out there.'

By the time they returned to the table, Sally and Laura had kissed and made up over another shot of tequila and were talking about Laura's younger boyfriend, or her 'man-child', as Sally called him. Annie hung around for another half an hour before making her excuses.

'Sorry ladies but the party's over for me,' she said, grabbing her jacket. 'Enjoy the rest of your evening.'

Laughing off their protestations, she kissed them goodbye and made her way outside. It was still warm and the streets were crowded. There were people everywhere, chatting in groups, waiting for friends or dashing to make trains or late dinner reservations. As she walked towards the Tube station, Annie pulled her phone out of her bag and saw that she had a missed call and a voicemail from her dad. She put the phone to her ear and listened to his message.

'Hi love, it's me. I finally heard back from our old GP in Northampton. I'm afraid they don't have Mum's records anymore; it was too long ago. Apparently, they only keep them for ten years. Sorry Annie, I know you wanted more information. Give me a call when you get this.'

Annie was disappointed. She had another midwife's appointment in a couple of days, and she'd been hoping to have some answers. A thought hit her, out of the blue. *Do they really destroy records after ten years? Could this be a cover-up? Or have I been watching too many ITV conspiracy dramas?*

It took her by surprise because she had never questioned what happened to her mum before. But now, after years of taking the scant information she had been given at face value, a seed had been planted in her mind and it was starting to grow. She wanted to know more. But how?

She knew so little about her mum that she wasn't sure where to begin. All she had to remember her by were her dad's stories and a couple of grainy photographs. How much had changed; these days your life was splashed all over the internet for the world to see but her mum had practically disappeared without a trace. They had moved away from Northampton soon after she died because Annie's dad had wanted them to have a fresh start and Annie had never been back to the city where she was born. It was as though her life had started in Hertford and everything before that didn't exist. She couldn't blame her dad for wanting to put it all behind him but now she felt frustrated that he hadn't held on to more of her mum in some way. Surely, he would have known that at some point, Annie would start asking questions. Yet they had only known each other for three months when her mum became pregnant, and nine months later she was dead. *Not much time to make memories*, Annie thought. *At least not without a smartphone.*

She looked at the time. It was nearly ten-thirty, too late to call her dad back now. It would have to wait until the morning. Her phone pinged with a message from Gabe.

Hey babe, how's it going? Having fun? Xx

She replied to say that she was on the way home, pocketed her phone and continued walking towards the station.

At least they had an exciting morning ahead. She and Gabe were going to view what she now thought of as *their* house. Lil had insisted on accompanying them so that it was all above board, and it was strange, knowing that she was going as a buyer rather than an agent. Gabe's parents had already agreed to give them the additional money they needed for the deposit and they had met with a broker who was arranging their mortgage application. Everything was happening so quickly that she could hardly believe it. Just a few months ago, she and Gabe were coming to terms with the fact that there may be no children in their future. Now here she was, pregnant and viewing houses for sale. Two such important milestones in her life. Yet, instead of looking to the future, she found herself thinking about the past more and more.

She reached the Tube station and paused outside to look around one last time. There were people as far as the eye could see, each one with their own life, their own hope, joy and sorrow. She was just one tiny little dot in a huge sea of humanity. A statistic. Just like her mum had been. With a final glance across the crowded concourse, she made her way inside.

The next morning she woke up to discover a message on her phone from Caz, which had been sent at 2.43am. Reaching for her glasses on the bedside table, she peered sleepily at the phone.

Oh my God. You missed the drama! We ended up going to a salsa club and Sally disappeared off with some hot Cuban guy. We think she's run away! Poor Marcus the Sharkus. Drunk. Love you xxxxxxx

'Blimey,' she said.

'What's up?' Gabe asked, rousing himself from sleep.

She showed him the message.

'I've met Sally several times and that seems highly unlikely,' he said, frowning.

'Knowing Sally, she probably cornered the poor bloke in a quiet spot somewhere so that she could talk to him about secondary school catchment areas and eleven-plus exams.'

'I hope they all got home okay.'

'I'm sure they did. Anyway, are you excited about the viewing this morning?'

Gabe stretched sleepily. 'Yeah. But I'm serious about looking at other properties too, Annie. I know you've got your heart set on this one, I'm not daft, but we're not going to be hasty and buy the first house we see, okay?'

'You forget that I do this for a living. This is literally, like, the thousandth house I've seen.'

'You know what I mean.'

'I do. But seriously, this is a good opportunity. I never thought we'd be able to afford something like this, I still can't believe that we can.'

'We don't know that yet. The seller would have to agree to an offer, and we need to work out how much we'd have to spend on the house to modernise it too.'

'I know, I know.'

'So, we're agreed right? We're not going to do something stupid like buy this house without looking at other properties first, okay?'

'Agreed.'

Two hours later, as they stood in the damp, smelly kitchen, Gabe turned to Annie and said, 'I think we should buy this house without looking at other properties first.'

'I know, right?' she replied, grinning at him.

'You could extend here,' he said, pointing at a wall. 'Then we'd have an awesome open-plan kitchen and living room. We could have bifold patio doors here.'

'That's a great idea,' she said, deciding not to tell him that she had already worked all of this out weeks ago, when she first saw the house. She turned to Lil, who was looking at Gabe like an indulgent parent. Like most ladies of a certain age, Lil had a soft spot for him.

'What do you think, Lil?' Gabe asked her.

'I think it's a good opportunity. It has huge potential and it's a lovely neighbourhood. It's a big undertaking though and with a baby on the way, it's a lot to take on. It's imperative that you do your sums and think very carefully about it before you make an offer.'

Gabe nodded thoughtfully and looked at Annie. 'She's right,' he said. 'It's a big project.'

'We can do it, Gabe, I know we can.'

They laughed at each other, delirious. 'Shall we do it then? Shall we make an offer?' he asked.

Lil looked exasperated. 'What did I *just* say?' she reprimanded him.

'Oh come on, Lil. Life's short. Sometimes you've got to take risks,' Gabe said.

'As a sales negotiator, I should be putting pressure on you right now, telling you that the house is in demand and that you need to act quickly. But as your friend, I urge you to talk it over, sleep on it. And if you want to put an offer in, we can do it on Monday morning. Okay?'

They both nodded reluctantly, knowing that she was right. 'Thanks for the viewing, Lil,' Annie said as they made their way out of the house.

'I have to admit, it was a little strange, showing you two troublemakers around a house. But it was kind of nice too,' Lil replied. 'Anyway, are you planning on doing *any* work today, Annie?'

'Of course,' Annie said, giving Gabe a kiss goodbye. 'I've got my first viewing in Burleigh Gardens at ten. See you back at the office later.'

As she showed people around their potential new homes, she couldn't stop daydreaming about hers. She knew that Lil was showing other people around it that weekend and she was fearful that someone would beat her to it and put in an offer they couldn't match. By the time she got back to the office she was practically bursting to know how Lil had got on. But she was nowhere to be seen and Brian had left for the day so she couldn't even distract herself by winding him up. She spent the next hour writing up her notes and waiting for Lil to arrive, until finally she gave up, locked the office and began to make her way home. On her way, she called her dad.

'Hi love, is everything okay?'

'Yes, it's fine, Dad, I just wondered if you were free for me to pop round for cup of tea?'

'Now?'

'Yep, now.'

'I'd love to see you but it's a long way to come for a cup of tea. Are you sure you're okay?'

'I'm peachy. What's wrong with a daughter wanting to have tea with her dad?'

'Nothing at all.'

'Right you are, I'll be over in an hour or so.'

She hung up and picked up the pace. She wanted to talk to her dad about the house but, more than anything, she was eager to ask some more questions about her mum. He had always been happy to talk about her, telling Annie stories whenever she asked; about how they met, how they got together.

He had told her that her mum was working in a nightclub and he had taken one look at her mixing cocktails behind the bar and had known she was the one for him. He sat on a stool and waited for hours until she finished work so that he could walk her home. The next day, he took her out for fish and chips on the beach and from that moment on they were inseparable. Two lost souls, he always said, brought together by love. A few months later, Eve found out she was pregnant and they got engaged. Mike, who was working as a teacher, got a job at a school in Northampton and they relocated. Almost a year to the day that they met, Annie was born and Eve died. No room in the world for both of them, it seemed.

After that, the stories always moved on to Mike getting to grips with being a single dad, heart-warming tales of learning how to change a nappy or of dancing to Aerosmith with Annie in his arms late at night, when she was fussy and wouldn't sleep. Of him wearing a fairy princess outfit on a trip to the park because three-year-old Annie had dressed him that morning and insisted that he didn't take it off all day. Of him crying one afternoon during a visit to the hairdresser because he couldn't braid Annie's hair properly for school, until the owner took pity on him and spent hours showing him how to do it.

Their family album was crammed full of such precious moments, snapshots of time preserved forever, but there were few records of the events that led up to them. Annie's own pregnancy had triggered new, unanswered questions and she could only hope that her dad would be able to answer some of them for her.

When she got home, Gabe was on the sofa playing a computer game, a cold beer on the table beside him. She stuck her head around the door.

'Hey, I've decided to pop over to Dad's for a bit,' she said.

'Want some company?' he asked, his eyes glued to the computer screen.

'No, you're all right, I'll be home for dinner, but I might be a bit later, okay?'

'No worries, have fun.'

She blew him a kiss and made her way back downstairs to the car. The Saturday afternoon traffic was light, and she reached her dad's house in no time. By the time she had parked and climbed out of the car, he was at the door waiting for her.

'Hi love,' he said, giving her a hug.

'Hey dad. Is Val home?'

'No, she's on a flower-arranging course today so it's just the two of us.'

'Lovely,' Annie said, pleased. She rarely got her father to herself these days.

She took her shoes off and curled up on the sofa waiting for him to make the tea. She was oddly nervous and she wasn't sure why. As soon as he sat down opposite her, she started telling him about the house first, and all their plans for it if their offer was accepted, warming up to what she really wanted to talk about, the true purpose of her impromptu visit.

Finally, she got to the point. 'I wanted to ask about Mum, if that's okay,' she said.

'Sure,' he replied.

'Starting with what happened on the day she died.'

Her dad shifted in his seat. With a stab of guilt, she realised she was making him uncomfortable by bringing it up again, but it was something that she needed to do.

'Okay,' he said. There was a long silence until eventually he started talking. 'Everyone said it should be an easy labour. Your mum was young and healthy. But you didn't want to come out, Annie. You were all snug as a bug in your mum's tummy and staying put. Time was ticking by, so they decided to induce the labour, for your own safety.'

Annie nodded at him to continue.

'From the start it was a difficult labour. It felt like it was going on forever. I think it was about forty-two hours. Your mum was amazing, she was a Trojan, but by the end of it she was so tired. She hadn't slept for so long and she was in a lot of pain. You can't imagine it, Annie.'

He looked mortified as he realised that in a few months' time Annie would be doing a lot more than imagining it. 'So sorry, Annie, that was careless of me.'

'It's okay.'

'Anyway, eventually you arrived and, my goodness, you were the most beautiful little thing I'd ever seen. They checked you over and then passed you to Mum. She was so proud, Annie. I've never seen her that happy. I was the same, I thought I was going to explode with joy.'

He paused, took a sip of tea. 'Your mum was looking pale but I assumed she was just exhausted. I mean, who could blame her after all that? I asked to hold you and when she passed you to me, I could see that her arms were shaking as though it was a huge effort. It was then that I noticed the midwife standing at the end of the bed and I remember thinking that she looked worried.'

He looked at Annie, as though he didn't want to continue.

'Go on,' she said.

'After that it was a flurry of activity – doctors rushing in, people crowding around your mum. I was clutching on to you, wondering what on earth was happening. I thought once the baby was born that was it, nothing to worry about anymore. But I was wrong. After that, everything's a blur. They bustled me out of the room and I paced the corridors with you in my arms. I think that was the moment when I realised that something had gone terribly wrong.'

Mike looked down, clutching his tea with both hands. 'They took me to a room and gave me some milk in a bottle to see if you were hungry. And that's where I was, giving you your first feed, when the doctor came in to see me.'

'And what did they say had happened, exactly?'

'They said she had a massive post-partum haemorrhage. She lost so much blood her body went into shock and they did everything they could. Then they started talking about how it was more common after inductions and difficult labours and so on, but by then I was barely listening.'

'Do you remember anything else? Any more details at all?'

He shook his head. 'No. I'm sorry. But it was nearly thirty-five years ago and I was all over the place. It's possible they said more at the time, but it didn't register.'

'Was there ever any talk of negligence? Of suing the hospital?'

'No. It was just one of those things, Annie, which you pray will never happen to you, but tragically it did. I don't think it's helpful to even think like that, especially not now.'

'Sorry, Dad.' He was right, she was already digging up the past, there was no point in sinking the shovel in further. She changed tack. 'What happened after that?'

'You stayed in the hospital for a while, and then we went home. I learned very quickly how to be a parent.' He smiled. 'And the rest, as they say, is history.'

History indeed. But with gaps, like an old jigsaw puzzle that Annie used to play with as a child. At the time she didn't mind that there were a few pieces missing. Now she desperately wanted to find them and complete the puzzle.

'What about her family or friends? I know you told me that she was estranged from her parents but there must have been other people in her life?'

He shook his head sadly. 'There was one guy she used to work with, Barry, who she was close to when we lived in Brighton but he died in a car accident. It was awful, he was only twenty-three. Other than that, she didn't keep in touch with anyone when we moved to Northampton.'

'What about the funeral? Did anyone else come?'

'Annie, I don't know if I can talk about this anymore.' Mike was looking down at the floor, refusing to make eye contact. His reaction surprised Annie because he had never clammed up on her before. But she had never asked him these questions before either.

'I'm sorry Dad, have I upset you?'

When he finally looked up she saw pain in his eyes. 'Why are you asking all this now?'

Annie thought about it carefully before she answered. 'Becoming pregnant, knowing I'm going to be a mum, I think it's made me more curious about my own mum.'

'Oh love, I understand that. I'm so sorry your mum can't be here with you.'

Annie knew from the tremor in his voice just how much he meant it. 'And I want to know more about what happened to her on the day she died,' she continued. 'In six months' time, I'm going to be giving birth too and I feel like I need to know all the facts.'

'All you need to know, love, is that it's not going to happen to you.'

'But you don't know that do you, Dad? Not really.'

'Trust me, please.'

She dearly wanted to, but she wasn't a little girl anymore. She knew enough about the world to understand that bad things happened and that her father couldn't keep her safe from them.

'I've been doing some research about accessing someone's medical records after they've died,' she said. 'You were right that GP records are only held for ten years, but apparently hospital records can go back further. So, I was thinking that the hospital where I was born might have more information about what happened to her. You can apply to get the record in writing but apparently it's better if the executor or administrator of Mum's estate does it. Is that you?'

He nodded. 'Yes. We made a will when Mum got pregnant.'

'Will you look into it for me? Write to the hospital and see if they have records?'

He sighed. 'What else is there to know, love? I've told you everything.'

'Please, Dad? For me?'

He nodded. 'Of course, leave it with me.'

She smiled, relieved.

'Anyway,' Mike said, slapping his hands on his legs. 'Tell me more about this house then.'

Annie took the bait, knowing that she had probed her dad enough for one sitting. It had clearly been distressing for him. She started filling him in on her dreams for the house and by the time she was ready to leave, they were back to their usual, easy patter.

He walked her to the car and hugged her on the pavement, holding on to her tightly, like he didn't want to let her go. 'I love you so much, Annie.'

'Ditto, Dad.'

'I'm sorry.'

Annie stood back. 'What for?'

He shrugged. 'Maybe I've made mistakes in the past, not done things right.'

'Don't be daft, you're the best dad in the world. It's my fault, I shouldn't have brought it all up.'

He looked at her for a long time. 'Annie, the past is the past. What matters now is your future. You, Gabe, and the baby. Don't forget that.'

'I won't.' She got into the car, waving as she drove off. At the end of the road, she glanced in her rear-view mirror. Her dad was still standing on the pavement, watching her.

CHAPTER SIX

Annie paced across the park, holding her phone in a vice-like grip. A watched pot never boiled, and a watched phone certainly never rang. Eventually she slipped it into her bag but she kept glancing down at it. She was working the late shift and wasn't due in the office until midday, but she was finding it increasingly difficult to kill time while she was waiting for *the* phone call.

They had put in an offer on the house on Monday, but the seller was away for a long weekend and he wasn't available to talk to Lil until the next day. It had been the longest wait of Annie's life, but she knew that Lil was planning to speak to him that morning and would call her as soon as she had news. She also knew, by eavesdropping on Lil's phone calls while pretending she was busy, that another couple had been interested in the house too. It wasn't fair on Lil to ask too many questions, so she had kept her head down, but it had been torture.

Her restless pacing was making her sweaty, so she sat down on a bench to cool down. She had a view of the playground below and she watched toddlers and preschoolers dash across the tarmac, racing towards swings and slides, while their parents hurried along behind them, ready to scoop them up if they fell.

It was a curious thing, she thought. She'd lived in the area for years and had been to the park countless times, but she had barely noticed the playground before, as though it was a secret world that only became visible once you had children. She'd probably be a regular there soon enough. As she watched a group of mums chatting, she felt a strange sensation in her stomach, like butterflies fluttering around. She put a hand to her tiny bump.

'Is that you, little one?' she asked. She'd felt the fluttering before but this time it was much stronger. For the first time she knew for certain that it was the baby moving, rather than indigestion or an overactive imagination, and it was thrilling. She closed her eyes and tried to concentrate, becoming so lost in her thoughts that when her phone finally rang she nearly jumped out of her skin. She scrabbled around in her bag to retrieve it before she missed the call.

'Hello?' she said, breathlessly.

'He's accepted your offer,' Lil said, wasting no time in getting down to business.

'Oh my God!' Annie put her hand to her mouth.

'Another couple put in an offer too, but they haven't sold their flat yet. When I told the buyer that you were chain free and ready to go, he decided to go with you but on the agreement that you can exchange and complete in six weeks. As you already know, the house belonged to his parents and he's keen to sell as soon as possible as he needs the cash to pay for their sheltered accommodation. What do you think?'

'We can do it,' Annie said confidently. 'We've got everything in place.'

'Are you sure you want to do this, Annie? It's a super house but it'll need a lot of work. And you've got plenty going on right now.'

'I know, Lil, but that house belongs to us, I can just feel it.'

'Okay. I'll revert to the owner and send you and Gabe a confirmation email now,' Lil said, sounding frightfully professional.

In the background, Annie could hear Brian squawking. 'Thanks, Lil. Thanks so much.'

'Don't thank me yet. You've got a long road ahead of you,' Lil said. Then she softened. 'But congratulations, Annie, I'm delighted for you both, I really am.'

As soon as Lil had hung up, Annie called Gabe, who answered immediately. Clearly she wasn't the only one who had been waiting anxiously for their phone to ring all morning.

'We got the house!' she told him triumphantly.

'Bloody hell!'

'I know!'

'This is it, Annie. This is the start of our new life as a family.'

'I *know!*'

'But the celebrations will have to wait as I'm in the middle of a meeting and my boss is giving me the evil eye as we speak. Gotta go.'

'Chat later,' Annie said, and hung up.

She put the phone in her bag and watched the playground again. The sky was starting to look ominous and parents were gathering up their offspring and preparing to leave before the rain came. Annie looked at the time. She still had another two hours before she was due at work, and she was desperate to talk to someone about the news. She sent Caz a message to see if she was free and her friend replied within a few minutes.

I am but I need to get out of this house! I'll come to you. Meet at that café near your work in half an hour?

Annie wrote back that she'd see her there, and then she put her phone away and stood up. Droplets of rain were starting to fall now, a prelude to the inevitable downpour, so she put her hood up and started making her way towards the café to wait for Caz.

'So what's the gossip with Sally?' Annie asked, looking at Caz from across the table. On her friend's lap, baby Harry was gurgling and giggling at her.

Caz rolled her eyes. 'All a fuss about nothing. She was outside with the Cuban dude smoking his dodgy cigarettes the whole time, which she thought was the height of rebellion of course, but it's not quite the same as snogging him up the wall in a dark alleyway.'

'So, what do you think about the whole Marcus thing?'

'Well, I wouldn't stand for it,' Caz said matter-of-factly. 'But there's no telling Sally so we just have to leave her to it. As long as she's happy, that's the main thing.'

'Is she, though, do you think? Happy?'

Caz looked thoughtful. 'She manages. And that's probably the best we can all hope for really.'

'You should frame that and sell it as an inspirational quote.'

Caz grinned. 'Anyway, what about you? What's happening?'

Annie filled her in on the house news first and then, after some whooping and clinking coffee cups, moved on to the conversation she'd had with her dad at the weekend.

'He seemed really uncomfortable,' she told Caz. 'It's the first time I've seen him like that. He's always been so happy to answer my questions about Mum before.'

'It's a bit weird for him though, isn't it? I mean, he lost his fiancée in childbirth and now you're up the duff. Perhaps it's worrying him more than he's letting on.'

'Maybe,' Annie admitted. 'I just think, though, if your partner died unexpectedly in hospital, wouldn't you have questions? Wouldn't you want some sort of inquiry?'

Caz shrugged. 'Things were different in the eighties. They weren't so litigious. And everyone knows that women die in childbirth all the time.' She clapped a hand to her mouth. 'I'm talking about in the past, and in other countries. You have nothing to worry about.'

'So everyone keeps saying.'

'But you don't think so?'

'I don't know, it's just playing on my mind, this event looming in my future, like a mountain. And the closer it gets to my due date, the bigger it becomes.'

'Have you spoken to the midwife about this?'

'To be honest, I see a different midwife at every appointment so it's hard to develop any sort of rapport. But I haven't mentioned it, no.'

Caz looked at her sternly. 'You need to bring this up at your next appointment. Don't sweep it under the carpet, it'll make it worse. You need to know what your options are, what can be done to reduce the risk and so on. If you feel in control, then it will help with the anxiety.'

'How do you mean?'

'Well, for example, if you tell them you're feeling anxious about the birth, which is understandable, they may suggest an elective caesarean.'

'I thought you had to bribe the entire maternity ward with gold to get one of those.'

'They do try to steer you towards a natural birth,' Caz admitted. 'But in your case, you have a valid reason to ask for an elective. Speak to the midwife, okay?'

'I will,' Annie promised.

'And as for your dad not wanting to talk about it, I think you just need to go gently on him. It's a strange time for him. Happy on one hand and sad on the other.'

'I know, I just wish that there was someone, *anyone*, I could talk to from Mum's past.'

'I understand. Let's hope your dad manages to get hold of those hospital records so you at least have some answers. Now, polish off that croissant so we can take a walk past this epic house I've been hearing all about before you have to go to work.'

By the time they finished eating the downpour had passed, and the late summer sun was already burning the clouds away. They strolled to the house and stood in front of it, staring at the overgrown garden and rusty gate. Even Harry, sitting in his buggy and kicking his chubby little legs around while he sucked on a rice cake, looked startled by it.

'What do you think?' Annie asked, nervously.

'It's amazing,' Caz said. 'Seriously, it's brilliant. I know it needs work but you can see the potential. And it's huge compared to the flat!'

'I know, right?'

'Look at you, all grown up,' Caz said, looking at her proudly.

'Check me out, I'm an adult,' Annie said.

'Are you sure you don't want to get married too, just for the craic?'

'I'm not sure how much of a craic it would be getting married when pregnant. Anyway, Gabe's not up for it *at all*.'

'But what about you?'

'I don't care, honestly,' Annie said. 'This is what I want. A wonderful partner, a family, a house to call our own. This is what matters.' She looked at her phone. 'Christ, I'd better get to work, I'm due there in three minutes. Are you all right to make your own way back to your car?'

She said her goodbyes to Caz and power-walked back towards the high street. When she entered the office, breathless, Lil and Brian both stood up and started clapping.

'Make way for the homeowner,' Brian declared, grandly.

'Well not quite yet,' Annie replied as she gave him a high five.

'As good as,' Brian told her. 'Congratulations, darling.'

'Cheers love.'

Lil shook her hand. 'You're my favourite customer,' she whispered into her ear.

'Thanks so much for your help, Lil, we really appreciate it.'

Lil gave her arm a squeeze and went back to her desk. Annie logged on and tried to focus on her work. She had viewings lined up for most of the afternoon and into the evening. But she couldn't help herself sneakily going on to Instagram and searching for accounts about house renovation projects. She followed a few and then forced her attention back to her diary.

After work, Gabe was waiting for her with a bottle of alcohol-free sparkling wine, which he popped as soon as she walked through the door.

'Booze-free wine?' Annie said, observing the bottle with distaste. 'You're really spoiling me!'

'Well, it's better than nothing,' Gabe said, pouring them both a glass. 'By the way, Mum and Dad are coming down this weekend.'

'So soon after their last visit?'

'Mum wants to see the house. I think she's checking on her investment.'

Annie was alarmed. 'But what if she hates it? What if she withdraws their financial support?'

Gabe put his arm around her. 'Don't worry, Mum would never do that. She knows it's up to us which property we buy. She just wants to have a look, that's all.'

Annie wasn't convinced. 'But she'll have an opinion, won't she?'

'Yes, she will,' Gabe agreed, 'but I'm sure she'll love it and if she doesn't now, she definitely will by the time we're finished with it.'

'Okay.' Annie couldn't wipe the frown from her face.

'Seriously An, stop fretting. It'll be fine.'

'I'm so incredibly grateful to your parents for helping us out, it's amazingly generous of them, but sometimes I wish we could have done it on our own.'

'You and me both,' Gabe agreed. 'But such is life. So, let's drink this delightful wine, which tastes like piss, and enjoy our evening.'

'Cheers to that.'

CHAPTER SEVEN

Annie tried not to wince as the cold gel hit her stomach. She smiled at the sonographer and then relaxed and turned her attention to the screen. It was her twenty-week scan, the moment when they would finally find out the sex of the baby, and she couldn't wait.

'Right,' the sonographer said. 'I'm going to check some things out first and this can take some time so I may go quiet for a while. At the end, I'll have a look and see if the baby is in the right position to determine the sex. Sometimes they don't like to play ball.'

He got to work, running the probe across Annie's rapidly expanding belly. Annie stared at the screen but, just like last time, she had no idea what she was looking at. It reminded her of those 3D pictures that were so popular in the nineties; some people saw the hidden image immediately and others couldn't make it out no matter how hard they tried. She gave up and turned to look at the sonographer instead, who was focused intently on something.

Then he spoke. 'I'm just going to pop out for a moment to get a colleague. I'll be back shortly.'

Panic-stricken, Annie looked at Gabe but he smiled back at her, oblivious. He hadn't understood what Annie had realised immediately: it wasn't standard protocol to call a colleague into a scan. Something was wrong. The sonographer slipped quietly out of the room before she could bombard him with questions and Annie grabbed Gabe's hand and gripped it tightly. 'Something's wrong,' she told him urgently.

Gabe frowned. 'What do you mean? How can you tell?' He looked at the screen, trying to see whatever it was that Annie was referring to.

'It's not that, Gabe, it's the sonographer. He's gone to get a doctor. They don't normally do that. He's seen something that has concerned him.'

Gabe's eyes widened. 'I didn't know that,' he said.

'Gabe, what if there's something seriously wrong?' Worst-case scenarios flooded Annie's mind. The baby had died. It had a rare syndrome, or a serious heart condition. It had a genetic condition. Her palms were sweaty. What if it wasn't about the baby at all? What if it was her? Had they seen something unusual during the ultrasound? Something that might make childbirth dangerous? Something that could kill her?

'What's taking so long?' Annie demanded. 'Why isn't he back yet?'

'Don't panic,' Gabe said, the tremor in his voice betraying the calmness of his words. 'You know how busy doctors are. He's probably just waiting for his colleague who's with other patients.'

Scenarios kept coming at her. What if the doctor told Annie that she could die giving birth? Would she risk it, to bring this miracle baby into the world? Or would she put her own safety first? And then another, new thought. Had her own mother been in this very position? Had they known all along that giving birth would be dangerous, but Mike had never told Annie because he didn't want her to blame herself for what happened?

Had her mum's death been all her fault?

She was escalating now, her thoughts spiralling out of control. Her heart was racing and she wiped her sweaty palms on her dress. *Please let the baby be okay. Please let me be okay.* Just as she thought she couldn't take it any longer, the sonographer returned with a woman.

'What's wrong?' Annie asked, before she had even had a chance to introduce herself.

'Annie, I'm Savi, and I'm a senior sonographer. My colleague has asked me to come and take a look at something for him. Is that okay?'

'What's wrong?' Annie repeated.

'Matt would just like a second opinion.'

Annie reluctantly lay back down on the bed so that Savi could put the probe on her belly again. She was gripping tightly on to Gabe's hand and she ignored his wince.

A few minutes passed, minutes that felt like hours. Then Savi nodded, satisfied, and looked at Annie and Gabe. 'Everything looks fine,' she said.

Annie stared blankly at her, unable to process her words. She had been gearing up for the worst and now her brain couldn't register that the news was good. 'Are you sure?' she asked.

'Yes. Sometimes a sonographer sees something during their routine checks that could potentially be a cause for concern, but it's not conclusive. So, they ask a colleague to come and take a look, for a second pair of eyes. I've had a good look and I'm happy with what I've seen today.'

'Are you sure?'

'Yes.'

'You scared the hell out of us!' Annie said, half laughing, half crying.

'I'm sorry we worried you, but rest assured that all looks well. Now, Matt told me that you want to know the sex of the baby. Is that right?'

Annie glanced at Gabe and they both nodded.

'Well, it just so happens that I'm getting a rather good view now,' Savi said, pointing to something on the screen.

Annie screwed up her nose. 'Sorry, but you're going to have to spell it out.'

'It's a boy,' Gabe said quietly. 'It's a boy,' he repeated, louder this time.

'Full marks to you,' Savi said. 'Well spotted.'

'We're having a boy?' Annie asked, in wonder.

Savi smiled. 'You're having a boy.'

Afterwards, they sat side by side on a bench outside the hospital entrance.

'Well, that was terrifying,' Gabe said.

'I thought that was it, Gabe.'

'Me too.'

'I'm sorry I scared you.'

He took her hand. 'It's fine.'

'But it's not fine, is it? I totally freaked out. I don't know what's wrong with me.'

'Don't be so hard on yourself, Annie, it was a difficult moment. We've wanted this baby for so long and it's understandable that you panicked when you thought there was something wrong.'

'I know, but even now that we've been told everything is

okay, I'm still thinking, *What if it's not okay? What if they missed something?*'

Gabe squeezed her hand. 'They didn't miss anything, okay? Our baby is safe and well.'

'But the first sonographer obviously saw something on the screen that worried him. What if he was right and the other one was wrong?'

Gabe shook his head vehemently. 'Savi was the more senior of the two, the other one looked like he'd only just left school. He's probably only been in the job for five minutes. If the senior sonographer says there's nothing to worry about, then there's nothing to worry about.'

'What about me though?'

'What do you mean?'

'This stuff with Mum. It's freaking me out big time.'

'But didn't your dad say there was nothing for you to worry about?'

'Yes. But he doesn't actually know that. He's not a doctor. He just wants to make me feel better.'

'No, he's not a doctor, but we've just been in a hospital full of them.'

'What's your point, Gabe?'

'My point is that you are in good hands. The midwives know about your family history, you have regular appointments. You're seeing the consultant next week to discuss your birth plan.'

'I know all that.'

'So, you need to try and relax, Annie, it's not good for you or the baby to be stressed out.'

Annie sighed and nodded.

Gabe stood up. 'I'm going to work from home for the rest of the day. I really don't fancy going into the office after all that. Do you have to go in, or can you chill out for a bit?'

'I've got to go in. We've got a meeting in an hour and then I've got viewings all afternoon.'

'Okay,' he said, reaching out a hand to pull her up. 'I'll drop you. We should call our parents first though and let them know that everything's okay.'

'Oh gosh, yes, you're right.'

But the truth was that although she should be relieved and elated, instead she was drained and struggling to stay positive. As she dialled, she looked over at Gabe who was already chatting to his mum, a huge smile on his face as he told her they were having a boy. It was as though he'd completely forgotten what had happened at the scan already. She envied him, his ability to let go so easily while she was still gripped by fear.

'Annie?' At the sound of her dad's voice, she forced herself to sound upbeat.

'Yes, it's me, Dad.'

'How did it go?'

'All good, it's a boy!'

'A boy! Wow!'

'Yeah.'

'Are you okay, love? You sound a little flat.'

She felt tears threatening again and tried to swallow them down. 'We had a bit of a scare at the scan, that's all. It turned out to be a false alarm.'

'What was it? Is the baby okay? Are you okay?'

'We're fine,' she said, her voice shaky. Gabe had finished his call and was watching her.

'Shall I come down? I can be there in an hour?'

'No, honestly, Dad. We're both safe and well. Ignore me, I'm just pregnant and hormonal.'

She heard him exhale. 'Okay, will we see you this weekend for lunch?'

'Absolutely, we're both looking forward to it.'

She rang off and followed Gabe to the car park.

'Shall we go out for dinner tonight?' he asked, taking her hand. 'Celebrate the good news?'

She didn't feel like celebrating, she just wanted to crawl into bed and go to sleep. 'Maybe another time, Gabe? I'm exhausted.'

'No problem, Netflix and chill it is.'

He dropped her outside the office, and she waved until his car disappeared round the corner. Then she went in, plastering a false smile on her face as she did.

'How did it go?' Lil asked.

'Good,' Annie replied, before bursting into tears.

Lil rushed over to her. 'What is it? What's happened?'

'Nothing's happened,' Annie said. 'I'm just being silly. I don't know what's wrong with me.'

'Sit down,' Lil instructed. 'Tell me everything.'

'I thought there was something seriously wrong for a while but there isn't. He's fine and I'm fine. I'm just all over the place because of these damn pregnancy hormones. I can't stop crying.'

'He?' Lil asked, raising an eyebrow.

'Yes, he.'

'That's wonderful, Annie. A little boy.'

'It *is* wonderful. That's why I can't figure out why I'm not more ecstatic.'

'It sounds like you've had a bit of a shock, that's all. Don't worry about it. You'll feel better once it's worn off. The main thing is that you and the baby are fine.'

Annie blew her nose and nodded, soothed by Lil's calming presence. 'Thanks Lil. I'm a bit embarrassed now. I don't think I've ever cried on the job before.'

'Don't worry about that, we all have our moments. Now you sit there while I make you a cup of tea. Brian will be back soon and then we'll have our team meeting, if you feel up to it?'

'Of course, Lil. I'm absolutely fine now, thank you.'

Before she moved away, Lil hesitated. 'I'm always here if you need me, Annie, okay? If you ever want to talk or anything. I know I'm your boss but I'm also your friend.'

'I do know that, thank you.'

Lil gave her shoulder a squeeze and disappeared to put the kettle on. Annie swivelled on her chair restlessly, trying to gather her thoughts. She was doing a full three-sixty when Brian arrived.

'Trying to make the baby dizzy?' he asked.

'Something like that.'

'Go on then, spill the beans.'

'It's a boy,' Annie said, grabbing the scan photo and showing it to him. By the time Lil returned, Brian was loudly declaring that the baby was going to be extremely well-endowed, just like his father. As Lil chastised him for being highly inappropriate in the workplace, Annie felt the knots inside her loosen. She smiled at Bri and Lil, slowly relaxing again. Perhaps it was all going to be okay after all. She picked up her notebook and made her way over to the meeting table. But no matter how hard she tried, she couldn't stop reliving the moment when the sonographer left the room, leaving her imagining the worst and not knowing what to do about it.

And she knew, despite Savi's reassurances afterwards that everything was as it should be, that she wouldn't be able to stop fretting for the next twenty weeks.

CHAPTER EIGHT

Annie woke with a start, her heart racing. She tried to move but her limbs were frozen. She was paralysed, her brain having woken up before the rest of her body. All she could do was lie still, trapped between dream and reality, until it caught up. Slowly she came round and remembered that she was at home in bed, safe and exactly where she should be.

Gabe was sleeping soundly beside her, one arm thrown above his head, undisturbed. Sunlight was peeking through the slats of the blinds in their bedroom and the birds were beginning their dawn chorus in the trees outside. She lay in bed for a few more minutes until she was fully awake, and then she got up quietly, put her dressing gown on and padded into the kitchen to put the kettle on.

She'd had a bad dream, a horribly vivid one, where she was in the hospital giving birth. She was screaming and Gabe was telling her to push. She shouted back that she was trying, but it wasn't working. Doctors crowded all around her like a rugby scrum, shouting in unison at her, telling her it was urgent. She pushed with all her might and then the pain stopped.

She looked down, excited to meet her son but there was

nothing there. No sound of crying. No baby. And then in the corner of the room, she noticed a figure, watching her. She squinted, trying to make out who it was, until the figure came into focus. It was her mother and she reached out a hand to Annie, beckoning her to come, and Annie had felt herself being pulled towards her against her will.

That was when she had woken up and she was struggling to make sense of it all. Was it just a silly, harmless dream, a culmination of her growing anxiety, or some sort of premonition about what was to come? Years ago, she had read an article in a magazine about a woman who said she could predict the future from her dreams. At the time, Annie had dismissed it as nonsense, yet the article had clearly resonated with her because now she couldn't stop thinking about it. She pictured the woman standing in the corner of the hospital room, whom she had known was her mother even though she had never properly met her. How had she known that? Was it instinct or had her mind based the image on the only two photos she had of her mum?

Annie went into the living room and pulled the old red-and-gold family album from the bookcase. She had looked at it many times before, but not for a long time. Sipping her tea, she opened the album and flicked through it, gazing at old photographs of her as a baby. There were dozens of them; Annie lying on a playmat, kicking her legs. Annie crawling. Annie learning to walk. Annie clutching onto a teddy bear. There were some of Annie with her dad, awkward selfies or photos taken by friends or kind passers-by. Finally, she reached the photos she had been looking for, of her mum, right at the back. They weren't great quality, taken before digital cameras and smartphones allowed people to snap away until they got the perfect picture. They had both been taken at the same time. Her mum was obviously pregnant and was sitting on a sea wall, looking at the camera, a smile playing on her lips. She was petite and slim, and her long dark hair framed her pale face. Annie studied the photographs for a good few minutes.

Why were there only two photos of her mum but so many of Annie? She had asked her dad before, and he told her that he didn't own a camera until she was born. Were there other photos out there? Framed pictures of a younger version of her mother still hanging on the wall of her parents' house, a shrine to the child who left home and never returned? Or did they erase her from their lives, the wayward daughter who they no longer associated with? What had happened between them that Eve had wanted to cut all ties to her family?

She closed the album, knowing that she wouldn't find the answers in there. Then she made herself another cup of tea and sat down at the small table overlooking the back garden. The garden belonged to the tenants of the ground-floor flat and their two young children often came out to play in the afternoons, a boy and a girl, clattering around on their ride-on toys. But it was far too early in the morning for children and the only inhabitants of the garden were the squirrels dashing this way and that, the birds high up in the trees, and a neighbour's ginger cat, carefully observing the activity and considering whether to hunt or head back inside for a nap.

In the summer months, when she was stuck at the top of the house, sweating in the stifling London heat that rose up through the floors, Annie envied the neighbours down below for having a garden. She couldn't believe that in a few hours, she and Gabe would have one of their own too. They had exchanged contracts a few days ago and all they needed was one email from their solicitor confirming that they had completed on the sale and the house would be theirs.

By this time next year their little boy would have arrived and although he would be too young for ride-on toys, Annie could lie out on the grass with him, under the shade of the apple tree, and watch the birds. But then she looked around the flat, with its higgledy-piggledy layout and draughty sash windows, and a wave of nostalgia came over her. It was time to move on but, still, this flat had been a happy home, full of memories and laughter. When they left, they would be starting again, creating fresh memories, and she hoped they would be happy ones too.

'A beautiful family home.' That's what Diana had said when she came to see the house for the first time. Annie had been pleasantly surprised because she had been gearing up for disaster. She had been terrified that Gabe's notoriously hard-to-please mother would disapprove and declare the property entirely unsuitable for her beloved son and grandchild. Although Gabe had assured Annie that the decision was theirs, she knew Diana held some sway and she couldn't bear the thought of losing the house when they were so close to getting it. However, when she showed Diana around it, putting on her best show and acting more like an estate agent than a daughter-in-law(ish), she or the house had clearly won Diana over.

'You've done well, Annabelle,' Diana had said as she stood in the middle of the living room surrounded by peeling wallpaper, a dusty fireplace and a faded, dirty carpet. 'With some TLC you can turn this into a beautiful family home. Congratulations.'

Annie had stared at her, momentarily speechless by this unexpected show of positivity, and Diana saw her gaze and rolled her eyes. 'I'm not a complete snob, you know.'

'I know, I'm so sorry, I didn't mean to offend...' Annie began.

Diana held up her hand to stop Annie's protestations. She looked wistful then, lost in her own thoughts, and then she turned to Annie with a smile. 'Actually, it reminds me of the first house that Bruce and I lived in. It was trouble from the start, with a leaky roof and terrible damp in the bathroom but oh, I adored that house. We lived there for six, maybe seven years and by then business was doing well and we could afford to upgrade.'

Diana paused. 'I will always remember that house so fondly. It was one of the happiest times in my life. You see, Annabelle, you don't need home gyms or swimming pools in the garden to be happy. Home is simply where the people you love the most are.'

But gyms and swimming pools help, Annie thought, thinking of Diana's current, sprawling house. Then a different image of Diana formed in her mind, one of a young woman raising three children single-handedly while her husband was out working all hours to get a business off the ground so that he could provide for his family. She imagined Diana painting walls and trying to remove stubborn damp while a baby cried in the background. It hadn't always been fancy houses and housekeepers, she realised, and it made her warm to Diana.

'Come upstairs,' Annie said. 'I'll show you which room will be yours when you come to stay.'

'About that,' Diana replied. 'I came on a bit too strong. Bruce told me off afterwards. I'm sure you don't want me cluttering up your house; you and Gabriel need to find your own feet.'

By now Annie was so disconcerted that she began to wonder if someone had taken the real Diana and replaced her with an imposter. 'Actually, I think I'll be grateful for the support. I will literally have no idea what I'm doing, it's a bit terrifying really.'

'None of us do when we become mothers. We learn on the job. If I can be of any help then of course I would be delighted but I certainly don't need my own room.'

'Come and check it out, nonetheless.'

Since "le grand tour", as Diana had called it, something had shifted between them. There was a softening at the edges of their relationship, a considerateness that hadn't been there before. They had started texting each other instead of using Gabe as the middleman. Diana had sent her some magazines in the post about babies and interiors that she thought Annie might like. The ceasefire had been short-lived, though, because a few days ago Diana had called Gabe, demanding to know why they wouldn't just consider a simple registry office wedding so that at least the baby wasn't born out of wedlock. She had then sent him a link to an online photo album of his ex, who had got married the previous weekend. Gabe had laughed at his mother's audacity and then gone off to make dinner, whereas Annie had obsessed over the photos, looking at the beautiful bride and wondering if she would ever be as good as her, or good enough for Diana.

But a wedding was the last thing on Annie's mind. They had builders and decorators lined up to get working on the new house as soon as they had the keys. They had decided to stay on in the flat for a few more weeks while the bulk of the work was carried out so they didn't have to live in a building site but there was so much to do and so many decisions to be made. And that was on top of getting ready for the baby and making sure they had all the things they would need before he arrived: pram, cot, blankets, baby bath, nappies, to name a few.

The previous evening, they had been to visit her dad for dinner and when they were leaving, he had slipped an envelope into her hand.

'What's this?' she asked in surprise. Her first thought was that it was her mum's medical records and her heart soared in anticipation.

'Open it later, love,' he said quietly.

She had done, in the car on the way home, and discovered a

cheque written out to her. She had immediately called him. 'Dad, what's the moolah for?'

'It's just a little something to help you and Gabe buy some things for the house and the baby. It's nothing really, I'm sorry I can't contribute like Diana and Bruce have.'

Annie's heart had broken for her dad. She hadn't even considered how he felt about Gabe's parents' financial contribution and the fact that he was unable to do the same.

'You didn't have to do that,' she told him.

'It's nothing,' he said again, sounding embarrassed.

'It's everything. And by the way, have I mentioned that you're going to be an awesome granddad?'

'Once or twice,' he said with a chuckle.

'There we are then.'

Annie had clutched the cheque all the way home, touched by her dad's gesture, and had gone to bed with a smile on her face. But just a few hours later, the nightmare had woken her up and now, on what was supposed to be an exciting day, it was all she could think about. Giving up on the idea of going back to bed, she headed into the bathroom for a shower instead, trying to wash away the dream, to cleanse herself of dark thoughts, so she could enjoy the day ahead.

They were tucking into a pizza when they finally got the confirmation. They had taken the day off work and had spent most of the morning feeling restless and trying to distract themselves from checking their emails every three minutes. Eventually they decided to go out for a walk and some lunch to keep themselves busy and Annie's phone pinged just as their food arrived.

'Ooh, I've got an email,' Annie said, opening it as quickly as her fingers would allow. She scanned the message. 'It's done,' she declared. 'We can pick up the keys whenever we like.'

They both stood up and started shrieking at each other, oblivious to the other lunchtime diners who were staring at them curiously over their garlic bread.

'We did it, Gabe!' Annie said.

'Christ, we really did.'

'Shall we sack off dessert and go pick up the keys?'

'Hell yeah.'

They scoffed down their pizza as quickly as they could and made their way to the office. When they arrived, Lil and Brian were both dealing with clients, so they hovered in the doorway. It was a surreal moment for Annie, who was so used to being the agent and not the client that she wasn't sure what to do with herself. She fidgeted with her hands and tried not to look nervous. After what felt like hours, the clients left and Lil came over to shake Annie and Gabe's hands.

'I imagine you're here for the keys?' she said, looking at Brian, who nodded and went into the back room before emerging again with a cake.

'Congratulations,' they shouted in unison and Lil stood up and clapped as Brian put the cake down on the table. In the middle of it, below the words 'New Home' was a set of keys.

'Wow, cheers Lil and Bri, you're the best,' Annie said, grinning.

'We *really* are,' Brian replied, as he started cutting the cake into pieces. 'Now tuck into some of this delicious cake, courtesy of Ian, and then be on your way to your new palace, so that you can take loads of photos for Instagram and make all your mates jealous.'

When they arrived at the house, someone had already put up balloons and a congratulations banner across the doorway. Gabe and Annie stood, hand in hand, and looked at it.

'Brian and Lil's work?' Gabe asked.

'Must have been.'

'Shall we go in then?'

'I think we probably should.'

Annie started to make her way towards the front door, but Gabe stopped her. 'Hang on a minute, I know we're not married but I have to carry you across the threshold.'

'Gabe, I'm five months pregnant.'

'Ah, don't worry, it'll be fine.'

And with that, he picked her up, tried his best not to wince, and staggered towards the front door, while she laughed at him. *Time for a new start,* she thought. *New memories. A new family album.*

'Wait,' she cried. 'Let's get a selfie!'

'Annie, I love you but I think my back's about to go.'

'Two seconds.'

She fished out her phone and held it above them, taking a snap of her in Gabe's arms, by the front door. And then, giggling, they made their way inside.

CHAPTER NINE

A few weeks later Annie was back in the new house, this time with her hands on her hips and a furious expression on her face, wondering where the bloody hell the builders had disappeared to. She was about to call and give them a piece of her mind when her phone rang.

'Hello?' she said distractedly, realising that they had most likely knocked off early and gone to the pub for Friday afternoon drinks. Which was delightful for them, but not so delightful for Annie and Gabe, whose house was still very much in a state of disarray.

'It's me.'

'Oh, hi Dad.'

She loved her father, but she wasn't in the mood to chat. She and Gabe had to move out of their flat the following weekend and as she looked around at the chaos, dirt and mess in the house, she strongly suspected that it wouldn't be ready in time. Everyone had warned her that work always took longer than estimated, but she had clung on to the hope that in their case, it would all work out okay. She kicked herself for being so naïve and tried to decide which was the lesser of two evils: moving into a building site or shacking up with her dad and Val for a few weeks.

'I'm afraid I've hit a dead end with Mum's medical records. I got a letter from the hospital today to say that they don't have them anymore either. It was all too long ago. I'm sorry.'

Given the afternoon she'd had, Annie didn't think her heart could sink any further, but now it was hurtling to the deep south. She had been pinning her hopes on this line of enquiry, hoping that it would finally give her the answers that she craved. Now she was bitterly disappointed.

'Did the letter say whether we could try anything else?'

'I'm afraid not.'

'So that's the end of it then? Forget all about it, like it never happened?' She was being narky, but she couldn't hide her disappointment. Part of her was angry with her dad too. Why didn't he know more? Why didn't he try harder?

'I know you're disappointed love, I really am sorry.'

'I have to go, I'm in the middle of something.'

She hung up, trying to justify her stand-offish behaviour to herself, but the guilt niggled. She shouldn't have taken it out on her dad, she'd have to call him back later to apologise. She was just tired and ratty. She couldn't remember the last time she'd had a proper night's sleep, not just because her growing bump was making it harder to find a comfortable position, but because of the nightmares that had become a regular occurrence. They were always the same and she would wake up in a state and lie awake for hours afterwards, trying to calm herself down, thinking about what it all meant. That, combined with the many other millions of things whirling around her head, didn't make for a peaceful night's slumber.

She was beginning to feel the effects now, an irritability that she couldn't shake off, but she didn't know what to do about it. In the past she would have popped an over-the-counter sleeping pill to take the edge off, but that wasn't an option during pregnancy. And despite her promise to Caz that she'd talk to the midwife about her anxiety, she still hadn't done it. She didn't know what was stopping her, whether it was a fear of being judged or an inability to verbalise what she was feeling but burying her head in the sand was her preferred option.

With a final, disgruntled look around the kitchen, she let herself out of the house, eager to get back to the flat and have a moan to Gabe. He was far more relaxed about things than she was, and his calm reassurance was just what she needed to hear. He would make her feel better, she was sure of it. She hurried back up the hill towards the flat and was home in less than ten minutes, letting herself in through the front door and slamming it behind her.

'Hi honey, I'm home!' she called.

There was no response and she wondered if Gabe, who had said he was working from home, had gone to the office after all. She walked into the living room and started when she saw him sitting on the sofa. He was staring vacantly into the distance with a glum expression.

'Are you okay?' she asked, shrugging off her jacket.

'Not really.'

'What's happened?'

'I've been told that I'm at risk of redundancy.'

Annie gasped. 'Are you serious? Why?'

'Restructure,' Gabe said simply, offering no more information.

'Oh my God, Gabe.'

'I know.'

'We've just bought a bloody house!'

'I know.'

'And I'm going on maternity leave in a couple of months!'

'I know all of this, Annie.'

She sat down next to him and took his hand. 'You're right, I'm sorry.' She tried a different approach, telling him what he needed to hear. 'Look, I know this is unexpected, but we'll make it work, okay? Let's not panic. Maybe you won't even be made redundant.'

'They're getting rid of the whole team. They're going to outsource all their design work. It's not their fault, business is slow, so they've got to make cuts. I'm as good as gone.'

'You'll find another job easily. A talent like you? Anyone would be lucky to have you.'

He didn't crack a smile. 'At least we're moving out of the flat next week. There's no way we can justify paying both rent and mortgage anymore. And we've got hardly any savings left.'

'But you'll get a redundancy package, right?'

'I've been doing some research and I reckon I'll get a week for every year I've been working there, which means ten weeks' pay. I mean, I gave my all to that goddam place for a decade and that's all I get.'

He thumped the coffee table with a closed fist, making Annie jump. She had never seen him this angry and dejected before. 'Gabe, calm down, it'll be okay.'

'But what if it's not? I mean, we're having a baby, we've just bought a house, I'm meant to be providing for my family and I can't even do that. What kind of man am I? I'm a failure.'

'Okay, well firstly, we're not living in Victorian times. It's both of our responsibilities to provide for our family. We're a team, okay? Secondly, you're an extremely talented guy and you'll get another job quickly, I just know it.'

He looked at her with the most hopeless expression she had ever seen. 'What if I don't?'

It didn't bear thinking about. Even if she went back to work and Gabe looked after the baby, her salary alone wouldn't be enough to cover the costs. Could they really be at risk of losing the house so soon after getting it? After putting weeks of blood, sweat and tears into making it liveable again? She squeezed his hand, looked him squarely in the eye and said, 'You will.'

But in bed that evening she lay awake, fretting. After tossing and turning for a while, Gabe eventually drifted off but she had no such joy. Her thoughts were in overdrive, flitting between Gabe's redundancy, all the work that still needed doing to the house, their depleted savings accounts, irrational worries over whether the baby was moving enough (he was), and the elephant in the room, her impending birthing experience. *One thing at a time*, she told herself.

Would Diana and Bruce step in and support them financially if things got bad? She knew it would be a bittersweet pill for Gabe to swallow, especially as he already felt like a failure, but surely it was better than losing the house? However, she didn't know how much money they had available to give. They were well off, but their income wasn't infinite. Bruce was retired and they had three children to think of. And Annie's dad would want to help but he couldn't afford it.

Giving up on sleep, she got up and went to the kitchen to get a glass of water. Gabe didn't stir as she left, and she envied his ability to sleep so soundly, even in the face of a crisis. As she sat down, she felt the baby wriggling. He was always more active at night.

'Hey fellow, are you ready to party now?' she said to her bump. He kicked in reply.

She loved it when he moved, knowing that he was growing bigger and stronger every day. The weeks, which had gone slowly in her early pregnancy, were now flying by, bringing her ever closer to the day when she would finally meet him. She should be full of joy and anticipation. She should be glowing. Instead, she sat alone in the dark, lost in even darker thoughts, haunted by her past and now worried about what lay ahead in the future too.

'Dad, can I have a root around in the attic after dinner?'

Annie's dad looked up in surprise. 'What for?'

'I thought there might be some old paperwork or letters or something. About Mum.'

He frowned as he chewed on one of Val's roast potatoes, dripping in oil and irresistible. 'I don't think there's anything like that, love. I threw a lot of stuff out when we left Northampton and the rest went when Val and I moved here.'

'I remember seeing some old boxes that went straight into the attic when you moved in though. There might be something in them.'

He was hesitant. 'I don't think you should be going up there in your condition.'

'It's okay, it's just a ladder. Anyway, Gabe can help.' Annie looked at Gabe who shrugged. He'd been subdued all week, ever since he heard the news about his redundancy. She had been doubling down on the positivity, trying to keep them both upbeat, but it was taking its toll on her too and she was physically and emotionally exhausted.

'How about I bring some boxes down for you?' her dad suggested. 'Then you can look through them in the comfort of the living room.'

'I want to go up there myself, Dad.'

Her dad glanced at Val, possibly for backup, but she only shot him a look which Annie read as, *Don't look at me – I always thought your daughter was strange.* Eventually he shrugged.

'Fine, okay. But please be careful, for goodness' sake.'

Annie was triumphant. This was it, she could feel it. So far, she'd hit nothing but dead ends but perhaps this would finally lead to some answers that would help her learn more about her mum.

She was on her feet before Gabe had even finished chewing his last potato. He looked at her with a sort of weary resignation and she smiled at him, trying to make him complicit in her adventure, but he just looked away and followed her up the stairs. *Am I being selfish,* she thought, *making this all about me when I should be focusing on Gabe?* But the attic was tantalisingly close now and she was being drawn to it, unable to resist.

Gabe reached up to open the hatch, pulling down the ladder.

'I'll go up first and check everything's sound,' he said, climbing up and turning on the light when he reached the top. After a minute he stuck his head back down. 'Come on up.'

She made her ascent, slowly and carefully. When she reached the top, she looked back down the hatch and saw her dad on the landing, staring up at her. She gave him a little wave and then turned away, looking around the attic until she spotted the boxes, stacked in a corner.

'Those are the ones,' she said to Gabe, and he went over and unstacked them for her, ripping the brown tape off and opening the flaps. The boxes smelt musty and damp. She sat on the attic floor and started pulling things out of the first one. There were all sorts of things in there; old photos of her dad as a boy; his graduation certificate; reams of boring paperwork. After rifling through it all, she put everything back, pushed the box to one side and moved on to the next. This one contained old jumpers and scarfs, men's clothes which she presumed were her dad's. With rising disappointment, she discarded the box and tried the third. It was filled from top to bottom with stacks of books. She considered pulling them all out and flicking through them to look for old letters or photos trapped between the pages, but she was fast losing enthusiasm for her mission. Her earlier excitement had ebbed away, leaving her with the sinking feeling that she wasn't going to find anything in these old boxes after all.

The final one contained baby and children's clothes and toys. As Annie waded through the contents, vague memories from her childhood came back to her. A soft toy elephant that she'd cuddled to sleep every night for years. A T-shirt that she'd loved. Normally she would have enjoyed the trip down memory lane but all she felt now was disappointment. She was about to give up and put everything back in the box when she spotted something at the bottom, a little wooden box that she hadn't noticed at first. She reached down and pulled it out. It was a jewellery box, with a pale, smooth cover and gold embossed on the top. Annie couldn't remember having seen it before, but it must have been hers. She tried to picture her childhood bedroom, her beloved dressing table, but she was sure that the box had never been on it. Slowly she undid the clasp and opened it up, gasping with pleasure when her ears filled with a tinkling musical melody and the little ballerina inside started pirouetting on her needle.

'It still works,' she said, turning to Gabe, who was on the other side of the attic, looking through Mike's old records.

'Was it yours?'

'It must have been. I don't remember it though.'

'Listen, Annie, I'm busting for a wee. Will you be okay on your own for a few minutes?'

Annie nodded and looked back at the contents of the jewellery box, pulling them out one by one; a tiny hospital bracelet with her name on which she must have worn when she was first born, a ringlet of hair taped to a postcard and then, underneath them, a handful of photos.

The first one was of a tiny baby, presumably Annie, taken in hospital. She must have only just been born and she was wrapped up in a blanket, fast asleep. There was someone's hand resting on her tummy. It was a sweet photo and she couldn't work out why it was hidden away in a box rather than in the family album.

The next photo was of her mum. She was sitting on a sofa, wearing jeans and a jumper, and she was staring at the camera with a look that clearly said, *Why are you taking my photo right now?* But what disturbed Annie the most was her mother's black eye. With her long, dark hair tied back in a ponytail there was no hiding how nasty the injury was. Annie stared at the photo, trying to make sense of it. What on earth happened to her? And was it just the injured eye that made her look so unhappy? She looked thinner too, gaunt almost, so different to the glowing pregnant woman in the photos that Annie had of her, that it was hard to believe it was the same person. She wondered if it was taken before her parents had met or after.

She flicked to the next photo. This one was of her mum and dad walking on the beach. Whoever took the photo had been far away and Annie had to squint to see her parents' faces in detail. She frowned. It wasn't her dad after all. It was a man she didn't recognise. He had his arm around her mum and they were both laughing. She looked younger, happier.

'Found anything?' Gabe asked, as his head popped up through the hatch.

Annie nodded mutely, still trying to grasp the meaning of the photos. Gabe sidled up to her and looked at them over her shoulder.

'Is that your mum?' he asked.

'Yes, I'm pretty sure it is.'

'You don't look like her. What happened to her eye in that photo?'

'I have no idea.'

Gabe looked around the attic. 'Did you find anything else?'

'No, nothing.'

'Sorry, I know you were hoping for something more. Are you all done up here now?'

She nodded, slipping the photos into her pocket. In a way Gabe was right, she hadn't found what she had been looking for, but she had stumbled upon something else that she sensed was important. She just wasn't sure why yet. She put everything else back in the box and stood up.

'Let's go,' she said.

She made her way slowly back down the ladder, stumbling slightly on the last step before regaining her balance and landing on the floor with a thud. Her dad thundered up the stairs.

'What happened? Are you okay?' he asked, his voice full of concern.

'Yes, don't worry, just a slight loss of balance, no harm done.'

'I knew you shouldn't have gone up there...' he began but she cut him off.

'Dad, I'm fine. But I do need to talk to you.'

She pulled the photos out of her pocket and handed them to him. 'What are these?'

He took them from her and flicked through them, the colour draining from his face. 'Where did you find these?' he asked.

'In an old jewellery box.'

'I had no idea we had these.'

'What happened to her eye?'

His face temporarily clouded over and then cleared again, and he looked at Annie with a smile that didn't reach his eyes. 'When she was pregnant, your mother insisted on climbing up the stepladder to put some decorations up and I told her that it wasn't a good idea in her condition. She lost her balance and fell. Fortunately, you were both okay but it gave us quite a shock. Now you can understand why I was so worried about you going up into that damn loft.'

'She doesn't look pregnant. There's no bump.'

'It was in the early stages, before she was showing.'

'And what about the next photo? Who is that man with Mum?'

Mike squinted as he looked at the photo. 'Oh yes, I remember him. That's Barry, the guy I told you about, Mum's friend from the club where she worked when we first met. He was a nice bloke actually. He died in a car accident, such a terrible thing.'

Annie took the photos back from him and pointed to the one of her as a baby. 'When was this photo taken?'

'Oh yes. Look at you! You must have only been a few hours old.'

'Was I in the hospital?'

'Yes, I think you were.'

'Whose hand is it on my tummy?'

'Oh gosh, I can't remember. Probably a nurse.'

They were all reasonable explanations but one, pressing question remained.

'Why haven't I seen these photos before?'

'I didn't even know they existed, love. I mean, I must have done at some point but I had totally forgotten about them until now.'

'All these years, I thought we only had two photos of Mum, and these were up in the attic the whole time. What else have you been hiding from me?' Anger was bubbling up inside her now with such force that she couldn't keep it down.

'Annie!' He looked devastated. 'This is a misunderstanding, that's all. Look, let's all go and have a cup of tea, okay? We can talk.'

They made their way downstairs, the tension between them almost palpable. As they walked into the kitchen Val looked up, a jug of cream in one hand and a cake knife in the other.

'Dessert is ready,' she said, observing their stormy faces. 'What on earth has happened?'

'Annie's found some old photos of Eve,' he told her.

'Are you okay, Mike? You look very pale. Sit down. You must think about your blood pressure.' Val was fussing around him, as though Annie didn't even exist.

'I'm fine, Val,' he said, looking at Annie, clearly hurt.

Val turned to Annie. 'So what has happened? Why have you two fallen out?'

'I don't understand why these photos were kept hidden from me all this time,' Annie said.

'Hidden or simply lost in an old box in the attic?' Val retorted, with her hands on her hips.

Val was probably right but Annie was irked that she was getting involved in family business. The stress of the past few weeks was also catching up with her. 'Look, Val, keep out of it, this is between me and Dad.'

'If it involves your dad, it involves me. You've clearly upset him.'

'What about me? Doesn't it matter if I'm upset?'

She had never argued with Val before but now she was squaring up to her, preparing for battle, years of suppressed feelings and forced politeness rising to the surface.

Gabe stepped in between them. 'Okay, we all need to calm down. This has got out of hand.'

Annie started to argue but Gabe put his hand on her arm. 'Leave it, Annie.'

Furious at everyone, she reached for her coat, hanging over the back of a kitchen chair. 'I think we should go.'

'Annie, please,' her dad began, but she ignored him,

shrugging on her coat and making her way towards the front door. She wanted to get away from that stupid, chintzy house, away from Val with her sickly desserts and frilly tablecloths, away from her dad who she so rarely rowed with that even though she was angry with him she still couldn't bear to see his forlorn expression.

It wasn't until she was in the car driving home in silence, Gabe sitting beside her in the passenger seat, equally silent, that she realised she had forgotten to bring the photos with her.

CHAPTER TEN

The next morning, she woke up with a sense of dread, like she had a hangover despite having not touched a drop of alcohol. She groaned and turned over to Gabe, who was already awake, sitting up in bed and looking at job listings on his phone. She was shattered, having tossed and turned for most of the night, before finally nodding off just before dawn.

'How are you?' Gabe asked, looking down at her.

'Regretting my life choices.'

'What do you mean?'

She sat up, next to Gabe. 'I think I overreacted last night. I feel bad about getting cross with Dad now; I think I really upset him. It was just a shock, finding those photographs.'

'Just call him and apologise, he'll be fine.'

'I will,' she said. If only it was that easy. 'And sorry if I took it out on you too.'

'Don't worry about it.'

'Anyway, how are you? Seen any good jobs advertised?'

'A few,' he said. 'I'm going to apply to some today.'

'Good.'

They sat for a few minutes, in a silence more

companionable than the night before, both scrolling on their phones, Annie gently stroking her bump with one hand.

'Gabe,' she said suddenly. 'I've been thinking about signing up to one of those websites. You know, the ones where you can work out your family tree.'

'How come?'

'I was thinking maybe I could track down Mum's parents or something.'

'Didn't she fall out with them big time as a teenager and cut them out of her life?'

'Yes.'

'So, what are you hoping to gain from it?'

'I don't know. They raised her; perhaps they can tell me more about her. Dad barely knew her for any time at all, really. I'd just like to know a bit more, that's all. Is that so wrong?'

Gabe frowned. 'No, but you're opening up a can of worms. Your mum was estranged from her family. For all we know, they may not even be aware that she died. If you rock up on their doorstep now, not only are you throwing their lives into turmoil but there's a chance they'll be hostile towards you and how will that make you feel? I can't see it ending well.'

'Maybe not,' Annie conceded.

'They may not even be alive anymore.'

Annie nodded, deflated.

'And anyway,' he continued, 'you're emotional enough as it is.'

She seized on him immediately. 'What do you mean by that?'

'You're not yourself, Annie. You're not sleeping, you're tearful all the time. I know that being pregnant is an emotional rollercoaster but it's starting to feel like more than that.'

'Well in my defence, there's a lot going on. We're moving

house, you're at risk of redundancy. Oh, and did you forget that I'm pregnant and my mother died in childbirth?'

'I'm not having a go, Annie,' Gabe said. 'This is what I'm talking about. You're so touchy and sensitive. I'm just worried about you, that's all.'

'Well, I'm worried about you,' she retorted. 'You've been miserable ever since you found out about your job. I know how stressed you must feel but we have to stay positive, Gabe. There are loads of jobs out there, I know you'll get another one soon.'

'It's easy for you to say that; you're not the one sending out job applications and getting nothing back. You're not the one who still has to go to work every day and pretend that everything is fine while knowing that the axe could fall at any moment. You're not the one who is forty-two years old and still reliant on their own parents to buy them a house.'

'Gabe, we've been over this a million times. Do you know how many people I've sold a house to who have had financial support from their parents? Dozens. Hundreds. It's just how it goes. Don't fixate on it, just appreciate that we're lucky to have the option and move on.'

'You don't understand.'

'I'm trying, I really am.'

They looked at each other, so caught up in their own issues that they were finding it increasingly hard to offer much comfort. Annie reached a conciliatory hand out and stroked his arm. 'Let's not fall out, Gabe. Stronger together, right?'

'Stronger together,' he agreed. But he didn't smile.

'Anyway, it's Sunday and the sun's shining for once. What shall we do today?'

'Job hunting,' Gabe replied, glumly.

'Not *all* day, give yourself a break. How about a nice long walk and a pub lunch?'

'I think we need to lay off the pub lunches for a while,

Annie. And takeaways for that matter. And pretty much everything else that's fun in our life.'

'Well, walking doesn't cost a thing, so how about we chuck on our hiking boots and take an urban stroll around north London?'

'I'm sorry, I'm not in the mood. I just want to get logged onto my laptop and start applying for jobs. Being proactive makes me feel better about the whole situation.'

'Sure,' she said. 'I think I'll pop over to the new house and do a spot of gardening, seeing as the weather's nice. If you fancy a break, come down and join me?'

'Maybe,' he said, and then added, 'Just stay off any stepladders, all right?'

She saluted him, trying to lift the mood. 'Yes, sir.'

By the time she'd showered and dressed, Gabe was ensconced at the table with his laptop, a steaming cup of coffee beside him. She kissed the top of his head and slipped quietly out of the house. It was brisk outside, but the glare of the morning sun cheered her up. She considered calling her dad to apologise but she wasn't quite ready to have that conversation yet, so instead, she tucked her hands into her pockets and crunched through the leaves towards the house.

She was furiously pulling out weeds, enjoying taking her stress out on the garden, when her phone pinged. She grabbed it, hoping it was from Gabe to say he was on the way, but it was Caz.

Big news! Sally has kicked Marcus the Sharkus out!!! Xxx

Stunned, she hastily thrashed out a reply.

Nooooooooooo. Are you free to chat?

Caz called her within seconds.

'What's happened?' Annie demanded.

'I don't know the full story; you know what Sal's like. But apparently she told him to do one until he was willing to *be more present*.'

'Blimey.'

'Tell me about it. I didn't think our Sal had it in her.'

'The poor kids though.'

Caz scoffed. 'He's a loser and they're better off without him.'

'I'm not sure that's fair, Caz. Or true.'

'Maybe not but I've been up all night with a teething baby, I've got PMT and I think Noah's got tonsillitis, so I'm not feeling very charitable right now.'

'Ouch.' Annie winced. 'That sounds like the hat-trick from hell.'

'Yep. Anyway, how's you?'

Annie braced herself to tell Caz everything; about the photos, her dad's reaction, her uncharacteristic storming out of the house. But as she opened her mouth to speak, she heard a chorus of frantic crying in the background.

'Oh God, sorry, I've got to go,' Caz said. 'Both boys are wailing. Chat later.'

Annie put her phone away and sat on the broken garden step for a while, thinking about Sally and what she must be going through. With everything that had been going on recently, she hadn't made much of an effort to check in on Sally and find out how she was getting on. Was Caz right? Were she and the kids better off without Marcus? She'd grown up with one parent and she'd turned out okay. But that hadn't been a choice. She put her hands on her bump, thinking about her exchange with Gabe that morning and the row she'd had with her dad the previous evening. *I must do better*, she thought. *I must be better*.

As if on cue, the baby started kicking, and she smiled. 'Hey fella, nice to hear from you.'

He kicked again, sending a ripple across her stomach.

'Woah there, I know I put an extra sugar in my tea this morning but there's no need for circus tricks.'

As she chatted with her bump, she got the strange sensation that she was being watched. She looked around the garden but there was no one there except a pair of squirrels chasing each other around a tree trunk. Without warning, her hairs stood on end.

'Gabe?' she called, hoping that he would emerge from the house, waving. But there was no reply. She looked up at the house next door, scanning it until she saw a figure standing at one of the windows looking down at her. Her heart started pounding in her chest, her adrenaline kicking into gear. *It's the shadowy figure from my nightmares.*

The window flew open and a friendly, middle-aged woman stuck her head out and waved at her.

'Sorry to startle you, duck,' the woman called down. 'I was just dusting the cobwebs and I spotted you down there. You must be the new neighbour.'

Annie came hurtling back to reality, her adrenaline already realising that it was a false alarm and disappearing as quickly as it had arrived. She waved back at the woman and felt ridiculous for freaking out. *What the hell is wrong with me?* She put her hand up to her face to shield her eyes from the sun and called back, 'Hi, yes, that's right.'

'I'll be down in a jiffy!' the woman replied. She closed the window and appeared a couple of minutes later, peeking over the low fence from the garden next door.

'I'm Linda,' she said, thrusting a hand over the top of the fence for Annie to shake.

'Annie.'

'Congratulations,' Linda said, observing her bump. How many weeks?'

'Twenty-nine.'

'Ooh, not long to go then, duck. Is it your first?'

'Yep.'

'I've got five,' Linda said proudly. 'All grown up now, mind.'

'Five? Wow.' Annie thought that one sounded like hard enough work.

'I'm a childminder now,' Linda continued. 'If you ever need any help with your little one...'

'Good to know,' Annie said, already thinking about how handy that could be when she went back to work. She liked the look of Linda, with her kind face and cheery smile.

'I bet your mum can't wait to be a granny.'

It happened all the time, presumptions, which Annie usually corrected quickly without a second thought. This time, though, it stung. 'Actually, my mum's not around anymore.'

Linda looked crushed. 'Oh duck, I'm so sorry. I've put my big foot in it.'

'It's okay,' Annie said, smiling weakly at her. 'It's not your fault.'

'Come round,' Linda said. 'Come and have a cuppa and a biscuit, you look like you need it.'

Annie hesitated, trying to think of a reason to refuse before realising that there weren't any. And that she'd quite like the company. 'Thanks, I will,' she said.

She made her way back round to the front of the house, where Linda had already opened the door and was waiting for her. She ushered Annie in, showing her to the kitchen, where the heady aroma of something delicious baking hit her immediately.

'It smells amazing in here,' Annie said.

'Bread,' Linda replied. 'I bake it fresh for the kids.'

'Lucky kids.'

Linda set about making tea, adding extra sugar to Annie's mug and placing it on the table in front of her with a few cookies. 'If you don't mind me asking, what happened to your mum?'

'She died giving birth to me,' Annie said.

'Oh, duck.' Linda reached out and put a hand over hers. It was strangely comforting. She'd known this woman for less than ten minutes, but she already felt safe in her company.

'What about your dad? Are you close with him?'

'Very,' Annie said. 'Well, usually. We had a bit of a row last night.'

Linda shrugged. 'That's family for you. Where does your dad live?'

'Hertford, not far. He's really excited to be a granddad.'

'My Clive, bless his soul, he loved being a grandfather,' Linda said. 'I lost him six years ago. Cancer.'

'I'm so sorry,' Annie said.

'After he went, I felt so lost. That's when I started childminding. Having children in the house brought it back to life again. It brought me to life too. There's something about children; they have this wonderful power to make us feel joy again, to give us hope.'

'Tell that to my friend Caz. She's got two under three and they're turning her hair grey.'

'Well, it's not easy, not at first,' Linda said. 'Babies are hard work. But I'll be right next door if you ever need anything, okay?'

'Thanks,' Annie said gratefully. Her phone started ringing and she looked at Linda apologetically. 'Sorry, excuse me a second.'

She went out to the corridor and answered. 'Hey.'

It was Gabe. 'Where are you? I'm at the house.'

'I've popped next door to meet our new neighbour, Linda.'

'I was worried about you. I didn't know where you were.'

'Sorry, I'll be over in a second.'

She returned to the kitchen. 'I've got to go.'

'No problem, duck, you get on.'

She walked back round to the house to find Gabe pacing around, agitated.

'The builders are way behind schedule,' he said.

'I tried to warn you,' she replied.

'Why is nothing going right at the moment?'

'Oh Gabe.' She put her arms around him. 'Well, I have some good news. Our new neighbour is a childminder and she's lovely. We might have already found our childcare for when I go back to work.'

'If we can afford childcare.'

'Come on,' Annie said, trying to rally him. 'It's going to be okay.'

His shoulders sagged. 'Sorry I'm such a miserable old Scrooge.'

'Don't be sorry. You're under a lot of pressure.'

'Anyway, are you hungry?'

'Famished. Shall we go home and make some lunch?'

'Good idea.'

They walked home, both lost in their own thoughts. Gabe was probably thinking about CVs, covering letters and having it out with the builder on Monday morning. And Annie was thinking about her reaction to Linda in the window and why she had worked herself up into such a state. It was as if she'd seen a ghost, which was just plain stupid because ghosts weren't real. She thought about her nightmares, her mother in the corner, calling her. Then she shook her head, trying to physically remove the intrusive images from her mind. *Ghosts are not real.*

CHAPTER ELEVEN

Annie stood in the doorway of a hospital room. In front of her, a woman was on a bed, giving birth, and she was screaming. Annie wanted to help the woman but she was rooted to the spot, unable to move or speak. She sensed that she didn't belong there but she couldn't leave either, like she was trapped in an alternate world. She thought she was invisible to the woman but then she looked up and stared at her with terrified eyes, and Annie realised who it was. It was her mother and she had a black eye. 'Help me,' she said to Annie. 'Save me before it's too late.'

Annie woke with a start. She turned to see if she had disturbed Gabe, but he was snoring peacefully, having devoured the best part of a bottle of red wine the previous evening. She slipped out of bed and went into the kitchen to make herself a hot chocolate, craving the comfort it had brought her when her dad used to make it for her as a child. As she sat down on the sofa and took a few sips, the baby started wriggling around.

'You like hot chocolate, eh, little bean?' she said to her bump. He kicked his agreement.

'We should both be asleep right now,' she reminded him,

stroking her belly over her pyjamas. 'But no chance of that with you doing acrobatics at two in the morning.'

He kicked a few more times, causing ripples across her stomach. At least someone was in a good mood. After a few minutes, though, he went quiet. She waited for a while to see if he started up again, but he seemed to have fallen asleep after his short, sharp burst of energy. A wave of loneliness came over her. She missed his company, even if he wasn't the best conversationalist. Not wanting to be alone in the darkness anymore, she put her mug in the sink and crawled back into bed, cuddling up as closely to Gabe as her bump allowed. She eventually drifted off into a deep, dreamless sleep and woke to the sound of Gabe's alarm clock. Tired and groggy, she put a pillow over her head and tried to go back to sleep but a few minutes later she heard him place a cup of tea on her bedside table and felt him sit down on the bed next to her.

'I'm lying in,' she told him from under the pillow.

'Don't you have an eight thirty meeting on Mondays?'

'Fuckety-fuck,' Annie said, reluctantly ripping the pillow off her head and dragging herself up into a sitting position.

'Bad night's sleep again?' Gabe asked, handing her the tea.

'Afraid so. How are you doing?'

'Okay,' Gabe said. 'I'm not looking forward to going into work today. I just want it all over and done with now. I've checked out of that place already.'

'I don't blame you.'

'Don't forget to call your dad today, okay?'

'I will,' she promised. She watched as Gabe headed to the bathroom and then she grabbed her phone and checked Instagram. She'd posted a couple of photos of the new house the previous evening and she had thirty-two likes. She sipped her tea and scrolled through her feed, until she was awake enough to get up and dressed. As she was locking up the flat, her dad called. She considered letting it ring out but she knew she had to face him eventually.

'Hi, Dad.'

He didn't beat around the bush. 'I'm calling to say sorry. I honestly had no idea that I still had those old photos. It breaks my heart that I upset you like that.'

'I'm sorry too. I shouldn't have had a go.'

'If I've been acting a little strange, or reluctant to talk, it's because I've been thinking a lot about the past recently and it's not that easy for me to revisit.'

'I get that. But is there anything you're not telling me? Perhaps something that you didn't want me to know about as a child in case it upset me?'

After a few seconds, he said, 'No, Annie, there's nothing.'

'Are you sure because I'm a big girl now and I can take it. And to be honest, Dad, I'd really rather know the truth.'

When he spoke again, he sounded distant. 'We've all done things in the past that we regret. Some more than others.'

Why was he talking in riddles? 'What are you talking about, Dad?'

His tone changed, without warning. 'Annie, you need to stop pushing me on this. There's nothing to tell you, how many more times can I say it?'

'But Dad...'

'There's *nothing*.'

She sighed. 'Fine.'

'So, are we okay? You and me?'

'I guess so.' She was just about to ring off when she remembered something. 'Can I keep those photos? Of Mum?'

He hesitated for a split second. 'Sure, they'll be waiting for you next time you come over.'

'Thanks.'

'I love you so much, Annie, you know that, right?'

'Of course I do.'

'If there's ever anything I can do to help at all, well... I'm here, okay?'

'I know.'

Annie hung up. Perhaps she was being cruel, pushing her dad like she had. She'd been so fixated on her own need to know more that she hadn't considered the impact on him. Something still bothered her though. The black eye, the other man. Her dad had explanations for them all, but it didn't quite add up. There was more to it than he was telling her, she could feel it. But if he was keeping secrets from her then why? Who was it that he was trying to protect?

'Annie, if I have to tell you one more time to stop lifting boxes, I'm going to lose my mind,' Gabe said as he passed her on the garden path, heading back towards the car.

'Last one, I promise,' Annie called back, as she carried the box through the house, up the stairs and into what would be the nursery. Against all odds, the builders and decorators had finished in time and the room, like the rest of the house, sparkled with fresh paint and fitted carpets. The new radiators they'd had installed had been turned on full blast to warm up the house after months of lying empty and the brand-new bathroom gleamed. Annie stood in the room for a moment, breathing in the smell of new house, and sighed with satisfaction. Then she made her way back downstairs to see what she could do to help.

The removal men had already done most of the heavy lifting, but she and Gabe had brought over a few bits and bobs in the car. She started to make her way outside to grab some of it but she was intercepted by Gabe, who scowled at her. 'Back inside,' he ordered.

She turned around and made her way to the kitchen instead. There was plenty to do in here, so she began pulling crockery and cutlery from the boxes and washing them up. She was elbow-deep in suds when she heard someone calling from the open front door.

'Coo-eeeee,' Brian said, walking down the hallway and locating Annie in the kitchen.

'Hey Bri,' Annie said. 'Make yourself useful and unpack that box for me, will you?'

'Not until I've had a good nose around your new pad,' he replied. He disappeared again, returning a few minutes later. 'It's amazing, Annie. Well done.'

'There's still loads more to do.'

'Yeah, but you've made a good start.' He lowered his voice. 'How's Gabe?'

'He's okay. He's finally agreed terms with his current boss and he finishes on Friday. He's had a few calls with recruiters and applied for some jobs but nothing concrete so far.'

'Are you guys going to be okay for money?'

Annie shrugged as she rinsed a fork. 'I hope so.'

Brian put a hand on her shoulder. 'You need tea. Where's the kettle then?'

'Aren't you supposed to be working today?'

'I've got a gap between viewings.'

'That box over there,' Annie said, pointing. But I don't think we've got any milk.'

'Well, it's a good job I'm here then,' Brian said, reaching into his bag and pulling out a bottle of fresh milk, along with two huge Tupperware pots. 'Gifts from Ian. Lasagne and chilli.'

'Oh, he's a saint. Thank you so much.'

Brian located the kettle, filled it up and plugged it in, before diving back into the box to look for teabags. 'And how are *you* doing?'

'Glad to be in. A bit knackered though.'

'You look terrible if you don't mind me saying.'

'Thanks Bri, that's really cheered me up.'

'I thought pregnant women were supposed to glow.'

'So did I. Turns out it's a ruse to con women into making babies.'

'You need some sleep. You've got bags so big under your eyes that you could fit a week's worth of shopping into each one.'

'As much as I'm enjoying this pep talk, any chance we can talk about something else?'

'Sure,' Brian agreed. 'Are you still obsessing over your dead mother?'

'Brian!' Annie was outraged.

'All this stress, it's not good for you, honey. You need to relax. Maybe you should take some time off work. Go chill in a spa or something.'

'Don't you start; Lil's already been on about me having some time off too.'

'We care about you.'

'I know you do. But to be honest, being at work is the only place where I can forget about everything else going on. It's basically my version of a spa.'

'God help you, honey, if you think Lillian Gold Estate Agents is a spa.'

'You know what I mean. Everything else is so up in the air, it's my only constant.'

'Well, Ian has a theory anyway, about those photos you found of your ma.'

'Go on.'

'The strange man, the black eye. What if she had a violent ex who your dad rescued her from?'

'But if that's what happened, why wouldn't he just tell me that?'

'Because he wants to protect you from the horrible truth. He doesn't want to tarnish your memory of your mum.'

'But I have no memory, that's the problem.'

'Look, all I know is that your dad loves you and that if – and it's a big if – he's keeping secrets, it's for your own good. I think you've got to trust him and let it go.'

'You're probably right.'

'And in the meantime, take a load off.'

Annie looked around at the chaos. 'Easier said than done, mate.'

'Lil's talking about bringing someone else in. Not just for your maternity leave but permanently. Things are picking up again.'

'That's good news, let's hope they're as good at making a brew as you are.'

'They're never going to fill the Annie-shaped hole that you're leaving behind though.'

'I'm not going forever, Bri, just for maternity leave. And it's still weeks away.'

'Ten weeks,' he said huffily. 'Not that I'm counting.'

Later that evening, as Annie and Gabe waited for Ian's homemade lasagne to heat up, Annie created a nursery mood board on Pinterest. But her mind was elsewhere as she considered her conversation with Brian. It seemed like everyone was telling her to let the past go, to look forward not back. So why couldn't she do it?

The timer pinged and Annie stood up, still lost in her thoughts. She opened the oven and reached in to pick up the lasagne and then screamed and recoiled, dropping the dish with a clatter. Looking down at her hands in horror, she realised that she'd forgotten to put oven gloves on. The shock was quickly replaced with searing pain, which burned through her flesh. Gabe looked up from his phone, saw her expression and almost flew across the table in his attempt to get to her as quickly as possible.

'Put them under water,' he instructed, pulling her towards the kitchen sink and turning on the tap so that the tepid water poured over her reddening hands. 'What happened?'

'I don't know,' she spluttered. 'I was preoccupied, and I just shoved my hands into the oven and picked up the lasagne without even thinking about it.'

'We should go to hospital.'

'No, don't be silly, it'll be fine.'

But he was already on his phone, googling *burns and pregnancy*. 'It says here that you should always seek medical attention if you burn yourself while pregnant,' he said.

'Gabe, I'm not going to hospital for a small oven burn, okay? Look, my hands are fine.'

He wasn't convinced. 'Well, I'm going to run to the chemist for some antiseptic cream at least. And if it gets any worse, we're going straight to A & E.'

'Fine,' she said.

He grabbed his keys and headed for the door. 'Will you be okay on your own?'

'Of course, I'm not a child,' she told him. He nodded and left.

Annie looked down at her hands. How could she have been so careless? What if she'd hurt the baby? She closed her eyes and prayed for him to kick or move – any sign that he was okay.

'I'm so sorry little man,' she said to her bump. 'Mummy's an idiot.'

The baby kicked in response to her voice, a gentle chastisement, like he was saying, *It's okay, but don't do it again.*

By the time Gabe returned, breathless from running and armed with enough medical supplies to bandage her from head to toe, she had calmed down.

'How are they looking?' he asked, putting the cream, bandages and paracetamol on the table and examining her hands.

'Not bad.'

'They haven't blistered. Keep them under the tap for another five minutes or so and then we'll put some cream on them. Do you want any paracetamol?'

'Gabe,' she said, ignoring his question. 'I've been thinking about Mum.'

'Right.'

'I keep getting this weird feeling that there's something Dad's not telling me. I can't let it go. Ian has this theory, do you want to hear it?'

Gabe's expression hardened. 'Not really. We've been over this a thousand times. Your dad's told you everything he knows and I don't know what more you want him to say. You've got to let this go, Annie. No wonder you're having silly accidents.'

'What do you mean?'

'You're so distracted. It was only a matter of time before something like this happened.'

Annie didn't know whether to be apologetic or apoplectic. 'Are you saying I'm a liability?'

'Yes, you are at the moment. And it's not just me who's noticed.'

'What's that supposed to mean?'

'Your dad called me. He's worried about you. And Brian had a quiet word on his way out earlier. Everyone can see that you're not yourself.'

'Oh, so you're all talking about me now, are you?'

'We're just worried about you, Annie. You've got a lot on your plate.'

'I'm doing my best, Gabe.'

His expression softened. 'I know you are. But please, let me help you. Starting with these hands.'

'Fine,' she said, tetchily. She let him dry her hands carefully and apply cream to them and then she sat back down at the kitchen table while he finished dishing up the now soggy lasagne. They ate in silence and when they were finished, Gabe washed up while Annie went upstairs to use the bathroom. She sat on the side of the bath, feeling about as bereft as she had ever felt. Then she closed her eyes as the first tear fell. Once she'd started, she couldn't stop. She cried for the stupid argument she'd had with Gabe which had ruined their first night in their dream home. She cried for her burned hands. She cried for her careless stupidity which could have hurt the baby. She cried for Gabe's redundancy. And, finally, she cried for a mother she had never known but who she now craved with every bone in her body.

CHAPTER TWELVE

Annie looked out of the window at the snow, falling gently to the ground and coating the parked cars with a sprinkling of white dust. She wondered if it would settle. It was only five days to go until Christmas and the prospect of it being a white one was sending the bookies into a frenzy.

'Annie, your blood pressure is a bit high.'

Annie turned to Louise, the midwife she'd met at her first appointment. She'd seen a series of different midwives since then and had been pleased to have Louise again.

'Have you been experiencing any headaches? Disturbed vision? Pain at the top of your tummy? Have you noticed any changes in the baby's movements?'

Annie shook her head in response to each question.

'Have you had high blood pressure before?'

'No, never.'

Louise observed her carefully. 'How are you doing, Annie?'

She laughed. 'Well, we've just bought, redecorated and moved into a new house in a matter of weeks and now my boyfriend has been made redundant. So, not great.'

'Oh gosh, that does sound a lot to take on. Last time we met,

I remember you told me that your mum had died in childbirth. Did you ever find out any more about that?'

'No. I tried, I really did, but it was so long ago that there's no paper trail anymore. My dad couldn't tell me any more about it either. Could this be related to my blood pressure?'

'Probably not. Stress can cause blood pressure to rise temporarily and from what you've told me, you've been up against it. I do, however, want to keep a close eye on it so I'm going to suggest that you come in more frequently to be monitored.'

'Why?' Annie's hand flew to her bump.

'High blood pressure can sometimes be serious in pregnancy. Currently you have mild hypertension, so there's no immediate cause for concern, but we need to stay on top of it. In the meantime, I want you to look after yourself. Slow down a bit, where you can. Make sure you take gentle exercise, like walking or swimming. Try some relaxation techniques.'

'I will,' Annie promised, thinking that was the end of it. But Louise continued watching her, as though she was trying to reach into her mind and see what she was thinking.

'Are you okay, Annie?' she asked. 'Is there anything you want to talk about?'

'I'm absolutely fine,' she replied brightly, giving Louise her best smile. 'Don't worry about me!'

Afterwards, she sat on what she now thought of as her usual bench outside the hospital. The snow seemed to have fizzled out already, over before it had even began. She wrapped her coat and scarf tightly around her and people-watched. It was the usual hospital crowd; visitors heading in with bunches of flowers or magazines tucked under their arms; nurses helping people in wheelchairs; the die-hard smokers huddling around the entrance, ignoring the no smoking signs.

Why hadn't she told Louise the truth? About her

nightmares, her insomnia and her escalating anxiety about the impending due date? Perhaps she could have helped. But the truth was that Annie could barely find the words to explain how she was feeling. Her emotions were so jumbled up inside her that they had wrapped themselves into a tight, impenetrable ball so that she no longer knew where one began and the other one ended. And what could Louise do, really? Magic the baby out of her without having to go through the act of childbirth? Find a secret vault that would provide Annie with all the answers to the questions she had about her mother?

Her bottom was beginning to freeze to the bench, and she could barely feel her hands, so she stood up and made her way back to the car. When she arrived at the office, Lil was there alone.

'How did it go?' she asked.

'Okay. I have high blood pressure,' Annie replied.

Lil frowned. 'That doesn't sound good.'

'It might not be as bad as it sounds. I just need to slow down a bit.'

'You should take some time off work.'

'We finish in a few days for Christmas anyway. I'll be fine until then.'

Lil stood up and walked over to Annie's desk. 'Your health is more important than work.'

'Don't you start, I've already had Gabe and the midwife on at me.'

'Well, I had some good news this morning. The new hire has just confirmed that he can start at the beginning of January, so we'll soon have an extra pair of hands.'

'That's great news. But I don't need any extra time off.'

'Well, take the rest of today at least. Do you have any viewings?'

'No, just follow-up calls.'

'Send me the details and I'll sort it out.'

Annie was about to protest but then she changed her mind. Maybe a few hours off would be a good idea after all. She could go for an afternoon swim; she couldn't remember the last time she'd been to the pool. And on the way home she could pop to the supermarket and buy some healthy food, seeing as she was under doctor's orders to look after herself better.

'Are you sure?' she asked Lil.

'Yes, I'm sure. Take tomorrow too, if you like.'

'I'll be back in the morning,' Annie said firmly, as she gathered her things. 'Thanks Lil.'

She walked home, wrapping her arms tightly around herself to keep warm against the winter chill, and was relieved when she finally reached the front door. A gush of warmth hit her as she opened it, and she sighed with pleasure. The house was starting to feel more and more like home every day. She took off her coat and shoes and headed into the kitchen to get a glass of water. As she was gazing out at the garden, which was still a tangled mess, her phone rang and she saw it was her dad, probably calling to confirm the arrangements for Christmas Day.

'Annie, I'm so sorry, something's happened,' he said when she answered.

'What is it? Are you okay?'

'Yes, I'm okay. It's just, we've lost the photos of Mum.'

'What do you mean lost them? They were just on your kitchen table.'

'I know but we think they got tangled up with some newspapers and magazines and thrown into the recycling. We've looked everywhere but they've vanished.'

Annie was instantly irritated, an emotion that was frighteningly easy to provoke these days. 'Well, that's very convenient.'

'What do you mean?'

'You didn't want me to find them in the first place and now they've mysteriously disappeared.'

'Oh Annie, this isn't a conspiracy theory, love. It was just a mistake. I'm sorry.'

'I bet Val's rubbing her hands together with glee.'

'What's this got to do with Val?' There was an edge to his voice now. Annie knew that she was going too far, pushing the wrong buttons, but she couldn't stop herself.

'Oh, come on, Dad. She likes to pretend that Mum never existed. So do you. It's like you've both erased her memory from the world entirely.'

'That's not true Annie...'

'Yes, it is!' Her voice was rising higher and higher now, she was on a roll and she couldn't stop herself even if she wanted to. 'If Gabe died, I would never do what you've done. I would make sure that our baby knew everything there was to know about him. I would show him photos, take him to see Gabe's family. His memory would live on forever.'

'That's not fair,' he insisted. 'I've always told you about your mum when you asked. But we never got the chance to make an awful lot of memories. That's not my fault.'

'Why didn't you try and contact her family when she died? Weren't you curious to know more about her? Where she came from? Didn't you want me to have some family?'

It was a conversation they'd had in the past, always amiably. But this time it was an argument.

'It's complicated, love.'

She seized on this. 'Why? *Why* is it complicated?'

There was a long pause. 'Annie, I've got to go, I'm sorry.'

He abruptly hung up, leaving Annie staring at her phone, wondering what had just happened.

A few minutes later the phone rang again. This time it was

Val, who rarely called. Against her better judgement, Annie decided to answer it.

'You've been upsetting your father and his blood pressure is very high at the moment,' she said.

'*My* blood pressure is high at the moment,' Annie bit back.

'You need to leave this alone, Annie.' It almost sounded like a threat.

'Why? What's it got to do with you?'

Val's tone softened. 'I know this is hard for you. For any child to lose a parent is just unfair, pure and simple. But your mother is long gone. Live in the moment, Annie, look to your future. Build a new family; you, Gabe and the baby.'

'And just forget about Mum, is that what you're saying?'

'No, that's not what I'm saying. Her memory is inside you. It always will be. But now *you* are going to be a mum and your son needs you. Focus on that, Annie. Let go of the past. Please.'

There was something about her tone that made it sound like she was pleading rather than asking.

'Do you know something?' Annie asked, suspicious.

Val sighed. 'All I know is that your father loves you very much and that he's heartbroken to see you getting upset like this. We both are.'

Annie sat down on the sofa. Suddenly she was exhausted. 'I've got to go, Val,' she said.

'Keep in touch, Annie.'

Annie threw her phone on to the table and lay down, resting her head on a cushion. The thought of swimming and a trip to the supermarket was a distant memory now. All she wanted to do was curl up and hide from everyone; the decorators who wanted invoices paid, Gabe with his enduring air of defeat, the midwife with her probing questions, her father with his half answers. She closed her eyes and, slowly, slipped into sleep.

When she woke, it was already dark outside. Groggy, she sat

up and checked her phone. She'd been asleep for three hours, a blissfully dreamless sleep. She rubbed her eyes and checked her messages – one from Caz and one from Gabe, who'd been for a job interview that afternoon. She read Gabe's first, eager to know how he had got on.

Total disaster, I wasn't what they were looking for and we all realised it after five minutes but had to stick it out for an incredibly painful forty-five minutes. Meeting James for a pint to drown my sorrows, won't be late. Xx

Poor Gabe. He really needed a win to give his confidence a boost. Annie had never seen him so downbeat before and despite telling him repeatedly not to take it personally, that he wasn't a failure, his melancholy hadn't shifted. She replied, sending commiserations, and telling him to enjoy his drink, and then read the message from Caz.

FML. Noah's got chickenpox and is in quarantine for the next five days and you can bet your arse that Harry will get it too. Plus, Sally's taken back Marcus the Sharkus. Sigh.

Grateful for a distraction and craving the sound of another person's voice, Annie decided to give Caz a ring. But the second that her friend picked up, sounding harassed and with the distinct sound of shrieking in the background, she knew there was no chance of a long, leisurely chat.

'Have I called at a bad time?'

'It's always a bad time in this madhouse. Don't worry about it. Are you okay?'

'Yeah, just fancied a chat.'

The screaming escalated and she heard Caz shouting at Noah to stop.

'Sorry,' she said to Annie. 'You'd think that having the pox would slow him down but apparently not. He's still a ball of energy and is currently using the baby as some sort of show jump.'

'No worries, so what's going on with Sally and Marcus?'

'*Noah*! If I have to tell you one more time to stop jumping over your brother, there'll be no iPad for a week,' Caz roared and then Annie heard a distinct thump as Caz's phone hit the deck. She waited for a moment or two to see if Caz picked it up again and then gave up and hung up. A few minutes later, she got a text message.

So sorry about that. That boy is driving me bonkers. You okay?

She typed out a quick reply.

Yeah fine, just fancied a chat. Can't wait to see you in a few days!

Annie and Caz always spent Christmas Eve night together; it had been their tradition since they were girls. This year they were both driving up to Hertford to stay with their families for a couple of nights and had arranged to meet for dinner in their favourite local pub.

But Caz's reply soon put an end to that.

Sorry, but looks like we won't be going to Hertford for Crimbo now because of this poxy pox. Reckon it's going to be a low-key affair this year, quarantining at home.

Annie's heart sank. Normally she looked forward to Christmas but with the ongoing tension between her and her father, she was dreading it this year. Seeing Caz was the only thing she'd been clinging on to. She looked around the living room, which seemed too big and empty with just her in it. She didn't want to be alone. As if on cue, her stomach rumbled, reminding her that she hadn't eaten in hours. She went into the kitchen, flicked on a light and opened the fridge to investigate her options before remembering that she was supposed to go to the shops. Unless she wanted dry cereal for dinner, which she very much did not, she'd have to order a takeaway. Then Gabe's words popped into her head, reminding her that they had to tighten their belts, followed by Louise's, telling her to look after herself better. Reluctantly, she was about to jump into the car and go to the supermarket, but then she had a better idea and called Brian.

'Fancy some company?' she asked when he answered.

'Sure,' he said. 'Ian's cooking pasta as we speak and there's more than enough. Everything okay?'

'Yep, Gabe's out and I'm not in the mood to be alone,' she told him.

'Well, come on over.'

She freshened up and grabbed her car keys. Brian and Ian lived about twenty minutes' drive away in Crouch End, a trendy suburb of north London. The rush hour traffic was still heavy and she crawled along, listening to festive songs on the radio, desperate to be in the warm, familiar comfort of Brian's gorgeous flat. The moment he opened the door and she inhaled the delicious smell of dinner coming from the kitchen, she felt better.

'Thanks for having me over,' she said, giving him a kiss on the cheek.

'No worries. What's your poison?'

'Have you got any herbal tea?'

'Honey, we're a gay couple. We have eleven different types of herbal tea.'

Annie laughed. 'You pick one for me.'

Brian returned a few minutes later with two mugs.

'What's on your mind?' he asked, cutting straight to the chase.

Annie told him about her appointment with the midwife and the row with her father. 'I feel like I'm constantly on edge, Brian, and now I'm terrified that my stress is harming the baby.'

'What does Gabe say about it?' Brian asked.

'I haven't told him about my blood pressure yet. He's got so much going on already, I don't want to stress him out more. He's not himself either but he won't talk to me about it. I feel like this pregnancy should be bringing us closer but we're actually drifting apart.'

'Oh, Annie. You and Gabe are the perfect couple. You've just got a lot of stuff on your plates but you'll sort it out, trust me.'

'I just don't understand what's happened to us. We've wanted this baby for so long, we've literally dreamed of this moment, and now we're both miserable. I mean I'm grateful and excited, don't get me wrong, I can't wait to be a mum, but I'm scared too. Bloody terrified.'

'I'm sure many parents-to-be are scared and you've got a whole load of family drama on top of that too. It's messing with you. Honestly, I think this all links back to your mum. Obviously it goes without saying that you're afraid of giving birth after what happened to her but it's more than that. You grew up without a mother, so you're worried you won't know how to be one.'

'Wow, you've just verbalised it way better than I ever could. But I think you're right, on both counts. I'm just not sure my dad and Gabe understand that.'

'So, talk to them, explain it. Give them a chance to understand. And in the meantime, take control of the situation. Speak to a professional about it; see what they say.'

'I did have an appointment with the consultant. She said that, given my family history and my anxiety about the birth, I could have an elective caesarean if I choose to. But that in itself carries a greater risk of haemorrhage. I just don't know what to do for the best.'

'Do whatever feels right in your gut.'

'That's the thing. I have no idea.'

'I don't know what to say. I'm the last person in the world to have any knowledge of vaginas.'

Annie snorted. 'Don't worry. I don't need your advice, just your listening ear. Thanks Bri, I really appreciate it.'

'You'll feel better when you make peace with your dad.'

'You're right and I want to, I really do. But I still feel like he's hiding something from me and I can't let it go. It's like he doesn't want me to know something and I don't know if he's trying to protect himself, my mum, or me.'

'And what's your evidence? Destroyed medical files and a bunch of lost photos?'

'I know, it sounds flimsy doesn't it? It would hardly stand up in court. It's just a feeling I have.'

'That you've never had in your life before, until now?'

'Okay, now you're making me sound like a total fruit loop.'

'You're not a fruit loop. I get where you're coming from. But I think you've trusted your dad up until this point. Maybe trust him now too.'

'Hmmm.'

'Look, from someone who has two emotionally unavailable parents, I say go home for Christmas, hug that dad of yours as tightly as you can and forget all about this. Because I promise you that having one parent who loves you is far better than none.'

'Oh Brian, I'm sorry,' Annie said. 'It must be hard for you at Christmastime.'

'It used to be,' Brian admitted. 'After I fell out with my folks, I spent the first few Christmases on my own, taking too many drugs or drinking myself into a stupor. Often both. But then I got a second chance.' He looked up at Ian who had drifted into the room and was now sitting on the back of the sofa, his hand resting on Brian's shoulder. Brian took it and gripped it tightly.

'Where are you two Christmassing this year?' Annie asked.

'We're off to Ian's folks in Scotland. I cannae wait. They're a right laugh.'

'I'm so glad you've finally found your people, Bri.'

'You've got your people too, Annie. Your dad. Gabe. Val the old gal. Me and Lil. Even Diana and that horny husband of hers.'

'Oh, don't get me started on them. They've already made us promise that we'll spend next Christmas, the baby's first, with them in Bristol. I haven't told Dad yet, he'll be gutted.'

'See, that's what I mean. You're in demand. You're loved. Don't forget that.'

Annie nodded. 'You're right, I'm sorry. I won't.' She raised her mug of tea into the air. 'Happy Christmas guys.'

Brian clinked her mug with his. 'Happy Christmas, honey.'

CHAPTER THIRTEEN

'Happy birthday, beautiful.'

Gabe sat down on the side of the bed and handed Annie a mug of tea. She sat up, disorientated from being woken from a deep sleep that she'd only just slipped into, and took the mug from him.

'Any exciting plans for the lady of leisure?'

Annie shook her head. Having a birthday in January had always been an anticlimax because everyone was partied out from the festive celebrations, but this year she didn't mind. She was hardly in the mood, or condition, to go clubbing. Still, she was beginning to wish that she'd made some plans as the prospect of a whole day on her own loomed ahead of her.

Christmas had come and gone in the blink of an eye. At the last minute, Annie had suggested that they spend Christmas Eve at home and drive up to see Mike and Val on Christmas Day instead of staying over. She told Gabe it was because Caz could no longer make their dinner but the real reason was that things were still not right with her dad and she just wasn't in the mood. Despite family issues playing on her mind, she had still been excited about waking up on Christmas Day in their new home, but Gabe had dampened her spirits.

'Don't spend too much money,' he had warned her. 'We can't afford it.'

'I know that, Gabe, I'm not off to Harrods with a platinum card, I just want to buy some decorations, a yummy Christmas Eve dinner from Asda and a present for the baby, okay?'

'Just don't go over the top.'

She had wanted to. She had googled beautiful babygros and eye-wateringly expensive artificial trees, but Gabe's voice haunted her, like one of Scrooge's ghosts. In the end they had dug out the tiny little fibre-optic tree that they had in the flat and put it in the bay window of their living room. She had stood there looking at it, thinking how sad and tiny it seemed, when Gabe came up behind her and put his arms around her.

'It will be different next year, I promise,' he said.

'It doesn't matter. It's only a silly tree.'

'I know you wanted something more, to mark the occasion.'

'What matters is that we're together in our very own home and that this little man in here,' she said, pointing to her tummy, 'is happy and healthy.'

Gabe had kissed the top of her head and drifted off to check his emails, but she had stood for a while longer, thinking of Christmases yet to come and hoping that they would be happy ones. She imagined their baby lying under the tree, kicking his legs. Their son, ripping open presents and looking up in delight while she and Gabe smiled down at him. Leaving a mince pie by the fireplace for Father Christmas and some carrots for his reindeers.

That night she had another nightmare. She gave birth but this time the baby was born safe and well and as she held him in her arms, she beamed with pride. Then she saw her mum, smiling and calling for her to come. Annie couldn't believe that she was alive, and she rushed towards her with joy, reaching out to her. But then her mother turned and walked away and when Annie looked back, she saw her own lifeless body lying on the hospital bed, Gabe crying next to it, and she realised she was dead. She had woken up in tears and it had taken a good few minutes for her to calm down and convince herself that it wasn't real, that she was still very much alive and the baby was kicking.

The next day they had both been subdued as they drove up to Hertford. In contrast to their paltry decorations, Val had gone all out. The tree must have been eight foot high and the spread on the table was enough to feed twenty people rather than four. Val clucked around everyone, anxious to fill any awkward silences, but her skittishness only made everyone even more nervous. Eventually Mike had gone outside for his annual Christmas Day cigar and after a few minutes, Annie had stood up quietly, shrugged on her coat and gone to find him.

'Annie,' he said, quickly stubbing out his cigar when he saw her.

'You don't have to stop.'

'It's okay. I hear it's bad for you.' He laughed. 'You look cold, shall we go back inside?'

'In a minute, Dad.'

'Okay love.'

They stood side by side, father and daughter, Batman and Robin, the bond between them flickering like electricity, trying to solidify again.

'I don't know what's happened between us, Annie,' he began.

'Me neither.'

'I'm sorry.'

'Me too.'

Their hands came together, bridging the gap between them. There was so much they wanted to say to each other, and so much they were keeping back. But in the end, neither of them spoke, and after a few minutes they turned and made their way back inside.

Bruce and Diana had visited for New Year, which had only made Gabe even more agitated. When Annie quizzed him about his deteriorating mood afterwards, he confessed that Diana had transferred some money into his bank account to tide them over while he was unemployed.

'Wow, that's so generous of her. I must thank her.'

Gabe was sullen. 'It's shameful, that's what it is.'

'What do you mean?'

'A grown man, a father-to-be, being bailed out by his mum yet again.'

'Being made redundant wasn't your fault. If your mum can afford to loan us some money until we're both working again then that's wonderful. Be grateful, not angry.'

'You really don't get it, do you?'

'I'm trying, I promise.'

Gabe had put his arm around her and given her a squeeze. 'Let's forget about it,' he said. But even though he hadn't mentioned it since, he was clearly still brooding over it.

A few days later Gabe got a call from a recruitment consultant offering him a temporary contract at a company in Slough, and although it was a two-hour commute by train each way, he'd accepted immediately. It meant that he had to leave the house by seven each morning and often didn't get back until after eight at night. When he returned home, he was drained, sullen and reluctant to talk about his day. It was painfully obvious that he hated the job, and the commute, but whenever Annie pressed him, he refused to discuss it.

'It's fine,' he always replied.

Fine. It's what they both said to each other all the time now.

Before she knew it, her birthday had come around, and

although she had the day off work, Gabe had to get on the road so that he wouldn't be late.

'Enjoy your day,' he said, as he stood up to leave.

'You too,' she replied.

She kissed him and lingered in bed for a few minutes. Then she got up and went downstairs to make herself some breakfast. As she ate, text and social media messages started coming in from friends wishing her a happy birthday. She replied to them all and then opened the small pile of cards that had been trickling in through the post over the last few days. While she was reading them, her phone pinged again. It was from Sal, sending birthday wishes. Annie read it guiltily. She still hadn't been down to visit Sal since all the trouble with Marcus, despite her promises to herself that she would make more of an effort. She typed out a reply.

So nice to hear from you! Don't suppose you're around today, are you? Would love to drive down and see you for a few hours x

Sal replied immediately.

That would be lovely! I'm home until 3pm, come whenever you like x

With a new sense of purpose, Annie heaved herself up from the kitchen chair and climbed back up the stairs. As she dressed, she thought about how much she was looking forward to a road trip. She could still fit behind the steering wheel, just about, but she knew that her driving days might be numbered. She put on some maternity leggings and a top, applied some make-up to hide the ever-growing bags under her eyes and climbed into the car, heading towards the M25. The traffic was heavy but she didn't mind. She turned up the radio and crawled along the motorway, and as she passed the exit for Heathrow Airport she had a strong yearning to jump on the first plane out of there, ideally to a paradise island, and leave all her troubles behind. But even if they could afford a holiday right now, she was too pregnant to fly.

It took her an hour and a half to get to Sally's and when her friend opened the door to greet her, Annie did a double take. She hadn't seen her since the drinks in London a few months ago and Sally looked like a new woman.

'Sal, you look amazing!'

Sally self-consciously tucked a strand of hair behind her ear. She'd had it cut to her shoulders, shorter than Annie had seen it before, and her new do had highlights running through it and a glossy sheen, which looked suspiciously like the product of a Brazilian blow-dry. She was also wearing a smart dress and tights, rather than her usual jeans and jumper. But what really caught Annie's eye was the striking lack of lines or wrinkles on her face.

'Have you had Botox?' she asked incredulously.

'Maybe a touch,' Sally admitted, as she ushered Annie in.

'I didn't know that was your thing!'

'It's not, I've never done it before, I just... I feel like I need to make more of an effort. You know, with Marcus. I've let myself go.'

'Well, firstly you're gorgeous just as you are and secondly you've got three kids, so who cares if you don't have time to wash and style your hair and pick out the perfect outfit every day?'

'Marcus cares.'

Annie bit her lip. She knew that bashing Marcus wasn't what Sally needed to hear, no matter how tempting it was. Instead, she adopted a more subtle approach. 'Marcus loves you, Sally. If you want to pamper yourself then that's fabulous, but do it for you, not him.'

'To be honest, this dress is quite uncomfortable,' Sally admitted. 'And I hate wearing tights.'

'Then take the damn things off and be done with it.'

Sally hesitated for a moment, before ripping the tights off her legs and sinking down on to the sofa with a satisfied sigh. 'That's better,' she said.

'Where's all this come from, Sal?'

'It's all this stuff with Marcus. We had a big row and I accused him of deliberately avoiding spending time with me. He replied that I had given up on myself and that all I did was nag him when he was here anyway, so who could blame him.'

'Sally, it's not okay for him to say that to you.'

'But he's got a point. I *do* nag him. And I can't remember the last time I wore mascara until I went and got some from Boots last week. When I met Marcus, I had a busy career and social life, and I wouldn't have dreamed of leaving the house without make-up on. Look at me now!'

'I *am* looking, and what I see is a beautiful, clever and remarkable woman who is working tirelessly to look after everyone else, and doing a bloody good job of it, mascara or no mascara.'

'Do you know, I've put on three stone since we got married?'

'That doesn't matter, Sally, as long as you're happy.'

'But, that's the point. I'm not.'

Annie was tempted to tell her that it was Marcus who was making her unhappy, not the extra pounds. But Sally was being more open and honest with her than she had ever been before, and Annie had to tread carefully so that she didn't put up her defences again.

'What do you think would make you happy?' she asked.

'I feel like I've lost my sense of identity. I'm just a mum and a wife now, that's it. I'm not Sally Roberts, head of HR, or Sally Roberts, full of ambition. And I want to feel wanted, desired. I can't remember the last time Marcus looked at me with desire.'

'Maybe you need a new challenge. Have you thought about getting a job?'

'I have, but it's been so long since I've worked anywhere, who would employ me?'

'Lots of people would, Sal, you just have to believe in yourself.'

Sally smiled at Annie. 'Thank you. Maybe you're right. Sorry to throw this all on you.'

'Not at all, I'm so glad that you've talked to me. I'm always here for you, Sal.'

'Anyway,' Sal said, slapping her now bare legs with her hands, signalling that the conversation was over. 'How are you? You look awful if you don't mind me saying.'

'Well, cheers,' Annie said with a laugh, trying to sound breezy. The last thing she wanted to do was burden Sally even more. 'I'm just tired. I'm not sleeping very well. You know how it is, with an ever-growing bump and having to get up to pee in the night every five minutes.'

'Oh yes, I remember it well,' Sally replied. 'I was a zombie by the end of all my pregnancies. And let me tell you now, it gets a lot worse when the baby comes.'

'Well, this is *just* what I need to hear right now.'

'I'm sorry, but it's important that you're prepared. Babies are hard work, far more than you think. The sleep deprivation is horrific, you'll have absolutely no idea what you're doing and your breasts and bits will hurt like hell, making even the simplest of things, like sitting down, an ordeal. And kids don't get any easier when they get older either.'

'Christ, Sal, don't ever teach antenatal classes. You'll have all the mums-to-be wailing before they've even reached their second trimester.'

'Honestly, I love my children but there are days when I wonder what I've done.'

Annie was taken aback. She'd always thought Sally was the epitome of an Alpha Mum, one of those types who was born to have a brood. To hear that she regretted becoming a parent was like hearing that David Beckham never really wanted to play football.

Sally immediately started to backtrack. 'Forget I said anything,' she told Annie. 'I'm just going through a strange time. I didn't mean it.'

But the conversation stayed with Annie after she had left Sally's. Of all her friends, Sally was the one who seemed to have it all sorted; three happy, well-behaved children who were always smiling in the photos she regularly posted on Facebook, a beautiful house, a family dog. To hear how different the reality was to the picture that Annie had painted in her mind was disconcerting. As she drove home, Annie considered her future – Gabe, miserable in a job he didn't like, miles away from home, never around to see the baby. And her, home alone with a newborn, with no idea how to look after him. Maybe Gabe was right after all, perhaps having Diana to stay would be a good thing. Even if she constantly chastised Annie for getting everything wrong, which she probably would, surely any company was better than nothing?

I wonder if Mum would have been a hands-on grandmother? she thought. *Would she have offered to come and stay when the baby was born? Or would we be so close that we lived in neighbouring streets*? She imagined her mother holding the baby, smiling, showing Annie how to change his nappy or bathe him. But without warning the picture in her mind switched to the one from her nightmares, of her mum lying on a hospital bed, crying and begging for help.

Why were these nightmares haunting her, stealing her

sleep? What did they mean? They were messing with her head, distracting her from all the good things in her life. Each time she had one it took her longer and longer to detach herself from it. And she was tired, so damn tired, that every day was an effort. Even now, she could feel her eyelids closing and she fought against it, trying to focus on the road. She turned the radio up and opened the window a bit, forcing herself to concentrate. But it was getting harder, the effort more exhausting. The song on the radio echoed around the car, the patter of the rain on the windscreen becoming increasingly hypnotic. Her head fell forward and she jerked herself upright again. She didn't notice that the car in front of her had stopped until it was too late to do anything about it.

CHAPTER FOURTEEN

Annie glanced up at the sound of a curtain being pulled open and Gabe rushed into the cubicle, looking like he'd run all the way to hospital from his office.

'Are you okay? What happened?' he asked.

'I'm fine, honestly. I was in a crash on the motorway but that sounds a lot more dramatic than it was. It was an incredibly slow-motion one because there was so much traffic.'

'Is the baby okay?'

'Yes. They're still monitoring him, which is why I'm attached to this machine, but I've had a scan and everything is absolutely fine.'

'Thank God you're okay,' Gabe said, sitting down and holding her hand. 'How did it happen?'

'I lost my concentration for a second and the next thing I knew, I'd rear-ended someone. The driver was okay, not even a scratch, but I'm afraid I've caused some damage to both cars.'

'Don't worry about that; that's what insurance is for. My main concern is you and the baby.'

'Well, Gabriel, be concerned no more because we are tickety-boo.'

Gabe scowled at her. 'This isn't a joke, Annie.'

'I know that.'

'I don't know if you do, actually. What were you doing driving on the motorway anyway?'

The tone of his voice made Annie defensive. 'Well, rather than spend my birthday alone, I decided to go and visit my friend. I didn't realise driving while pregnant was a crime?'

'You know I'm not saying that. But you're exhausted, you're not yourself...'

'So, you're saying I'm unfit to drive?'

Gabe looked away. 'Yes, maybe that's what I'm saying.'

'It's not up to you though.'

He looked at her again, eyes blazing. 'Well, it can't be up to you, can it? I feel like I can't even trust you anymore, Annie, like I don't know what you'll do next. All this falling out with your dad, your burned hands, and now this. I'm scared that you're going to hurt the baby.'

It was like she'd been slapped. 'I would never hurt the baby,' she said, through gritted teeth.

'I'm not saying you'd do it deliberately; I just think that you don't know what you're doing at the moment. When is your next midwife's appointment?'

'Next Monday.'

'I'm coming with you and I'm going to make sure you tell the midwife what's been going on. This isn't normal. You need some help.'

'What about your work?'

'Screw work.'

'I'll speak to the midwife, I promise, you don't need to come with me.'

'I love you, Annie, but I don't believe you anymore. I'm coming with you and that's all there is to it. And until then, you are *not* driving.'

'I think our car would agree with that anyway, Gabe, given the state of it.'

'God, I hope the insurance pays out.'

Annie fiddled with her hands guiltily. Gabe was right, she *had* become a liability and through her own carelessness she had put their baby at risk again. She hated herself.

'I'm so sorry, Gabe,' she said, weakly.

He lay down on the bed beside her and put his arm around her. 'I'm sorry too. I saw something like this coming and I should have intervened sooner.'

'What do you mean?'

'Ever since you got pregnant you've been spiralling. It's so obvious now that pregnancy would trigger you, given what happened to your mum, and we should have been more prepared. Your dad's in bits about it, by the way. He blames himself.'

'You've spoken to him?'

'We've been talking quite regularly; he's really worried about you. And Lil called on the way here to see how you were. She was the one who suggested I make sure you speak to the midwife about what's been going on. She thinks you need some more support.'

'Wow, I didn't realise that you've all been talking about me behind my back.'

'We're not ganging up on you, Annie. We all love you. We want to help you.'

'If you genuinely want to do that, Gabe, you can help me figure out what this secret from my past is because until I know for sure, I don't think I can let it go.'

Gabe sighed. 'Not this again.'

'There's something odd going on Gabe, I *feel* it.'

'You're right, Annie, there is.' Her heart soared as she thought he finally understood. Then he added, 'There's something going on with you. And we need to fix it, before anyone gets hurt.'

Before she could respond, the doctor appeared at the curtain and smiled at her before looking at the machine. 'How are the patients?' he asked.

'Ready to go home, I hope?' Annie replied tentatively.

'Everything looks good, so I'm happy for you to be discharged but I want you to call your maternity team today. And no more driving if you're feeling tired, okay, Annie?'

Annie nodded, relieved.

'Where's the car?' Gabe asked.

'It's been towed to a garage,' she replied.

'I'll call a taxi.'

'We can get public transport, Gabe, I know a taxi won't be cheap.'

'We're getting a taxi.'

On the way home they sat apart, looking out of their respective windows at the driving rain. But their physical distance was nothing compared to the huge, gaping emotional gulf that seemed to be getting larger, not smaller. Annie thought back to the day when she discovered that she was pregnant and how excited they had both been. It had been such a wonderful, shared moment and she had never felt so happy. What had happened to them since then? Pregnancy was meant to be one of the greatest times of her life. On the contrary, it seemed hell-bent on destroying her.

The next day, she met Caz in a café and told her what had happened.

'Jesus, Annie, I've heard of baby brain, but you're taking it to a new level. What's going on?'

Annie rested her head on the table. 'I don't know,' she said.

Caz reached over and touched her arm. 'I hate to see you like this.'

Annie lifted her head again. 'I'm so tired I can barely think. Everyone keeps telling me how hard it's going to be when the baby comes and half of me thinks, *How on earth will I manage if I can't even cope with being pregnant?* while the other half thinks, *What if something happens to me and I never get to find out?* I'm all over the place, Caz, and I can't seem to stop spinning.'

'Have you spoken to anyone about it yet?'

'Gabe's insisting that I talk to the midwife. He's basically marching me to my next appointment to make sure that I spill the beans. But I'm not sure it's going to help.'

'What do you think would help?'

'Honestly, I have no idea, but I think it all comes down to Mum.'

'I can't begin to imagine what you're going through and how difficult this must be for you. Remember me telling you months ago that it would hit you like a ton of bricks? Well, this is your ton of bricks right here. The question is, what can we do about it?'

'I just wish I knew if Dad really was holding something back or if he's told me everything he knows. If those photos really did conveniently disappear or if he got rid of them.'

'Look, I've known Mr B for thirty years and I just don't see him harbouring some dark, terrible secret. The man's as straight as a die.'

'Do you think I'm losing the plot?'

'No, I think you're exhausted and overwhelmed. Gabe's right, you need to talk to the midwife. Enough holding it all in and pretending that you're okay.'

Annie had a thought. 'Maybe I just need some closure. Do

you know, I've never been to see Mum's grave? She was buried in Northampton, in the cemetery near the hospital. We haven't been back since I was a baby because Dad always said the city was too full of ghosts for him.'

'Do you want to go and see it?'

'Does that sound crazy?'

'No, it doesn't. Hey, why don't I come with you? We can make a day of it.'

'Are you sure?'

'Yes. Let's do it. How about next Saturday?'

'Okay. You'll need to drive, though, I'm banned.'

'It's a date. I'll pick you up at nine.'

As she made her way home, Annie tried to decide whether her newly hatched plan was a stroke of genius or another sign that she was losing it. But she had been haunted by her nightmares for long enough and it was time to confront her fears; to finally go and say goodbye. Then maybe that would be the end of it all and she could move on with her life.

When she got back, Gabe was hovering around the front door, like he'd been waiting for her.

'What's up?' she asked, taking off her coat.

'I've just had an email from a recruiter. I've been offered an interview at this amazing firm. It's more money than I was earning before and it's twenty minutes on the train into the office.'

'Oh Gabe, that's marvellous!'

'The thing is,' he said, looking shifty. 'The interview's on Monday morning.'

'So what?' Annie was confused.

'The same time as your *midwife* appointment?'

'Oh, don't worry about that, Gabe, this is more important. I'm fine to go along to the appointment on my own.'

'But I said I'd go with you.' Gabe was torn.

'I've told you that I'll speak to the midwife and I will, okay? In some ways it will be easier if I do it on my own, without you breathing down my neck.'

'Do you promise?'

Annie put her hand up in a salute. 'Yes, sir!'

'I mean it, Annie.'

She put a hand on his arm. 'So do I. Now, go and do whatever you've got to do to prepare for the interview and I'll iron your best shirt.'

Gabe grinned, looking happier than Annie had seen him in weeks.

'This is it, I can feel it. We're finally on the up.'

'Well it's about bloody time, isn't it?'

He dashed off to find his laptop and start researching the company and Annie went off to find the iron. But when she returned to the living room, he was lurking, looking shifty again.

'Perhaps I should iron my shirt?' he suggested.

'Why?' Annie was confused.

'Just in case you accidentally burn yourself again.'

'I'm perfectly capable of ironing a shirt, Gabe.'

'Even so, I think I'd like to do it.'

Annie glared at him, trying to decide whether to stand her ground or not. Gabe was talking to her like she was a silly little child and she didn't appreciate it. But what if he was right? Was she not to be trusted, even with basic household chores? If there was a trophy for who felt more like a failure in their house, she could no longer call it between her and Gabe.

But she couldn't be bothered to argue with him. She no longer had the energy or conviction. Wordlessly she handed him the iron and went upstairs.

CHAPTER FIFTEEN

Gabe checked himself in the mirror, fiddled with his shirt, and then turned to look at her.

'What do you think?' he asked.

'Hot.'

'I don't need to look hot, I need to look employable.'

'Well, actually that very much depends on who's doing the interviewing.'

He rolled his eyes. 'Your appointment's at nine-thirty, right?'

'Yep.'

'Okay, I'll call you as soon as I'm done with the interview to see how it went. Good luck.'

'Good luck to you too, babe.'

Gabe kissed her and left. Rubbing her eyes, she took a sip of the tea that he had left on her bedside table and checked the time. It was eight o'clock. She needed to get up if she was to be ready in time for her appointment. At thirty-six weeks pregnant, doing anything in a hurry was now impossible. But having only had three or four hours' sleep again she was so very tired.

She forced herself out of bed, taking her tea with her, and made herself some toast and peanut butter which she ate on the sofa. When she was finished, she rested her head against the pillow, steeling herself to get up and dressed – a simple act that now felt like climbing a mountain. The sound of people walking past the house, children chatting on their way to school, dogs barking, was soothing. Her eyelids felt heavy. *Just five minutes' rest, then I'll get in the shower.*

Annie woke to the sound of the doorbell ringing. Disorientated, she looked around, trying to work out where she was. Her eyes focused on the empty mug and plate on the coffee table. She stood up slowly and made her way to the door, where she was greeted by the postman.

'You must be due soon,' he commented, taking in her huge bump and dishevelled state, as he handed over a couple of parcels.

'Four weeks,' she replied. 'Hey, what time is it?'

The postman looked at his watch. 'Quarter past ten.'

Shit! She'd missed her appointment. She tried to think straight. Maybe if she called the hospital, they could fit her in later that day. She said goodbye to the postie and went back to get her phone, but before she could dial out, it started ringing and a photo of Gabe flashed up on the screen. With shaking hands, she answered it. 'How did it go?' she asked him.

'Really well!' Gabe sounded like his old, jovial self. 'We hit it off straight away and they seemed really positive about me. Now I just have to wait for the recruiter to call and give me their feedback, but they said they want to move quickly.'

'I'm so pleased for you, fingers crossed.'

'How did it go with the midwife?'

Annie paused. Gabe would be livid if she told him that she'd missed the appointment, but she couldn't lie to him either. 'Listen, don't panic.'

'What?' Gabe demanded, panicking.

'I kind of fell asleep on the sofa and missed the appointment.'

'Oh Annie.'

'I'm sorry, but I was literally about to call the hospital when you rang. I'm sure I can get another appointment later today.'

'Very convenient, isn't it?'

'What do you mean?'

'Come on, Annie, do you expect me to believe that you overslept? I knew you didn't want to go to the appointment, that you would do anything to avoid speaking to the midwife.'

'That's not what happened!'

'Sure Annie, whatever you say.' Gabe sounded defeated again. 'Listen, I have to go to work. They're still pissed off with me for leaving early last week when you had the accident and if I don't go in today, they've said there's no point going back at all.'

'That's a bit harsh!' Annie was incensed on Gabe's behalf.

'Yeah, well I've got no choice, have I.'

'Soon you'll have an amazing new job and you can take great pleasure in telling them to stick it.'

She expected Gabe to laugh, to tell her she was right. But instead there was silence.

'Gabe, look, I'm really sorry. This was not deliberate. I'm going to call the hospital right now.'

'Fine.'

She hung up, feeling wretched. How dare Gabe suggest that she had deliberately avoided seeing the midwife? The health of their baby was more important to her than anything in the world. With a hand on her bump, she dialled the maternity ward but it was engaged. She pressed redial three more times, determined to get through. *I'll prove Gabe wrong.*

On the fifth attempt, someone answered, and Annie explained what had happened.

'We have back-to-back appointments all day,' the receptionist said disapprovingly. 'How many weeks are you?'

'Thirty-six,' Annie explained. 'And I'm having regular blood pressure monitoring.'

'All I can say is come down as soon as you can and we'll squeeze you in, but you might be in for a bit of a wait.'

'That's fine,' Annie said. She went upstairs to get dressed, forgoing any attempt to shower or put on make-up. Then she called for a taxi and waited by the front door for it to arrive. On the journey into hospital the driver kept glancing at her in the rear-view mirror.

'You're not in labour, are you?' he asked, probably thinking of his leather seats.

'No,' she replied, stroking her bump. 'This baby's still cooking in the oven.'

'Is it your first?'

'Yes. Do you have children?'

'Four,' the man replied proudly.

'Four? Blimey!'

'It's a joy, being a parent,' he told her. 'You'll love it.'

I wonder if your wife agrees with you, Annie thought, imagining trying to wrangle four children. But she smiled sweetly at the man and said, 'Thanks, I'm really looking forward to it.'

When they arrived at the hospital she walked as quickly as she could to the maternity ward, stopping at reception, out of breath, to explain who she was.

'Oh yes, I spoke to you on the phone,' the woman said loudly. 'You're the one who missed your appointment this morning.'

A few heads whipped around to stare at her. It was probably the most exciting thing that the bored, mums-to-be in the waiting room had seen all morning. Annie wanted the ground to swallow her up. 'Yes, and as I said on the phone, I really am terribly sorry.'

'Well as you can see, we're extremely busy,' the woman said, gesturing at the packed waiting room. 'Take a seat and we'll call you as soon as we can.'

Annie shuffled nervously into the waiting room, sitting down in between two other women. One was on her own, reading a copy of *Glamour* magazine. The other had her toddler with her and was trying, unsuccessfully, to stop him from running off. She glanced at Annie with an expression which looked a lot like, *Why did I decide to have another one?* Annie smiled sympathetically and then got her phone out to distract herself from the knot in her stomach which was tightening at the prospect of bearing her soul to whichever lucky midwife it was this time.

An hour later she was still waiting and she was so desperate for the loo that she thought she might explode, but she was too scared to go to the ladies in case her name got called and she missed her only chance of an appointment. Sitting with her legs crossed, she saw a woman she hadn't seen before with a clipboard and prayed that it was her turn.

'Annie Branning?'

Annie waved and stood up, following the woman down a corridor and into a room.

'I understand you missed your appointment?' the midwife said, scanning Annie's notes.

'Yes, I'm so sorry, I'm not sleeping well, you see–' Annie began, but the woman interrupted.

'We're very stretched at the moment. We ask for at least twenty-four hours' notice if you can't attend an appointment, so that we can offer it to someone else.'

'Yes I understand, and again, I'm sorry–'

The midwife cut her off for the second time. 'Right, let's get started then.'

Ten minutes later, Annie was back outside in the corridor. The midwife had gone through all the necessary motions – checked her blood pressure and urine, measured her bump – and then as good as chucked Annie back out of the door again. There had been no chance to open up about how she was feeling, she was sure of it. She would have said something if she'd had the opportunity. But would Gabe believe her if she explained what had happened? She had always believed that she could tell Gabe anything and he would have her back, but she wasn't so sure anymore. When had the lines of communication broken down so badly between them?

After finally making it to the loo, she left the hospital and waited by the main entrance for her taxi to arrive. She was horribly late for work and she'd missed her first two viewings, but at least the new guy could cover for her. When she got to the office, Lil was there, waiting for her.

'I'm so sorry,' Annie gushed as she closed the door behind her. 'I've had quite the morning.'

'Annie, I think we need to have a chat,' Lil said, gesturing for Annie to sit down opposite her.

Annie's heart sank. 'I'm sorry,' she said. 'It won't happen again.'

Lil waited until Annie had sat down. 'I think you should start your maternity leave early.'

'How early?'

'From now.'

Annie's eyes widened. She had planned to work until a few days before she was due. Not only did they need the money, but she also craved the distraction of work to keep her busy. 'But I've only just come back after the Christmas break and the baby isn't due for another four weeks!'

'Annie, I can see the toll that this is taking on you. You're exhausted and you're stressed. It's not good for you or the baby – or our clients for that matter.'

'I'll be okay, I promise...' Annie began but Lil shook her head.

'You *have* to look after yourself.'

Annie hung her head. 'We can't afford it, Lil.'

'Don't worry about that, I'll cover it. You'll be on full pay.'

'You can't do that!'

'I can, and I will.'

Touched by Lil's generosity but terrified at the prospect of not having the daily constant of her work, Annie was torn. But even if she tried to protest, she would be fighting a losing battle; when Lil made up her mind about something, there was no chance of her changing it again. Reluctantly she nodded her agreement and promptly burst into tears.

'Oh Annie.' Lil rushed around the desk and took Annie into her arms, holding her tightly and shushing her, like one might do a child. 'It's going to be okay, I promise.'

'I'm sorry, Lil.' How many times had she said sorry today? She'd lost count.

'Now, don't ever say sorry to me. You have nothing to be sorry for.'

'Anyway, how do you think the new guy is getting on?' Annie asked, wiping her eyes, embarrassed about crying in front of Lil yet again and eager to move the focus away from her.

'He's doing well and he's very enthusiastic,' Lil said. 'Possibly a bit *too* enthusiastic for Brian. We're really going to miss you, Annie. It won't be the same without you.'

'I'm going to miss you too.'

Lil looked at Annie sympathetically. 'Are you okay, my love?'

'It's just been a long day. And now I'm worried that you

think I'm a massive liability and won't ever give me my job back.'

'Annie, you'll always have a job here. I promise. But now is the time for you to focus on yourself. Relax, go for walks, get a pregnancy massage. Enjoy yourself. You'll be busier than ever when the little one comes along.'

'You're right.'

'Is there anything you want to talk about? I'm a very good listener, you know.'

Annie felt so warm and safe in the familiar office. She looked at Lil's kind, attentive expression. She hadn't managed to confide in the midwife but maybe now was her chance to finally get everything off her chest; the nightmares, the argument with her dad, her growing obsession over what happened to her mum, the tension between her and Gabe, her fears about the future.

'Where do I start?' she began.

But before she could, the bell above the door tinkled and a couple walked in.

'We'd like to enquire about one of the properties we saw in the window,' the woman said.

Lil looked at Annie apologetically. 'Stay put, we'll continue this in a minute,' she whispered.

But the conversation with the couple dragged on and by the time they left, Brian and the new guy were back and were filling Lil in on their viewings. The moment had passed.

'Annie's going to be starting her maternity leave today,' Lil explained, looking over at her and giving her a reassuring smile.

'We'll miss you,' Brian said, in a way that made Annie suspect he already knew about Lil's plans. Had they been talking about her too? Probably, everyone else had.

'I'll miss you too,' she said. The phones started ringing and everyone dispersed. Annie spent the rest of the afternoon writing up her handover notes, and as she was leaving, Lil and Brian gave her a cuddle and made her promise to keep in touch.

So that's it, she thought as she closed the door behind her. *No ceremonious leaving lunch. No great send-off. I'm now on maternity leave. Right then.* For months she had imagined her last day at work to be some sort of momentous occasion and now it seemed like a huge anticlimax. She tried to think positively, to imagine the easy weeks that lay ahead of her with no stress and no responsibility. She could make sure that everything was ready for the baby. She could do some gentle swimming every day. Get her hair cut. Maybe even book a pregnancy massage, like Lil had suggested. But all she could see was day upon day of being on her own, lost in her thoughts and fears, while everyone else went about their business as usual. And she was dreading it.

CHAPTER SIXTEEN

The morning frost was still clinging on to the cars outside as Annie stared out of the window, waiting for Caz to arrive. She already had her coat and scarf on in anticipation.

'Are you sure you want to do this?' Gabe asked from the sofa.

'Definitely. I'll be back this evening,' she replied.

He nodded and turned to his laptop. He'd been invited for a second interview and was working on a presentation. She imagined that he'd probably still be sitting in the same spot when she got back from Northampton, with about five empty teacups on the table beside him.

'Caz is here,' she said, as she saw her friend's car pull up.

'Okay, good luck. Let me know how you get on.'

She gave him a wave and left, letting herself into Caz's car.

'Ready?' Caz asked.

'Yes. I found the address of the cemetery. I'll pop it in the satnav.'

'Right you are.' Caz pulled away from the kerb and started telling Annie about her recent conversation with Sally who, apparently, had given up on wearing dresses after a gust of wind and her hatred of wearing tights conspired to cause an incident at school, where she flashed her pants to the entire playground. Her mortified eldest child was still not speaking to her.

'She and Sharkus are having marriage counselling,' Caz confided.

'Good,' Annie said. 'I really hope they can sort it out.'

'What about you? How has your first few days of maternity leave been?'

'Okay,' Annie said. 'I've been bumbling about, doing a few bits and bobs.'

'How's things with you and Gabe?'

'We're both trying but sometimes it feels like we're strangers having a polite conversation. I don't think he understands why I'm doing what I am today, but he didn't push it. It's like he's treading on eggshells around me in case I crack completely.'

'He's got a lot going on too. But for what it's worth, I get it.'

'Thanks Caz. For being such a good friend. For coming with me.'

'Any time, babe.'

A sudden tightening in Annie's stomach made her gasp.

'You okay?' Caz asked, glancing at her.

'Yes, just a Braxton Hicks, I've had a few of them recently.'

Caz nodded and turned the radio up, and Annie looked out of the window, stroking her bump absent-mindedly. It was a typical winter's day, grey and cold. As they drove up the motorway, she peered into the cars they passed, watching the people inside, imagining who they were and where they were going. It was a game she had played since she was a child. Her stomach tightened again; it was not exactly painful, more uncomfortable. Ten minutes later it happened again. *These Braxton Hicks are intense*, she thought. She glanced over at Caz, wondering if she should say something, but she didn't want to worry her, especially while she was driving. And anyway, they weren't actual contractions; they were simply a practice run for the real thing.

They turned off the motorway and started making their way towards Northampton. As they drove into the city centre, Annie looked around, curious to see if anything jogged her memory. But she hadn't lived there since she was a baby and nothing about it felt familiar. Despite it being the place of her birth, she felt no connection to it at all.

'I think we're nearly here,' Caz said, as she pulled off the main road. They found a parking space near the cemetery and climbed out of the car, wrapping themselves up in hats and scarfs and making their way towards the entrance.

'So, whereabouts is your mum's grave?' Caz asked as they stood, rubbing their hands together and looking out at the sea of gravestones.

'I have no idea,' Annie admitted.

'Are you serious? There must be hundreds here. Why don't you call and ask your dad?'

'I didn't tell him that we were coming.'

'Why not?'

'I was afraid that he'd try to talk me out of it. He's already worried enough about me as it is.'

'How did you even know where she was buried then?'

'He's told me before that she was buried in the cemetery near the hospital.'

Caz looked at her with one eyebrow raised and for a second Annie thought that she was going to put her foot down and insist that they call Mike. Perhaps this had been a stupid, half-brained idea after all. But then Caz shrugged and said, 'Righty-ho then, we'd better get cracking.'

Annie smiled gratefully. 'Thanks, you have no idea how much this means...'

She didn't get to finish her sentence before a wave of pain hit her and she leaned forward, clutching on to her stomach.

'What the hell was that?' Caz asked. 'Are you having contractions?'

'They're just Braxton Hicks,' Annie said, with less conviction this time.

'Are you sure?'

'No, I'm not bloody sure!' Annie shouted, suddenly afraid. 'I've never had a baby before, have I?'

'Okay, calm down,' Caz said, looking around her. 'Well one thing's for sure, Annie, you're not giving birth in a frickin' cemetery, so I think we need to get you to a hospital.'

'No,' Annie said. 'Definitely not.'

'Definitely yes.'

'But it might be a false alarm! A lot of fuss about nothing.'

'And if it is, then they will send us on our way and we can come straight back here and start looking for your ma's grave, okay?'

'But,' Annie said, gripping Caz's arm tightly, 'I'm scared.'

'I know you are. But I'll be right with you the whole time.'

Caz took Annie's arm and they made their way back towards the car. Just as Annie was about to climb in, the pain came again and she had to stand with her hands on the roof of the car, breathing slowly, until it passed. Caz remained quiet but as soon as they were strapped in and back on the road, she glanced at Annie. 'You should call Gabe.'

'I'll wait and see what the doctors say first. I still think it might be a false alarm, I'm not due for another three weeks. I don't want to stress him out.'

'But he's an hour and a half away, so he needs a head start if you are in labour.'

'I thought first labours took forever, anyway?'

'Some do, some don't. Call him. Now.' Caz had adopted her

authoritative, don't-mess-with-me voice that was usually reserved for her children and wayward MPs. Annie obediently reached for her phone.

He answered after one ring. 'Are you okay?'

'Yes,' Annie began. 'I'm having a few twinges, so we're going to the hospital, just to be safe.'

'Twinges? What does that mean?'

'It might be nothing,' Annie said, trying to sound calm. 'I'll know more when I get there.'

'Send me the name of the hospital, I'm leaving now.'

'It might be nothing,' Annie repeated.

'And it might be something. I'm coming.'

'What about your presentation?'

'Fuck my presentation.'

He said it so passionately that Annie started laughing but then another wave of pain hit her and she cried out.

'Are you okay?' Gabe demanded.

'Yes,' she gasped. 'I'll text you now.'

She waited for the pain to pass and then she sent Gabe a message with the address of the hospital. It wasn't until she pressed send that the penny finally dropped about where they were heading. The same hospital where she had been born. The same hospital where her mother had died giving birth to her.

'I don't want to go in,' Annie said, standing outside the hospital entrance.

'I know, but you kind of have to, unless you want to give birth on the road.'

'You do understand what happened here, right?'

'I do, and I'm sorry we've had to come here but it was the nearest hospital.'

'Look, the pain has actually eased off a bit now. I reckon we have time to get home. I can call Gabe, tell him to meet us at the hospital in north London instead.'

As she said it, Annie felt a wetness creep down her legs, and she glanced down. Caz followed her gaze. The two women looked at each other.

'You know what that is, right?' Caz said.

'A pregnant woman who didn't get to the toilet in time?' Annie asked, hopefully.

Caz shook her head and reached out her hand. 'Come on, Annie. You've got no choice.'

She remained rooted to the spot. The nightmares that had haunted her for months now felt like they were coming to life. How had she ended up back here? What cruel twist of fate had brought her to this godforsaken place? The pain in her belly returned and she knew that she could no longer deny the inevitable. This baby was coming, whether she liked it or not. She took one last, lingering look behind her and made her way slowly inside.

Arm in arm, they followed the signs to the maternity ward. *Did Mum walk these same corridors*? Annie wondered. *Did she take the same route as us to get to the room where I was delivered*? She felt sick to the stomach and Caz squeezed her arm, gently propelling her along. When they finally got there, Annie paced around nervously while Caz explained the situation to the woman on reception. The woman glanced over at Annie and then picked up the phone to make a call.

Caz came up to her. 'She told us to wait here, someone will come out shortly. You okay?'

'No, not really. I'm *literally* living my worst nightmare. We should never have come here.'

'In hindsight, driving sixty miles to the place where your

mum died giving birth to you, when you're thirty-seven weeks pregnant, probably wasn't the wisest of plans.'

Annie started giggling, the nerves making her hysterical. Once she'd started, she couldn't stop. She laughed and cried until she was as doubled over as her bump would allow and tears were streaming down her face. Beside her, Caz was chortling quietly.

'Annie Branning?' A nurse asked, observing the scene with mild amusement. 'Follow me, please.'

They followed her into a room and Annie sat on the bed, trying to answer the nurse's questions in between contractions. Christ, it was getting painful. How much worse did it get? Then a midwife bustled in, took one look at Annie and said, 'Right then, let's have a look at you.'

Annie lay back and let the midwife examine her, praying that she'd shake her head and say that there was nothing going on down below at all and that Annie could go home. Perhaps a couple of paracetamol would take the edge off the pain. She looked down at the midwife to see if she could read anything from her expression but the woman remained poker faced. Finally she nodded, satisfied.

'You're five centimetres dilated,' she announced.

'Is that good or bad?'

'It means that you're in established labour and you need to go to a delivery room. And given how quickly your contractions came on, I'd say the sooner the better.'

'Oh my God,' Annie said, looking at Caz in horror.

'I'm going to see if we can take you down straightaway,' the midwife said. 'I'll be back shortly.'

She slipped out of the room and Annie gripped on to Caz's hand. 'Tell me the pain doesn't get any worse,' she pleaded. Caz pulled a face which told her everything she needed to know.

Her phone beeped and she looked down at the screen. It was from Gabe.

There's been an accident on the M1. Total gridlock. What's going on?

She started to reply but then another contraction came, this one even worse than the one before, and she cried out in agony, thrusting her phone at Caz.

'I'll text him back, don't worry,' Caz said.

By the time the contraction had passed, the midwife had returned. 'You're going down now,' she said. 'Your wheelchair's on the way.'

'I can walk,' Annie insisted, standing up and then sitting straight back down as another wave of pain came.

'I'm sure you can, but let's not make life any more difficult for ourselves than it needs to be, eh?'

Annie nodded, wondering how on earth she was going to get through the next few hours. 'How long have I got? My partner's on the way from London.'

'It's hard to say for sure. First babies often like to take their time, but your labour seems to be progressing quite quickly.'

'My first boy took forty-three hours,' Caz said proudly.

'Is that meant to cheer me up?' Annie gasped.

'Oh yeah, sorry.'

Annie's wheelchair arrived and she gingerly climbed in and let herself be pushed down the corridor towards the delivery room. She felt like she was in a horror movie; the walls were closing in on her and she was petrified of reaching the door in case the room turned out to be the one from her dreams. She could still see the shadow lurking in the corner and her stomach tightened with fear as well as pain. As they wheeled her through the door she closed her eyes, forcing herself to open them again once they were inside. She looked around and breathed a sigh of relief. The room had a huge bed in the middle, a bunch of machines, a birthing ball and lots of cupboards. It was large, sterile and completely different to her nightmares. Annie peered hesitantly into all four corners but there was no one there. The room was safe.

Another midwife was waiting for her. She helped Annie out of the chair, introducing herself as Hannah. 'I'm going to be looking after you. How are you doing?'

'Gas and air!' Annie managed to gasp, staggering towards the bed and standing beside it, not sure what to do with herself. It seemed that no matter what she tried, nothing made the pain go away.

'Of course,' Hannah replied, walking over to the gas and air machine and showing Annie how to work it. 'Wait until your next contraction before you have another go.'

Annie ignored her and inhaled deeply. Then she took another puff, and then another. And one more for good measure. Less than a minute later, she was off her face.

'Oh Hannah!' she said, between fits of giggles. 'You'd better make sure that I don't cark it today too, otherwise my poor dad's going to lose his marbles!'

Hannah frowned, confused, and Caz quietly filled her in on Annie's family history. As the midwife listened, her hand shot to her mouth. Then she turned to Annie. 'I've been a midwife for nineteen years and I'm going to take very good care of you and your baby today, okay? Nothing's happening to you on my watch.'

But the high from the gas and air had already worn off and despite taking a few deep drags, Annie couldn't replicate it again. The relief had been short-lived.

'Epidural!' she shouted, to no one in particular.

'We're a bit beyond that now, I'm afraid,' Hannah said.

'Drugs!' Annie demanded. 'Any drugs!'

Hannah put a comforting hand on the small of her back, rubbing it gently. 'Breathe, Annie, breathe through your contractions, in and out, in and out.'

Annie wanted to punch her in the face.

'I can't do this,' she said. 'I just *can't.*' She no longer knew which bit she was talking about.

'Yes, you can,' Hannah told her confidently.

'I definitely can't. Argh!' Annie writhed around in pain. 'There must be something wrong. It shouldn't be this painful. I think there's something wrong. You need to get a doctor.'

Hannah and Caz exchanged glances.

'There's nothing wrong, Annie,' Caz said. 'Labour hurts like hell. That's all there is to it.'

'Where the hell is Gabe?!'

'He's on his way, he'll be here, don't worry.'

Annie lay on her side, one hand clutching the gas and air mouthpiece, and moaned over and over again. 'Make it stop,' she begged. 'Make it stop.'

She had no idea how much time passed. It could have been five minutes, it could have been five hours. *I want it to end. I don't want it to end. I need to hold on, I can't hold on anymore.* She was aware of the midwife in the room, Caz by her side, talking to her, but she was in a world of her own. She was afraid, but not of a ghost anymore, of her own body. Was she up to this? Could she do it?

'I can't do this,' she cried. 'I can't do this anymore.'

And then five minutes later. 'I need to push!'

The midwife examined Annie. 'You're fully dilated, Annie, you're right, it's time to push.'

'I want Gabe!' she screamed. 'I want Gabe!'

'Annie, try to put all your energy into pushing rather than screaming. Push, push.'

The contraction stopped, a few seconds of blessed relief,

and then a new one came. She screamed again, ignoring the midwife's advice. It was a constant cycle; pain, push, stop; pain, push, stop. It seemed like it would never end. Yet there was something else going on too. Through the agony, she was also empowered. Because, she realised, she was doing it. She was giving birth and it was both horrific and life-changing, but she was doing it. She was no longer afraid, she was determined and she was ready to meet her son.

'Okay Annie, I can see baby's head, listen to me very carefully now. It's crucial that you push when I tell you to and stop when I say stop, okay?'

And then, a few moments later. 'Annie, I'm just going to call someone.'

An emergency bell sounded. Annie looked at Caz in panic.

'What's going on?' Caz demanded, understanding immediately that Annie was unable to speak but needed a voice.

'I just need a bit of assistance getting baby out. His shoulder is stuck.'

'No,' Annie cried. This was it, the thing that she had feared for months was finally coming true. There was something wrong. The baby wasn't going to make it. She wasn't going to make it.

'Don't panic, Annie, just breathe, don't push, okay? Listen to me, Annie.'

Someone rushed in. Then someone else, who introduced himself as a consultant.

'Annie,' he said, 'I'm going to perform an episiotomy, you probably won't even feel it but it will help to get your baby out quickly.'

She nodded, gripping tightly on to Caz's hand. And then they were telling her to push again and she was pushing with all she had, and crying and pushing and then suddenly the pain stopped. And then the room was filled with the sound of crying and her beautiful, slimy, wailing baby was placed gently onto her chest.

'Oh my God!' she said, looking down at him.

'You did it, Annie, you did it!' Caz was in bits.

Annie looked down at her little boy. She couldn't believe he was here. It had all been worth it, all that fear and pain, to experience this moment of pure euphoria.

'I can't believe it,' she said. 'I can't believe you're here.'

'Annie, we need to take baby for a short while, just to check him over. He'll be right back with you before you know it.'

He was gently lifted away from her and Annie followed the midwife with her eyes as she took him over to a little table, examining him and making notes. Everyone in the room was starting to look a little blurry. *I'm so tired*, she thought. *So tired I can barely focus.* She looked down at the end of the bed, smiling at the doctor. But he was concentrating on something.

'Is everything okay?' Annie asked. Then she smiled. 'I'm falling asleep.'

She heard a voice, it could have been Caz's. 'What's going on?'

Then another. 'She's losing a lot of blood.'

But a wonderful sense of calm had come over Annie and she didn't feel scared. She knew that everything was going to be okay. More than okay, it was going to be amazing.

She couldn't fight it anymore, the urge to sleep was too strong. *Just a little nap and then everything will be okay. When I wake up, Gabe will be here and we can start our new life as a family. I can't wait to see him and tell him how much I love him. We'll put the last few months behind us and have a fresh start.*

She took one last look at their beautiful baby and closed her eyes.

CHAPTER SEVENTEEN

35 YEARS EARLIER

Eve heard a baby crying, nearby at first, then further away until it was no longer in earshot. Where was she? Was this a dream? There were voices murmuring above her. She tried to listen, but it was difficult to concentrate. Then she remembered exactly where she was.

'Eve, love, can you hear me?'

Slowly, she opened her eyes. Mike was looking down at her, his face full of concern.

'She's awake,' he said.

She tried to speak but it came out as a whisper. 'What happened?'

'There was a complication. We almost lost you.' He could barely speak himself; he was as white as a sheet. 'I thought that was it, Eve, I've never been so scared in my life.'

It all came flooding back; the agony of labour, the relief after giving birth, the joy at holding her baby for the first time, and then something pulling her down into the depths of sleep.

She tried to sit up, wincing. She felt like she'd been hit by a bus; everything hurt. She looked down and saw that there were tubes attached to her. *Isn't that a bit extreme?*

Mike put a hand on her arm, stroking it gently. 'Just rest awhile, love, you've been through a lot.'

'Where's Annie?' she murmured.

'You just missed her, but the nurses will bring her back soon.'

A doctor appeared above her and introduced himself. 'Eve, you had a severe post-partum haemorrhage and you lost a considerable amount of blood. We had to put you under general anaesthetic and take you to the operating theatre for emergency surgery.'

Surgery? No wonder she felt so groggy. A look passed between the doctor and Mike and she sensed there was something else they weren't telling her.

'What is it? What's wrong?' she demanded.

'Just rest now, love, we'll talk later,' Mike said soothingly, still stroking her arm.

'No, I want to know. What's wrong? Is it Annie?'

The doctor looked at Mike, who nodded. He turned back to Eve. 'Your bleeding was severe and uncontrollable, Eve. In order to save your life, I performed an emergency hysterectomy.'

A hysterectomy? But she was twenty years old. She looked at the doctor, trying to make sense of what he was telling her, and then at Mike who was unable to meet her eye.

The doctor smiled. 'You gave us all a bit of a fright, young lady.'

Is that all he could say? Like she was some silly little girl who had fallen off her bike and hurt her leg? The man had just butchered her up and removed her reproductive system. None of it made any sense to her; women gave birth safely every day. Why had this happened?

'I don't understand...' she began.

'It's impossible to know for sure what causes a post-partum haemorrhage, but it's more common after a long labour like yours. The important thing though, Eve, is that you are fine now and you will make a full recovery.'

But she wasn't fine at all. The doctor seemed to be suggesting that her nightmare was over but to her it seemed like she was still living it. She was sore and uncomfortable, and she had just been told that she would never have any more children. She didn't even know if she wanted any but she didn't like the choice being taken away from her against her will. She was supposed to be young and healthy, but she felt a hundred years old. She had a strong urge to close her eyes and go back to sleep rather than attempt to process what she had been told. She was too groggy to move, too shocked to cry. Mike was still looking away, wiping his eyes. What was he upset about? He wasn't the one who had almost bloody died. He wasn't the one lying in a hospital bed.

There was a gentle knock on the door and a nurse appeared, wheeling a cot. Eve craned her head to see the baby, swaddled tightly in a blanket, sleeping peacefully. She waited for joy and elation to hit her again at the sight of Annie, like it had done in those glorious, heady moments after she gave birth, but this time she felt nothing. The nurse wheeled Annie over to the bed and Eve reached out and put a tentative hand on her small body, feeling the rise and fall of her chest as she breathed. She looked so tiny and helpless. Eve was a mother now, shouldn't she be instantly in love with her child? *You almost killed me*, she thought angrily and then at once she was appalled by her own thoughts. She heard a click and looked up to see Mike taking a photo.

'Not now,' she snapped. 'Put that thing away.' The last thing she wanted was to be reminded of this moment. He hesitated and then put the camera down.

'Of course,' he said, a fraction too brightly. 'There's plenty of time. Do you want to hold her?'

Eve shook her head. 'Leave her, she's peaceful, I don't want to disturb her.'

The doctor continued talking to her, telling her more about what had happened, her recovery, how long she would need to stay in hospital. She was barely listening. She just stared at Annie, wondering how on earth this strange creature could be her own flesh and blood.

'I'll be back to check on you later,' the doctor said, and then he left.

'How are you feeling?' Mike asked.

'Awful.'

'It's to be expected, your body's been through the wringer. Shall I go? Let you rest for a while?'

But the thought of being alone with Annie terrified her. 'Can you stay?' she asked. 'Keep me company?'

Mike smiled. 'Sure,' he said. He pulled up a chair and sat beside her, gazing at Annie. 'She's so beautiful, isn't she?'

'Yes.'

'When I thought you were going to die, I...' He paused, swallowed. 'I'm just so relieved that you're okay. Annie and me both need you, Eve. It doesn't matter that we won't be able to have any more children, because we have this one and she's perfect.'

He was trying to be positive, to look on the bright side like he always did, but she didn't know what to say to him, to explain what she was feeling. She wasn't even sure she knew herself. There was a numbness to her that wasn't down to anaesthetic or painkillers. She didn't have the words or the energy to verbalise it. In fact, she didn't want to talk to anyone. She turned her head away from him, closed her eyes and pretended that she had fallen asleep.

After a while Annie stirred and began to fuss, and she heard Mike getting up and going over to pick her up, talking to her in a sing-song voice. 'Come on, little one, let's go back to the baby ward and let Mummy rest awhile.' Then the door closed softly, and she was alone.

Once she was sure they were gone, Eve opened her eyes again. The only sound keeping her company now was the monotonous beeping of a machine. The tears began to fall, silently and steadily, and she made no move to wipe them away. How had she ended up here? A year ago, she was carefree and having fun, drinking all night and sleeping all day, nowhere to be but work and no one to worry about but herself. Now here she was, flat on her back in hospital, having nearly died giving birth to a baby she hadn't even wanted in the first place.

And it's all your fault, Mike Branning.

They had met a year ago. Eve was working at a nightclub in Brighton when Mike sat down on a vacant stool at the bar and ordered a drink. After she'd served him, he made no attempt to leave and rejoin his friends. In fact, he sat there all evening, watching her.

It wasn't the first time that a punter had taken a liking to her and she wondered if he was going to offer her a good time at the end of the evening. She'd probably accept, she decided, he wasn't bad-looking and she had nothing better to do. In any event it beat going home alone to her messy, unloved room in her shared digs. She stole glances at him and each time he looked away. But within a few minutes she could sense his gaze on her again. She basked in the pleasure of being an object of desire, sank a few shots for Dutch courage, flirted harmlessly with the regulars, and all the while he watched. At the end of the evening, when even the diehard clubbers had staggered home and the DJ was packing up for the night, he had remained glued to his stool, looking like he desperately wanted to strike up a conversation with her but didn't know where to start. Eventually she threw a tea towel at him.

'I'll wash, you dry,' she said, pointing at the rows of dirty glasses.

The conversation was awkward and stilted at first but gradually it began to flow. He was a secondary school teacher, he told her, and worked at the local comp. He had come out with some colleagues but he hated dancing, so he had left them to it on the dance floor and headed to the bar instead. He was a Brighton boy, born and bred, and his parents and little brother had died in a car accident when he was eleven, so he'd been raised by his nan who had recently passed away too. He still lived in her house, he said, and hadn't been able to bring himself to change a thing yet. The house was just as she'd left it the day she died.

Eve imagined a young man living in an old soul's house, surrounded by chintzy ornaments and china teapots, and felt a bit sorry for him. She sensed he was lonely. She was too, but she drank her way through it and surrounded herself with people every night until she felt loved again. It was a sticking plaster which always peeled off by the morning, but it was better than nothing. Better than sitting around in a museum to your nan, in any case.

When she finished her shift, he asked if he could walk her home. She nodded and he followed her out of the club and on to the street. Her friend Barry, who worked the door, raised an eyebrow at her and she gave him a look, which said, *It's okay, he's nice*. Barry shrugged and turned away. She set off in the direction of her digs and then, on impulse, decided to head to the beach instead. She loved being by the sea in the middle of the night, while the innocents slept. There were sometimes a few drunken stragglers hanging around, but it was largely peaceful, with the gulls for company. She threw herself down on to the cold, damp pebbles and he sat beside her, close enough for her to feel the warmth of his body but not so close that they were physically touching. *A respectful distance*, she thought. He didn't want sex. So, what *did* he want?

'Why are you here?' she asked him.

'Here at the beach?' He was confused.

'Here with me.'

'Because I like you.'

'Why?'

He laughed. 'I just do.'

Eve didn't have a lot of experience of being liked. She didn't think her parents liked her very much; her father had made that clear every time he got his belt out to her and whipped her for being a terrible girl, while her mother turned away and let him do it. Every Sunday they went to church to repent for their sins and then as soon they got home, her father would start totting up his weekly sin tally all over again, so he had something to cleanse himself of the following week. Her friends had acted like they liked her, but they had been quick to turn their backs when all the trouble started. Her head teacher definitely hadn't liked her when he expelled her from grammar school after she was caught kissing her maths teacher in a storage cupboard. She was a troublemaker and a slut, he had told her, and her sort didn't belong in his school. That night, her father beat her black and blue while her mother stayed in the kitchen, making dinner with the radio turned up loud. That was the day he threw her clothes into a bag and kicked it – and her – out on to the street, slamming the door behind her.

The so-called boyfriends who had stolen her heart, stomped all over it and then given it back in a crumpled mess when they got bored of her, hadn't liked her much either. Even the perv of a manager at the nightclub where she was working had his own agenda, which he made clear every time he patted her bottom or squeezed past her behind the bar when there was plenty of space to get by. So, she wasn't sure what to make of this studious, unassuming man sitting beside her on the beach, asking for nothing from her but her company.

Eventually she stood up, brushed off her coat and said, 'I'm going home now.' He got up and followed her and when they reached her door, he asked if he could see her again.

She looked at him, long and hard, and then said, 'Come by tomorrow. We'll go for chips.'

He smiled, waved and then he was gone, leaving her standing on the doorstep, watching him go.

He turned up the next morning at eleven o'clock. She was still in bed when she heard a knock on the door and she looked out of her window to see him standing outside, a bunch of flowers in his hands. She suppressed a smile, wrenched open the window and shouted down to him that she'd be out in ten minutes. She didn't want to let him in because he was respectable, and she lived in a dive. She washed quickly, slipped on jeans and a jumper and rushed downstairs before any of her housemates got up. He was sitting on the doorstep, waiting for her.

'You're keen,' she said, and he blushed.

She took the flowers inside, and then they headed towards the beach. They got some chips from a kiosk, wrapped up in paper and steaming hot, and walked along the seafront, talking about their past lives and future hopes. He was a few years older than her, and she wondered why he hadn't settled down already.

'I just haven't found the right person,' he said when she enquired.

He asked her about her life, where she was from, her family. She gave him the abridged version; strict parents, a bit of trouble at school, getting kicked out of home, a sympathetic family friend taking her in, managing to get a place at college to finish her exams. After that, muddling through for a while, dossing where she could and then, an overwhelming desire to escape from the miserable town where she had grown up and heading to Brighton on a whim.

'Do your parents know where you are?' he asked.

'No. They don't care. They never want to see me again and the feeling's mutual.'

She gave him a sideways glance to see his reaction. He seemed like a decent man, and she was obviously damaged goods. She braced herself for the inevitable excuses that she knew were coming; he'd completely forgotten he needed to be somewhere else; sorry but he had to go because he had lots of marking to do. But he just stopped and pulled her towards him. They stood there, in each other's arms, until at last she became embarrassed and pulled away.

'I think you're brave and strong,' he told her.

It was the nicest thing anyone had ever said to her.

They courted for five weeks. She called it courting because it was so different to anything she'd experienced before. They went out for meals or walks on the beach, sometimes to the cinema. They talked, and at the end of the evening he walked her home. He never came back to the club where she worked and she began to feel like she lived two separate lives. By night she batted her eyelids at men for free drinks, sank shots and danced on the bar for tips, but by day she was sober and uncharacteristically demure. She could be both devil and angel in a twenty-four-hour period but she was starting to prefer the angel version of herself and it was all down to him.

After a while, though, she became frustrated. It had been weeks and they hadn't so much as kissed. She began to fret that she'd read the situation wrong and that all he wanted was friendship. Or, worse, that he felt sorry for her. Had she been a fool to think that he could be attracted to someone as chaotic as her? She didn't even consider whether she was attracted to him because she liked who she was around him and that was what mattered. She decided that she needed to know, once and for all, and there was only one way to find out.

One evening, as they were walking home from the cinema, she stopped in the street and kissed him. He hesitated and then pulled away.

Mortified, she turned and legged it.

'Eve, stop,' he called, running after her, until he finally caught up with her.

'What do you want from me?' she demanded, simultaneously embarrassed and furious.

'I want you, Eve, I love you.'

No one had ever spoken those words to her before. She looked at him suspiciously. 'Why won't you even kiss me then?'

'I want to, I really do. Believe me. But people haven't been very kind to you in your past. I don't want to be like them. I don't want to take advantage of you.'

'You'll never be like them.'

'I just don't want you to do anything until you're ready.'

She looked him squarely in the eye. 'I'm ready.'

He smiled and took her hand, and they made their way silently back to his house. It was the first time she'd been there and it was almost exactly as she'd imagined it, with china ornaments littering every bookcase and a stone mantelpiece adorned with old family photos. He led her up to his room, which still looked like a teenage boy slept in it, and they fell on to his bed in a tumble of arms and legs. Afterwards, they lay side by side, under his duvet. She was relieved that the deed had been done. Alarm bells were ringing in the depths of her mind, warning her that she hadn't been aroused, that she didn't really fancy him, but she pushed them away. Where had sexual attraction got her in the past? Nowhere good. Mike represented something different to her; safety, security, companionship. And, she realised, she wanted that more than anything.

A few weeks later she quit her job at the club because her two lives were no longer compatible. The only person who was genuinely sad to see her go was Barry. He was the one who had got her the job in the first place and he had always looked after her, making sure none of the punters got too touchy-feely without her consent and escorting them out if they did, a big, burly hand on the scruff of their necks.

'Stay in touch, Eve,' he said when she left. 'And keep hold of that Mike, he's a good 'un.'

She got a job waitressing in a café, serving morning coffee to harassed-looking mothers and afternoon tea to elderly couples. She spent the rest of her time at Mike's house, encouraging him to put his stamp on the place, gently reminding him that his nan wasn't coming home. They went shopping together to buy new things; cushions, framed posters, and he always seemed so grateful that she was helping him. She rarely went back to her digs, where she knew she'd only end up getting drunk or high with her housemates. One evening, she confessed to Mike that she'd love to go back to college, and he encouraged her to apply. She got excited, ordering prospectuses, arranging to go to open days, choosing what to study. She wanted to run her own business, she decided, a little shop or a café. Mike put his safe, warm arms around her and told her that she'd be brilliant at it because she had a way with people.

When he asked her to move in with him, she agreed immediately and packed her bag the next day. In anticipation, Mike had cleared out a few drawers for her to put her belongings in and bought fresh sheets for their bed. It was sweet of him, and she was touched by the gesture. That night he cooked shepherd's pie and they ate it in front of the telly on matching trays illustrated with kittens. Afterwards he made them both a cup of tea in his granny's best china. She felt more like ninety-nine years old than nineteen, but he was making such an effort and it felt nice to be loved, so she pushed down any reservations she had about the set-up, settled in, and allowed herself to look forward to the future for the first time in a very long time.

Perhaps she would have gone to college. After that she could have gone to university or got an apprenticeship and worked her way up the ladder. Maybe she would have ended up leasing one of those gorgeous little shops that she loved down in The Lanes. For the briefest of moments, the world really had been her oyster. But then she discovered that she was pregnant.

It had been a surprise and not a good one, at least not for Eve. Mike had talked about them getting married and having kids one day, but it had felt like a million miles away. She was only just learning to look after herself, there was no way that she was ready for a baby, and she wasn't even sure that she wanted children anyway. Half of her wanted to have a kid to blot out the memories of her own childhood and prove there was a better way. The other half wondered if she was even capable of giving love. She and Mike had only known each other for three months and even though she knew deep down that he was a good person, she was scared that he would run a mile, leaving her penniless and alone with a baby to look after. She hatched a plan to get rid of it without him even knowing but every time she looked at his kind, honest face, she felt so terrible about it that eventually she couldn't take it any longer.

She broke the news to him one evening, as they sat in matching armchairs, sipping on tomato soup with cheese and bread. Her hands were shaking as she slowly put her spoon back in the bowl, turned to him and told him that she was expecting.

He stood up so quickly that he almost sent his soup flying, and his face lit up with pleasure.

'That's wonderful news,' he said.

'You're not angry?'

'Why would I be angry?'

'Because you barely know me.'

'I know all I need to know. We're meant to be, you and me. We're going to be a family.'

She tried to tell him how she felt; that it was too soon for a baby, she wasn't ready to be a mum, she wasn't sure if she would be any good at it. But he shook his head and told her that she was going to make a wonderful mother, he just knew it.

'I think we should consider an abortion,' she said.

He was horrified. 'No,' he said. 'No, we can't do that.'

No matter what she said, he had a counter argument. He made her promise not to have a termination. In the end he wore her down with his assertions that everything was going to be okay and that he would take care of them both. He loved her, of that she was sure, but it was more than that for him. His own family had been snatched away from him in the most heartbreaking and horrific way, and he was desperate to rebuild it again. He needed it.

The next day, he got down on one knee and presented her with his dead mother's engagement ring. It was beautiful and it fit her slim hand perfectly. She stared at the diamond glinting up at her and decided to accept. He was a good man and would look after her and the baby. She pushed all thoughts of college and having her own shop out of her mind for the time being and instead, set her targets on becoming a good wife and mother.

They had a small engagement party on the beach with just a handful of people, some colleagues of Mike's, Barry and his girlfriend.

Barry put his arm around her and told her he was happy for

her. She remembered his words, even now. *I'm so relieved that you've settled down, Eve. Mike's a top guy.* She smiled at him and for a moment, with the sun on her skin, the wind in her hair, and a baby in her tummy, she felt truly happy. She didn't even realise his girlfriend had taken a photo of them until she sent it to her in the post three weeks later with a handwritten note, telling Eve that Barry had died in a car accident and that the funeral would be the following Tuesday. Eve had collapsed into a chair and sobbed at the injustice of it. Then, when she was done, she had dried her eyes and put the photo in a jewellery box that Mike had bought her for her birthday. *Let it be a reminder*, she thought. *Life is cruel and unfair. I can't take anything for granted.*

A few weeks later, Mike was offered a job at a school in Northampton. He suggested that they rent a place at first and then if they liked Northampton they could sell the Brighton house, which had been left to him, and buy their own. It could be a fresh start for them, he said, somewhere they could put down roots. She agreed without hesitation. There was nothing left for her in Brighton anymore and at least it meant that she could walk down the street without bumping into some bloke who'd seen her make a fool of herself while drunk, or who'd kicked her out of bed after an awkward fumble.

On her last day in the city, she walked down The Lanes and imagined what might have been. Then she turned around and made her way home.

They moved when she was seven months pregnant, her bump now unmistakeable. He found them a nice little flat to rent, not far from Northampton city centre, and started his job the next day, leaving her at home on her own, with no friends and too pregnant to get a job. She busied herself playing wife-to-be, making the flat homely and getting the nursery ready. *It will be better when the baby comes,* she told herself. *Then I'll be busy and perhaps I'll make friends with other mums.* She pictured herself, pushing a pram around the park, chatting with the other, older women she'd watched out with their babies, but she couldn't see it. No matter that she was in a committed relationship with a ring on her finger, a good man and a nice home, she would always be the unmarried teenager who got herself knocked up in their eyes. She was the outsider, she realised, no matter where she went. She became bored and restless shut up at home, living for the moment when Mike got back from work and breathed life into the flat again. She was becoming dependent on him and she didn't like it but she didn't see that she had any other choice.

One evening, she woke up and the bed was wet.

'Mike,' she said, shaking him awake. 'Something's going on.'

He was up in seconds. 'Is it the baby?' he asked. She nodded and he sprang out of bed, threw some clothes on, and reached for the hospital bag that he'd had packed for weeks.

When they got to the hospital, the midwife confirmed that her waters had broken. But the baby wasn't keen on going anywhere in a hurry and in the end her labour was induced. It lasted for days. He was by her side the whole time, as she knew he would be. He was her cheerleader, her biggest fan. But with each contraction she became more fearful, more convinced that she had made a huge mistake. She didn't know how to be a mother. She didn't want to raise a child who might go on to make the same mistakes as her. She didn't want to be tied down. She didn't want to try to fit into a world where she didn't belong. She didn't love Mike Branning.

By then, of course, it was too late to do anything about it.

CHAPTER EIGHTEEN

Eve stared at the little bag by her feet and then at the bed where she had spent the best part of three weeks, recovering from her surgery. She resisted the urge to climb back into it and bury herself under the hospital-issue blanket. It was thin, scratchy, and uncomfortable but it offered a safety barrier between her and the outside world. A world which she didn't feel at all ready to face. She was like a rabbit caught in the headlights, not sure which way to go.

Mike appeared at the door, with Annie in his arms, and a wide smile stretched across his face when he saw Eve up, dressed and waiting for him.

'You must be so excited to be going home,' he said.

She nodded because it seemed like the right thing to do, but the truth was that she didn't want to go home. In the hospital, people looked after her. They looked after Annie too. They showed Eve how to feed her, bathe her, change her nappy, so that she was more of an observer than a participant and that was fine with her. Now she had to stand on her own two feet.

'Want to hold her?' Mike asked.

Eve shook her head.

'I know you're nervous but you're strong enough now. Don't worry, you won't drop her.'

'Maybe later,' she said.

'Okay, love. Shall we get off then?'

With once last glance around the hospital room, Eve picked up her bag and followed Mike out of the door. The nurses, who had all fallen in love with Annie, waved and called out goodbye as they passed. They must have looked like any other young couple, thrilled by their new addition and looking forward to going home and being a family. As they headed towards the hospital exit, a few people congratulated them in the corridors, and Eve smiled politely at them. She had been on autopilot ever since Annie was born, incapable of processing everything that had happened or of accepting that she was a mother now. There wasn't a single part of her that felt like a mother. Sometimes she wondered if she was in a coma and this was all a dream because she felt so detached from Annie, as though they were two strangers who didn't belong together. She half expected another woman to come bursting through the door at any moment and say that it was all a mistake, and *she* was, in fact, Annie's true mother. She prayed for it to happen.

In contrast, Mike walked around beaming at everyone, his heart so full of joy that she wondered if it might pop like a balloon. He told Eve constantly how proud he was of her, how much he loved her, how glad he was that she was okay. Unsurprisingly, he was wonderful with Annie and she was most settled and calm in his arms. Their bond had been formed within minutes of Annie being born, while Eve lay on an operating table.

The head teacher at the school where Mike worked had been supportive and told him to take as much time off as he needed, so he had been at the hospital almost all day, every day. He gave Annie the formula milk that the nurses mixed up for him, topped and tailed her in the little baby bath, and rocked her to sleep, singing toneless lullabies to her. The nurses adored him.

'You're such a wonderful father,' they crowed, watching him approvingly. 'A real natural.'

Every day Eve waited for her maternal instincts to kick in. She tried to replicate the emotions she'd experienced when Annie was first born. She waited and waited. But they didn't come. So, in the end it had been easier to sit back and let the nurses take over.

'You're tired,' they told her, giving her the get-out pass that she desired. 'You need to rest and recover from your surgery. Baby needs a happy, healthy mummy.'

At first, the nurses did all the night feeds so that Eve could sleep, but instead she lay in bed, awake, staring up at the ceiling and wondering what was wrong with her. Her breasts ached, they craved Annie, but the rest of her body did not. She allowed dark thoughts to spill into her mind; *Everyone was right all along. I am a bad girl. I don't even love my own child. That's why the doctor took my ovaries away, to make sure that I never have any more children. I'm cursed, just like Eve was.*

Mike knew something was wrong, but he glossed over it with flimsy reassurances.

'You've had major surgery, Eve. You're exhausted. Don't rush things. You and Annie have plenty of time to get to know each other. She loves her mummy.'

When the doctor told Eve that she was being discharged, probably expecting her to jump for joy, she was horrified.

'I'm not ready,' she began. 'I'm still recovering, I'm sore.'

'It will take a few more weeks to fully recover,' he agreed. 'But you'll be much happier at home, I'm sure. Annie needs to go home too, she's spent enough time in this hospital.'

And that was it. Her future decided for her by a doctor yet again.

Mike had been delighted when he heard the news. 'At last,' he said. 'The flat hasn't been the same without my girls.'

My girls. That's what he called them now. It was sweet but for some reason it made her angry. She wanted to punch him every time he said it, but she didn't know why.

The night before she was due to be discharged, Eve cried for hours but no one noticed. She was in a busy hospital, surrounded by hundreds of people, but she had never felt more alone.

When they arrived home, she felt no pleasure. He opened the front door and then looked back at her, a hopeful expression on his face, excited to see her reaction. There were balloons everywhere, on the floor, on the ceiling, pink ones, white ones, gold ones. He had taped a *welcome home* banner to the fireplace. On the coffee table was a giant stuffed rabbit holding a pink heart.

'Surprise!' he said.

He was expecting her to be thrilled and she tried to smile, but she couldn't manage it. His face fell and her heart went out to him but still she said nothing.

'You must be so tired,' he said. 'Why don't you go to the bedroom and rest. I'll settle Annie in.'

She nodded, relieved, and made her way slowly to their bedroom, not even bothering to pause and peer inside the nursery like she used to before Annie was born. She slipped off her shoes and climbed into bed, pulling the duvet up to her chin. And then she closed her eyes and shut out the world for as long as she could.

It hardly seemed possible that a newborn baby could have such a fervent opinion but within days, Annie had made it perfectly clear what she thought of her mother. She wailed every time Eve stepped near her and refused to take a bottle from her, no matter how hungry she was.

At first it didn't matter too much because Mike was at home and he could step in. He was so patient with them both, never accusing Eve of getting it wrong – which she was – but instead trying to show her how Annie liked to be held, fed, bathed. At night, when Annie cried, Mike was up and out of bed before Eve had even registered what was going on. She was relieved and grateful, but she also felt redundant, like they didn't even need her. Every time she tried to hold Annie, she would wail inconsolably until Mike, unable to listen to her cry anymore, scooped her back into his arms and Eve turned away, hiding her own tears.

They probably could have muddled along for a bit longer, pretending that everything was fine, but one day the inevitable happened. It was a crisp late winter's day and they had gone outside to get some fresh air. As they walked through the park, Annie wrapped up tightly in blankets and fast asleep in her pram, Mike reminded her that it would be their last day together for a while.

Her head whipped round to face him. 'You're going back to work tomorrow?'

'I have to, love. I've been off for too long as it is.'

'But how will I cope? Annie hates me.'

'Come on, Eve, she's a baby. She doesn't hate you.'

'Yes she does! She screams every time I go near her.'

'You've just got to get to know each other, that's all. You're her mummy, she loves you.'

Eve knew plenty about life to realise that just because you were flesh and blood, it didn't mean that you had to love each other. 'I don't know, Mike, can't you take a couple more weeks off? Please?'

He shook his head. 'I'm sorry love, I can't. The school have been amazing but they need me back. And we can't afford for me to lose this job.'

That night, Eve lay awake, her heart pounding. She had never been alone with Annie before and she had no idea how she would cope. She wanted to shake Mike awake and beg him not to go to work, to stay here with them, but she knew that his hands were tied. She considered getting a job herself, so that Mike could stay at home and look after Annie instead, but there was no way she'd find work that paid the equivalent of a teacher's salary. For a brief moment she even considered calling her mother and asking her to come and stay for a while, because surely any company was better than none? But then she imagined her father's reaction when he learned that she'd had a baby out of wedlock, and it was so terrifying that she quickly dismissed the idea.

She heard Annie fussing, a prelude to full-on tears, and she closed her eyes and pretended to be asleep until Mike got up without so much as a sigh of protest, as she knew he would. Guilt and shame were eating away at her because Mike had to go to work in the morning and she should be doing the night feeds, but she couldn't find the energy. She hated herself. She was afraid that she hated Annie too.

The following morning, they ate breakfast together while Annie kicked her legs about on a playmat on the floor.

'You'll be okay,' Mike said, finishing his toast and getting up to kiss her. 'You're a great mum.'

If she hadn't been feeling so bleak, she would have laughed at him. Mike bent down and gave Annie a tickle and then, with a final wave, he grabbed his coat and left. The door slammed shut and, on cue, Annie immediately started fidgeting and fussing. Eve watched her for a few minutes and then walked over and picked her up, jiggling her about like she'd seen Mike do. But instead of soothing Annie, it seemed to incense her even more. Her whimpers developed into full-on wails. Eve grabbed a bottle of milk that Mike had already prepared for her but Annie kept turning away, refusing to put the teat into her mouth.

'What do you want?' Eve demanded. But she already knew what Annie wanted. Her daddy.

She put Annie back down on the mat and dashed into the nursery to find a dummy, but when she tried to put it into Annie's mouth, she spat it out in indignant rage. She was almost tomato-coloured now, her tiny little arms and legs thrashing about madly.

Tears rolled down Eve's face. 'Please,' she begged. 'Please stop crying.'

She thought about calling the school where Mike worked and asking for him, but she realised with horror that he probably hadn't even arrived yet. He had left less than half an hour ago and she was already falling apart. *What is wrong with me? Why does Annie hate me so much?*

She picked Annie up again and paced around the flat singing lullabies, but her voice was manic and chaotic, not soothing. Annie's wails echoed off the walls, making them seem even louder.

Then Eve heard a rhythmic thumping coming through the walls. Their neighbour, a cantankerous woman who didn't like children, had been complaining about the noise ever since Annie got home from hospital. The woman had started banging her broom against the wall whenever Annie cried for longer than a couple of minutes. Mike had been round to apologise a few times, but the woman was not to be placated and Eve knew from the way that she scowled every time they passed in the corridor that she didn't approve of them. Working herself up into even more of a frenzy, she had visions of Mike coming home to an eviction notice and she rushed around the flat in a wild panic, trying to work out where to go. Then she remembered that Annie usually settled when they went out for a walk. She quickly gathered up the essentials and bundled Annie into the pram, walking briskly out of the flat and down the street.

But something was wrong. Annie wasn't settling at all, if anything, her cries were getting louder. Eve walked quicker, as if speed alone could lull Annie to sleep. She reddened in shame, avoiding eye contact with passers-by who she was sure were judging her. She walked furiously towards the park, praying to a god that she hadn't believed in for a long time, for Annie to just fall asleep, promising that she'd be a good girl, that she'd do *anything* if Annie would just stop crying.

'I think your baby's hungry, love,' a builder called out to her as she passed, laughing with his mates. In a previous life she would have given him some lip, told him to mind his own bloody business, but she was too mortified, so she kept her head low and shuffled past. Eventually she couldn't take it any longer and she turned around before she had even reached the park and made her way back home. She quickly let herself back into the flat and closed the door behind her, breathing a sigh of relief that she was out of the public eye and praying that their grumpy old neighbour had gone out. The thumping started up almost instantly and Eve's heart sank. Nowhere was safe, not even her own home. It was hopeless.

But then Annie's crying became a whimper until it fizzled out altogether. Still in her pram, she turned her head to the side and closed her eyes, her jagged breathing slowing down and becoming steady. She'd fallen asleep through sheer exhaustion. Eve's shoulders sagged with relief and she left Annie in the hallway, asleep in the pram, and went into the kitchen. She looked at the clock; it was ten o'clock. Another seven hours before Mike came home again. She should put some laundry on or tidy away the trail of destruction she had already managed to create, but she didn't want to. She couldn't even be bothered to make a cup of tea. Instead, she sat at the kitchen table, with her head in her hands, and waited for Annie to start crying again.

It was no wonder, then, that when Mike finally got home from work, scooping Annie up into his arms and whisking her off for a bath, that she craved a drink. Something to take the edge off the terrible day she'd had. She poured herself a vodka and Coke and sat down on the sofa, listening to Mike singing from the bathroom. She downed her drink and slipped into the kitchen to make herself another one. As the alcohol kicked in, it softened the edges of her frayed nerves and she finally relaxed. She closed her eyes and smiled with relief, until she remembered that it would be exactly the same tomorrow, the next day, and every day for what felt like the rest of her life.

When Mike returned from putting Annie to bed, she was still on the sofa, three drinks in. He sat down next to her and took her hand.

'How did it go, love?' he asked.

She should have told him the truth, but she couldn't bring herself to do it. So, instead, she shrugged and said, 'It was fine. I went to the park and got chatting to a couple of other mums.'

His face lit up. 'That's wonderful! I knew you'd make friends in no time. You stay here and rest awhile, I'll go and make us some dinner.'

In the kitchen, Mike was clattering around, humming to himself as he chopped vegetables. In the nursery, Annie was sleeping peacefully, calm – at least for the moment – now that her father was home. In the living room, Eve finished her drink and wondered if she could have another one.

CHAPTER NINETEEN

The days merged into one, an endless pattern of misery and monotony. Meanwhile Annie and Eve's relationship was barely improving. They were trapped in a vicious cycle where Annie sensed Eve's nerves and cried in her arms, reinforcing Eve's belief that she was a terrible mother. She had been rejected many times in her life, but it was brutal when it was by her own baby. Yet she deserved it because what kind of mother doesn't love their own child?

Through the haze of grey that clouded her life, she had started to view her past with rose-tinted glasses, reminiscing on what she now remembered as the good old days before she met Mike. Her selective memory blotted out the squalid digs and over-amorous punters, remembering only the fun parts of it. *I used to be such a laugh. Everyone loved me. What's happened to me?*

She got into a routine, survival by day and release by night. As soon as Mike got home, she would hand Annie over to him and go into the kitchen to make herself a drink now that she considered herself off duty. Beer, wine, vodka, whatever they had was fine with her. While Mike bathed Annie, Eve helped herself to another drink. Then another while he read Annie bedtime stories.

She looked forward to the sound of his key in the lock all day, every day.

Meanwhile, she fabricated stories. She told Mike that she'd made some new mum friends and that they went for walks together or met for cups of tea. The truth was that she spent her days in the flat, too afraid to go out with an unpredictable baby and face the judgement of the public. She was a prisoner trapped in her own home, with Annie as her ball and chain.

One Friday evening, after a particularly challenging day with Annie, she couldn't take it anymore. On a whim, she decided to tell Mike that she'd been invited out with her new mum friends.

'I completely forgot about it until now, but I have to be there in half an hour,' she lied.

'Of course, you should go,' Mike said. 'I'm so glad you're making friends.'

She quickly changed and left before he could see the guilt written all over her face at her deception. On the street outside she stood, shivering in the cold, and considered her options. There was a pub a few minutes' walk away and for want of a better idea she started heading towards it. The smell of alcohol and cigarettes, combined with the rush of warmth that hit her when she opened the door and stepped into the pub, was mesmerising.

She sat down on a bar stool and ordered a double vodka and Coke, drinking it quickly and looking around the room at the punters. There were a lot of student types hanging around and she remembered that the college was just down the road. To her left a group were chatting and laughing. They were probably around her age, and she looked at them with envy.

One of the girls in the group caught her eye and smiled at her.

'Have we met?' she asked.

'I don't think so.' Eve looked back down at her drink.

'Maybe I've just seen you around college?'

The possibility of an alternative life flashed before Eve's eyes, one where she was at college, studying business and still dreaming of running her own shop. She didn't see how it could ever come true now, but what was the harm in pretending, just for a few hours?

'Probably, yes, I do study there,' she said to the girl.

'Would you like to join us?'

'I'd love to.'

They got hammered that night. After a few drinks at the pub, they'd gone on to another, and then another, and eventually a club where they had danced until four in the morning. She staggered home, her heels clattering on the pavement, and vomited in a bush before letting herself back into the flat. Stumbling into the corridor she crashed into a wall and slithered to the floor, laughing hysterically. Annie started crying and Mike appeared a few seconds later.

'What the hell happened to you? I thought you were going out for dinner?'

'Oops, I forgot to eat,' Eve said, giggling.

'Well, that explains the state of you. So where have you been?'

'We ended up going clubbing. It got a bit wild.'

Mike observed her dishevelled state and looked like he was about to say something else but Annie's wails escalated and he dashed into the nursery instead. Eve staggered into the living room and landed face first on the sofa, passing out almost immediately.

When she woke up the next day, Mike had undressed her

and covered her with a blanket. Her head was pounding, and she thought she might be sick again.

'What day is it?' she croaked, when Mike walked into the room, holding Annie.

'Saturday,' he replied.

Thank God. Mike can look after Annie. She tried to sit up, but the room was spinning and she had to lie back down again. She hadn't had a hangover this bad in a long time. But she hadn't had such fun in a long time either. She should be feeling guilty about what she'd done, promising Mike that it was a one-off, but even in the state that she was in, all she could think about was when she could get away with doing it again.

The following Wednesday, she ran out of nappies and so, reluctantly, she had to take Annie out to the shops to buy some more. As she was pushing the pram up the confectionary aisle, praying that Annie wouldn't wake up and kick off, she spotted her new student friends. She spun around and walked hurriedly the other way, horrified that they might see her.

'Eve, is that you?'

She stopped in her tracks and turned around slowly. Emily, one of the girls from the group, was striding over to her.

'I thought it was you! Is this your baby?!'

'No,' Eve said. 'She's my older sister's. I'm looking after her for a couple of hours.'

'That's kind of you,' Emily said, peering into the pram. 'She's cute. Hey, we're going out again on Friday, fancy joining us?'

Eve's heart soared in anticipation. 'I'd love to,' she said.

'Great, meet in the same pub as before at eight?'

'I'll be there.'

She grinned all the way home, the two bottles of wine she'd bought clinking in her bag. It wasn't until she was nearly back at the flat that she realised she'd forgotten the nappies.

On Thursday she told Mike that she was going out again the following evening.

'With the same friends?' he asked.

'Yes. It's someone's birthday, that's why we're going out again so soon.'

'Is it going to be another big one, do you think?'

'Maybe,' she said, looking sheepish. 'But this is definitely the last one.'

'All right, love.'

At least I'm kind of telling the truth, she told herself. *I am actually meeting friends.* Friday dragged on and on, and Eve thought that it might never end. At five o'clock she declared it the weekend and went to the kitchen to pour herself a glass of wine. Then she put Annie on the floor in the bedroom and spent the next hour getting ready, doing her make-up and choosing what to wear. She was ready to leave as soon as Mike arrived home, even though she wasn't meeting her friends for another two hours. The sooner she got out of that flat, the better.

'Leaving already?' Mike asked, as he took his coat off.

'Yes, I've just given Annie a bottle,' she said, already heading out of the door.

'Aren't you forgetting something?'

She paused. 'What?'

'Saying goodbye to Annie?'

'Of course!' She turned and waved at Annie, who was smiling and gurgling at Mike. 'Bye, Annie.'

'Have a good time, don't be too late, eh?'

But she was already gone.

She sat at the bar, drinking alone and waiting for her pals to arrive. A couple of men tried to chat her up but although she let them buy her a drink, she quickly gave them the brush-off. She wasn't interested in men, she was interested in having fun with people her age, people who didn't have babies. By the time her new friends turned up, she was already tipsy. They got a round of shots in, downing them in one, and ordering another round. She listened to them talking about their studies, telling stories of college life, and although she laughed, nodded and pretended she knew exactly what they were talking about, she felt horribly excluded, so she drank some more to take the edge off. After a while, the room was swaying.

'Let's go dancing,' she said, and they all laughed and agreed.

At some point she lost them in the club, and she staggered around looking for them before she eventually gave up and went off to dance on her own, spinning her arms around and revelling in the sheer joy of being young and carefree again. She stayed there until the club closed and then she made her way home. The cold night air sobered her up a bit and she stood outside the flat, staring at the door, and realised that she didn't want to go inside. She lay down on the carpeted hallway of the communal area and fell asleep, which is where Mike found her the next morning.

After that, going out became her release. At first it was once every couple of weeks, then once a week. Soon she was going out as much as she could, making up all sorts of excuses until it became so ridiculous that even good-natured Mike couldn't let it go any more.

'Where do you go, Eve?' he asked her one evening as she was getting ready.

'What do you mean, where do I go?'

'Come on, Eve. It's not mum friends, is it? Is it another bloke?'

'No, Mike, it's not another bloke. I'm just letting off some steam, okay?'

'With who?'

She hesitated. She didn't want to admit that she often went out on her own, hoping to bump into some students up for a good time, and drinking alone if she didn't. Anything was better than being in the flat. But she didn't want him thinking that she was having an affair either.

'I go to a student pub,' she admitted. 'They think I'm a student.'

'But you're not a student. You're a mother, and Annie needs you. I don't mind you going out from time to time, but it's getting out of hand and you get so drunk that you can barely stand. Then you have to look after Annie the next day. It's not safe, Eve.'

She wanted to tell him everything then. How unhappy she was, how she still hadn't found a way to love Annie even though she'd tried. How she yearned for another life. How she hated herself for it. Instead, she slipped into self-defence mode because it was easier.

'I never wanted this life, Mike. I never wanted this baby. You made me have it. And now you can look after it.'

She got up, grabbed her bag and walked out, slamming the door behind her. That night she got so drunk that she got into a fight and ended up getting kicked out of the pub. The next morning she woke up feeling like she'd been hit by a lorry and although she couldn't remember everything about the previous evening, the few flashbacks she had filled her with shame. Mike was already awake and he was lying on his side, watching her.

'It has to stop,' he said quietly. 'I'm sorry, but it has to stop. You have a responsibility now.'

'I know,' she said, contrite. 'I'm sorry.'

She did as Mike asked and stopped going out. But she still craved the release that those nights out had given her, so she started drinking at home instead. Her evening tipples, as she called them, became more plentiful. Mike was watching her, keeping an eye on what she was drinking, so she started hiding booze in various places around the flat, where she could surreptitiously have a few swigs without him realising. He stopped leaving money in the kitty like he used to, so she had to ration her money, buying the cheapest booze she could find. After a while, she could no longer wait until Mike got home to have her first drink. The days were just too long. She lived for the moment when she could have her first taste – five o'clock, then four o'clock, then three o'clock. Soon she craved her first sip from the moment she woke up.

Annie was growing and changing all the time, her smiles increasing in frequency, her tears slowly being replaced by giggles. But they did nothing for Eve. She looked after her because it was her responsibility, but she got no joy from it. She was sure then that there was something so fundamentally wrong with her that she could never be saved.

One afternoon, after a difficult morning with Annie who was teething, Eve was so desperate to take the edge off that she overdid it and drank a bottle of wine. As she was walking back into the living room, she tripped over one of Annie's toys and hit the coffee table with her face on the way down, leaving her with a nasty black eye. When Mike came home, he was horrified.

'What happened?' he asked.

'I fell over one of Annie's toys,' she said. 'Silly me for not tidying up properly.'

He looked at her for a long time and then he silently walked over to Annie, picked her up and took her off for a bath. Afterwards, he put her to bed and came to sit down next to Eve.

'How long have you been drinking during the day?'

She was shocked, appalled, and ashamed. 'What do you mean? I haven't been drinking.'

'You think I don't know about your stash of vodka in the bathroom? Or our bedroom?'

She lowered her head, trying to think of an excuse. Finally, she said, 'Okay, they're mine but I only drink in the evening, after a long day. I'd never drink during the day.'

'I turned a blind eye at first. Lord knows why, but I did. I knew that you were finding motherhood hard, that you missed going out with your friends and having fun. I thought I was doing the right thing. But it's gone too far now, Eve. I think you need some help.'

'Mike, I'm not drinking during the day, I promise.'

'Your promises don't mean anything anymore because I don't trust you.'

'You have to trust me, Mike, I'd never let anything happen to Annie.'

He looked at her. 'We're going to see the doctor.'

'Oh, come on, Mike, it's just a few drinks, it's not like I'm an alcoholic.'

'It's not safe, drinking around Annie.'

'For the last time, I'm not drinking around Annie, I just fell over for Christ's sake,' Eve yelled, and Mike shushed her, pointing at the door to Annie's bedroom, which was ajar.

Then he nodded, defeated and afraid of further confrontation. 'Okay, Eve.'

After that, he started turning up at unexpected times – popping home during the day on the pretence that he'd left his lesson notes at the flat or returning early with a pile of textbooks, saying that a cover teacher was doing his afternoon lessons so he could catch up with his marking. Eve knew that he was trying to catch her out. She became more careful, making sure that she only drank enough to numb the sides, never enough that she got too drunk.

'Have you been home all day?' he would ask, as he picked

Annie up and showered her with kisses, barely able to look Eve in the eye anymore.

'No, we went to the park this morning,' she would lie.

But his frequent visits home weren't sustainable. A few weeks later he got offered a deputy head of department role and he couldn't get away with sneaking off any longer. Instead, he would call a few times a day, to see how she was getting on. Sometimes she didn't pick up the phone, so that he would think she had gone out. She became strategic with which calls she answered and which she didn't, plotting out her fictitious day so that she could fill him in on it when he returned. She had lived a lie for so long that it was too hard to tell him the truth now.

The school holidays were difficult. He was at home all the time and whereas before she was relieved to have him there to help with Annie, she now resented it because it meant that it was harder for her to drink. One afternoon he suggested that they take Annie to a farm to see the animals but she feigned a stomach ache and told him to go without her. As soon as he left, she grabbed the bottle of vodka she hid in her underwear drawer and made herself a drink. By the time he returned, she had brushed her teeth, taken a few swigs of mouthwash and was sitting on the sofa with a cup of tea. She was getting better at deception.

She always knew it had to end eventually, for better or for worse. It couldn't go on like that forever. But in the moment, it was easier to coast along a path of destruction than it was to address what was really going on.

One beautiful summer day, Annie was in a good mood for once and so Eve decided to brave the outside world and take her to the park. As she walked, with the sun on her face, she was optimistic for the first time in weeks. Part of the problem was being holed up in that dingy flat, she realised. If she'd just go out a bit more, maybe she'd feel more upbeat, less trapped. As she walked, she made a promise to herself that she'd make more of an effort from now on. They reached the park and Eve decided to go to the playground. Annie was sitting up now, and Eve had an idea to try her on the swings and see if she liked it. Perhaps she might even get chatting to some other mums, make some actual friends. It would be lovely to have someone to meet, a reason to get out of the flat, away from the hidden stash of vodka that called out to her all day, tempting her.

On the way to the playground, she passed an ice-cream van and she decided to treat herself to a 99 Flake. *Today is a good day*, she thought. She smiled at the man, ordered her ice cream and handed over some change. Behind her she heard someone shouting and then screams of horror and she spun around, curious to see what the commotion was. It was then that she realised the pram was no longer there.

She looked around frantically, trying to work out where it had gone and then she saw people running towards the pond at the bottom of the hill. With a growing sense of panic, she looked at the pond and saw her pram, upside down, in the water.

'Annie!' she screamed, dropping her ice cream and hurtling down the hill in a blind panic.

By the time she got there, several people had waded into the water and pulled Annie, and the pram, out of the water. Annie was soaking wet and screaming blue murder. A woman was holding her and jiggling her up and down, soothing her.

'She's mine,' Eve cried, 'the pram rolled away, is she okay?'

'She's fine,' the woman told her. 'My husband had her out in seconds.'

Eve was crying, her hands shaking, as she took Annie from the woman. Next to her some kindly passers-by were trying to clean up the pram, removing the debris and giving it a shake.

'She could have drowned,' Eve heard someone say. She reddened in shame.

The woman put a hand on her shoulder. 'It was an accident, love, don't beat yourself up. It could have happened to anyone. The main thing is that she's safe.'

Eve looked up at her, immensely grateful for her kind words, but then she glanced over the woman's shoulders at two mums with their toddlers, who had stopped to witness the drama. They were looking at her with horror and disgust. She wanted to hand Annie back to the woman and drown herself in the pond, there and then. Instead, she grabbed the pram, and without even saying thank you to the people who had helped her, she turned to leave.

'Do you need some help?' the woman, who had been nice to her, called. She shook her head as she walked away, the pram in one hand and a dripping wet Annie in the other. She found a quiet spot behind some bushes and changed Annie into a clean nappy and some dry clothes, before picking her up again and making her way home as quickly as she could. Annie stopped crying a few minutes later and started smiling and kicking her legs instead, all memory of her traumatic incident forgotten, but Eve couldn't get the image of the pram, upturned in the pond, out of her head. She had nearly killed her own baby. Mike was right, she couldn't be trusted. *I'm cursed,* she thought. *That's all there is to it. I bring misery and pain to everyone in my life.*

The minute she got back to the flat, she put Annie on her playmat and rushed into the bedroom to find her trusty bottle. She took a few deep swigs and then a few more. She could hear Annie waving her rattle about from the other room. She sat on the floor, leaning up against the bed, and took a few more swigs. Then she lay down on the floor, staring underneath the bed, wondering if she could hide there like she used to when she was a child. She spotted her jewellery box and reached for it, opening it up and watching the little ballerina for a while. There were a handful of photographs inside; the one of her and

Barry on the beach, an awful photo Mike had taken of her when she had the black eye even though she had told him she wasn't in the mood to have her picture taken. She had wondered at the time if he'd done it to remind her of the state she'd got herself into, perhaps to scare her into stopping. It hadn't worked. She flicked through them until she got to the one of Annie that Mike had taken in the hospital, shortly after Eve woke up from her surgery. She remembered the moment so clearly. The moment when she had expected to feel love but instead felt nothing. Back then she had thought there was still time for the love to grow. She closed the box and shoved it back under the bed. Then she put the bottle to her mouth and drank.

The next thing she knew, Mike was standing over her, with Annie in his arms.

'Annie was crying and she'd soiled her nappy. How long have you been asleep?'

'Not long,' she mumbled, trying to remember what had happened. Mike was looking at something to the side of her and she followed his gaze to the empty bottle of vodka. He shook his head in disgust and walked out of the bedroom again. She heard him running Annie's bath, singing to her, soothing her. She lay there listening to it all, but she didn't move. Eventually he returned, closing the bedroom door softly and sitting down on the floor beside her.

'How could you, Eve? You left a tiny baby to fend for herself.'

'I know,' she said, too tired and defeated to even try and defend herself.

'What happened?'

There was no way she could tell him about the pond incident, so she said, 'I don't know.'

'Well, I do. You got drunk again and passed out. In charge of our child. How could you do that?'

'Nothing happened to Annie. I'd never let anything happen to her.' But the words sounded hollow, even to her.

'This can't go on any longer. You need help. I've already spoken to the doctor and he said that there's an extremely long waiting list for residential treatment but I think we should go private, use the money from the sale of nan's house...'

What was this talk of residential treatment, like she was some washed-out alcoholic or crazy person? Eve looked at him, anger flaring. 'You've got no idea what it's like, Mike, stuck here in the flat all day every day with a baby who hates me. Nowhere to go, no one to see.'

'Annie doesn't hate you...' Mike began but Eve cut him off.

'She does! And the feeling's mutual.'

She was horrified by her own words, but it was cathartic too, finally verbalising the thoughts that had consumed her for months.

Mike looked like he'd been slapped in the face. His expression crumpled and she instantly regretted her cruel words, but it was too late to take them back. Instead, she buried herself deeper.

'And you? You're like a fifty-year-old man, padding around in your slippers, dinner from a tray every night. You're boring. No wonder I'm bored. No wonder I need a drink.'

'Why are you being like this, Eve? I don't understand.'

Eve was drowning in misery. She thought of her father, beating her and then throwing her out on to the street. She thought about her old headmaster's sneer. She thought of the boys who had used and abused her for their own ends. And then she thought of Barry, one of the nicest men she'd ever met, killed at the age of just twenty-three. Finally, she thought of Mike and Annie. She didn't belong in this world of innocents, she belonged in the shadows, with the other dropouts and misfits. Fairy tale endings didn't exist for people like her. Mike and

Annie were good people; they were not her people. She shouldn't be here with them, she realised that now, because if she stayed, someone was going to get hurt. She stood up and grabbed her jacket.

'Where are you going?' he asked.

'Out.'

'Eve, please, we need to talk. Please, I'm begging you, don't go out.'

She brushed past him and let herself out of the flat, not even caring about how dishevelled she looked. She walked down the street, glancing behind her to check that he wasn't following her. She headed straight towards the pub, fishing around in her pockets to see how much money she had. Enough for a couple of drinks at least, and if her student friends were there, hopefully they'd get a few rounds in. She wanted to get so drunk that she forgot all about what had happened – until she forgot who she even was. She wanted oblivion.

She entered the pub and went to sit down on a stool but the barman shook his head. 'I'm not serving you,' he said.

'Why?'

'Not after what happened last time. You're barred. You need to leave.'

'What are you talking about?'

The barman sighed. 'You seriously don't remember? Jesus, how hammered were you?'

Eve didn't know whether to object or apologise. All she really wanted was a damn drink. 'I've got no idea what you're talking about.'

'You started shouting and throwing punches around, telling everyone how privileged and spoiled they were. You even bit someone. You're lucky you weren't arrested. Go on, off you go.'

Eve reddened with shame. Vague flashbacks started coming back to her. She looked up and saw that a few people were staring at her. In the corner someone whispered something and the whole group sniggered. She recognised one of the girls as Emily, who she used to party with. She had thought they were friends but all she could see in the girl's eyes now was disdain.

The walls of the pub were closing in on her now, the sounds of people's laughter echoing around her until she couldn't breathe anymore. She stood up and ran for the door, desperate to get out as quickly as possible so that she never had to see those horrible people again. Out on the street, she fought back tears as she considered what to do next. She needed a drink more than ever. She headed round the corner to another pub that she'd passed a few times but never been in. It was a bit of a dive but needs must, so she steeled herself to walk in, taking a few deep breaths to steady her nerves and then pushing the door open. A few people looked up and gave her the once-over, but most ignored her, interested in one thing only and that was the drink in front of them. She breathed a sigh of relief. She'd be safe here, where no one knew her.

She ordered a drink from the bar and sat down at an empty table, necking it in one go. As soon as she had finished, she went back to the bar for another.

'Can I get that?' She looked up and saw a man sitting at the bar, looking at her. He had the sort of weathered face which made it impossible to tell if he was thirty or fifty.

She shrugged. 'Okay.'

He patted the stool next to him. 'Come and sit with me,' he said.

His name was Shane and he plied her with vodka and attention, making her feel special and desired again. It was obvious he'd lived, *really* lived, unlike boring Mike with his granddad slippers and TV dinner trays, she thought maliciously. It was unfair, but it made her feel better. It validated the betrayal which she already knew was coming.

When Shane told her there was a party going on at his house and invited her to come back with him, she only hesitated for a second before she nodded her assent. As they left, she noticed the barman watching her but then he turned away again, as if deciding that her comings and goings were none of his business.

The house was a ten-minute walk away, but it was more of a squat than a home. There were people everywhere, huddled in every room; drinking, smoking, shooting up. Some looked up and smiled or nodded at her but most of them ignored her. She took in the scene with a mixture of horror, fear and excitement. She'd never seen anything like it but she was drawn in, like a moth to a flame. For these people, she realised in wonder, were just like her; they belonged in the shadows, hidden away, unnoticed by normal people living their everyday lives. There was a voice inside her, warning her to turn and leave before it was too late, but she ignored it. She was drunk, she wanted to have fun and more than anything, she wanted to forget everything.

Shane handed her a bottle and she took a few swigs and gave it back to him. Then she started dancing, swaying around the room and Shane was watching her, laughing. Someone gave her a joint and she puffed deeply, almost falling backwards as the high hit her.

For a few minutes she felt a buzz more intense than she had ever experienced and she was wrapped up in a blanket of euphoria, but it was quickly replaced by a violent need to be sick.

She looked around at the sea of faces which were now blurred. The room was spinning and Shane was nowhere to be seen. She lurched down the corridor, holding on to the walls to stay upright, fearing she might collapse unless she found the way out into the fresh air.

Finally, she reached the front door and staggered down the

street, half running and half falling, until she tripped. Her head hit the pavement and she vomited until there was nothing left in her body. She lay there for a while and considered getting up and going back to find Shane, but everything hurt and she had no energy left. All she wanted to do was fall asleep, right there on the street.

She closed her eyes and blacked out.

CHAPTER TWENTY

When the police brought her home, Mike really did try to help her. He didn't shout and scream and tell her she was a disgrace. He took her to the doctor the next day and demanded she get some help. The doctor gave them contact numbers of organisations and local support groups, promised to make a referral but warned again of the long wait, and sent them on their way.

Mike ransacked the flat, removing every trace of alcohol he could find. He tried to book Eve into a private clinic, but she refused to let him spend his inheritance on her.

'I'm not worth it,' she said.

'You are to us,' he insisted.

She tried another tack. 'Give me one last chance and then I'll agree.'

School had just finished for the summer, which was a blessing and a curse. It meant that Mike was home to look after Annie because he no longer trusted Eve to be alone with her and she could hardly blame him. But it also meant that he hovered around all the time, watching Eve's every movement and making her feel even more claustrophobic than ever.

After the pond incident, it was safer to distance herself from Annie. Mike didn't understand and was clearly hurt by her indifference to their child, but it was the right thing to do, and if she was being honest, the easiest.

Meanwhile, Annie and Mike's bond went from strength to strength. She giggled and wiggled her arms around when she saw him. She was rolling now, and she would flip herself across the living room towards him, always wanting to be as close to him as possible. Often, he slept in Annie's room, on the floor by her cot, rather than in bed with Eve.

Meanwhile, she watched them, torn between jealousy and regret. She was an outsider in her own family now and it was all her doing, yet she resented it nonetheless.

Self-loathing, self-pity, shame, envy. It was exhausting.

She craved the buzz that alcohol gave her. She knew it was wrong, but she wanted it anyway. On Annie's half birthday, as Mike called it, he decided that they should all go out for lunch. It was a beautiful summer's day, not hot enough to be oppressive but perfect for a picnic in the park. Mike sang as he packed a bag with bread, ham, cheese and strawberries, but it sounded forced, as though he was pretending that they were just an ordinary family, looking forward to a pleasant day out together.

Eve put on a strappy dress and looked in the mirror, wondering how she had become so thin without even noticing. Her baby weight had fallen off her without any effort and now her collarbone protruded, and her face was gaunt. She rarely ate during the day; her only meal often the one that Mike made for them when he got home from work. Embarrassed, she popped a cardigan over her dress to hide her skinny frame.

'Ready to go?' Mike asked when she emerged from the bedroom. She nodded and he put Annie into her pram, handed Eve the bag and opened the front door. They walked to the park in silence, the easy conversation that used to flow effortlessly between them long gone. She knew he was trying but he was finding it increasingly difficult to communicate with her, to understand her, and so often he just gave up. When they arrived at the park, he suggested that they go to the pond first and feed the ducks but she shook her head fiercely.

'No, let's go over to the other side,' she said.

He shrugged and took the path that circled the perimeter of the park until they found a quiet spot near some rose bushes. He lifted Annie out of her pram and placed her on a picnic blanket, where she proceeded to start picking grass and trying to eat it.

'No, no, not for you, little love,' Mike said as he pulled the grass from her tightly clenched fists, laughing and trying to catch Eve's eye so they could share the moment. She looked away.

'I've been thinking about what to do when I go back to school in September,' Mike said, as he pulled the food out of the bag.

At this her ears pricked up. Summer stretched before them in a seemingly endless row of days, all the same. But at the end of it she had always known that he would go back to work, and she didn't know whether the prospect thrilled or scared her.

'I was thinking we should get an au pair. I don't think we can afford a full-time nanny but the au pair could help you look after Annie and do the housework. It would be a bit of a squeeze. Annie would have to come in with us to free up a bedroom. But I think it could work.'

He was watching her, waiting for her reaction. She was aghast at the idea of a stranger living in her house, observing her movements and reporting back to Mike.

'I don't think so,' she said.

They were silent for a few minutes until eventually Mike spoke. 'It wasn't really a question, if I'm being honest. I've already decided. We're getting an au pair.'

It was then that she understood what he was really getting at. He didn't want Eve to be alone with Annie, period.

'I haven't had a drink in days,' she told him. 'I'm trying my best.'

'I know you are, love, and I'm proud of you. But it's more than that. You don't even seem interested in Annie. You never want to spend time with her. I'm trying to understand it and be patient because you're going through a lot right now. Maybe you just need some time to take care of yourself for a while. I'm worried that looking after her will be too much for you.'

'You don't trust me with her.'

He looked down. 'No, I don't.'

If he knew what had happened to Annie the last time we were in this park, he'd trust me even less. She could barely bring herself to think about it. Anxiety started bubbling up inside her as she relived the moment that she saw Annie's pram, upturned in the water. God, she needed a drink.

'Eve, did you hear what I said?'

She came to and shook her head.

'I said that we could try an au pair for six months. Maybe by then you'll be feeling better. Isn't it your first meeting tonight? That's an important step in the right direction.'

The idea of going to an AA meeting appalled her. A few days off the bottle had made her see things in a new perspective. She couldn't be an alcoholic if she could go that long without having a drink and she didn't belong in a room full of low-life drunks who were pissed from the moment they woke up. She was just a young girl who liked to have a few vodkas and let off some steam once in a while. What was so wrong with that? But she had promised Mike that she would go to the meeting, and it was the only way she could save their relationship and be the mother that Annie needed her to be. The trouble was, she didn't know if that was what she wanted. Her fiancé didn't trust her and her baby hated her. She was struggling to even get out of bed in the morning. What she really wanted was to go out and get wasted. She thought about that night at Shane's digs, conveniently forgetting how it had ended and remembering only the feeling she'd experienced when she was as high as a kite, dancing as though her life depended on it. *Maybe I just need one more night out*, she thought. *And then I'll be done with it, once and for all.*

She turned and smiled at Mike. 'Yes, the meeting's tonight. I'm looking forward to it.'

He smiled back, pleased. 'That's great, love. Like I said, I'm really proud of you.'

That evening she didn't even feel guilty when she said goodbye to Mike and left the flat because she was doing what needed to be done and that was far better than any stupid AA meeting. One more blow-out and then she would really try to be the person that Mike and Annie needed her to be. She would find a way to love them and, through doing that, perhaps she would find a way to love herself too. She headed in the opposite direction of the community hall where the AA meeting was taking place, and walked purposefully towards the pub where she had first met Shane, hoping desperately that he would be there.

When she got to the bar, she pulled out the money she had stolen from Mike's wallet and ordered a drink.

'Has Shane been in?' she asked the barman.

He studied her carefully. 'How old are you anyway?'

'Old enough to be drinking,' she retorted.

'I'd stay away from Shane if I were you. He's not good news.'

'I didn't ask for your concern, mate, I asked if you'd seen him.'

The barman shrugged. 'Not for a few days.'

She drank up and ordered a second. By the third she'd made

up her mind. She left the pub and started walking in the direction of Shane's place, trying to remember the roads they'd taken to get there. But she'd been half-cut at the time and after a few wrong turns she ended up back where she'd started. Furious with herself, she was just about to give up and go back into the pub when she saw Shane sauntering down the street towards her.

He grinned when he saw her. 'Hey darling.'

He didn't ask what had happened to her the other night, why she'd disappeared. He didn't strike her as the sort of person who asked too many questions. Instead, he just said, 'Fancy a drink?'

'Yes.'

'Come on then.'

She went to head back into the pub, but he shook his head. 'Not tonight, let's go back to mine.'

She shrugged. 'Okay.'

They stopped at an off-licence on the way, and she spent all her remaining money on booze. Then they carried the plastic bags, clinking with bottles, back to the house. She was far less drunk than she'd been the last time she was there, and it wasn't how she remembered it at all. It was no longer the cool, smoky, atmospheric venue she had pictured it to be. It was dark, dirty, smelly and depressing; the sort of place most people would run a mile from. She hesitated in the corridor, wondering if she had made a horrible mistake by going there. *It's not too late, I can still turn around and go home, pretend I went to the meeting after all. Mike would never have to know.*

'You coming, darling?' Shane was already halfway up the stairs.

She felt the weight of the bottles in her bag. Someone had lit a joint and the smell of cannabis permeated her nostrils. She nodded and followed him up the stairs. *One last time.*

CHAPTER TWENTY-ONE

'Eve, you've got a visitor.'

Eve opened her eyes but made no attempt to move. She stared straight ahead at the wall in front of her, until her gaze fell on a long, vertical crack in the plaster. She studied it idly, following its journey from the windowsill as it meandered down the wall towards the floor.

'Eve?'

She didn't respond. She was lying with her back to the door; her body providing a physical barrier against the world. She willed the nurse to go away and leave her alone, but she could still sense her presence in the room.

Eventually, Eve relented. 'I don't want to see anyone.'

The nurse tutted quietly. 'Eve, your fiancé's here. Mike.'

'And I said, I *don't* want to see anyone.'

They fell into silence, except for the monotonous sound of hospital machines. Finally, Eve heard the squeak of the nurse's rubber-soled shoes as she walked away, no doubt shaking her head with disapproval. Eve continued staring at the crack. How long had it been there? How many poor bastards had lain in this bed looking at it for hours? Had they recovered from whatever ailed them and gone home or had they ended their journey here, in this soulless room?

When she had woken up in the hospital, her first thought was that she was dead. She imagined the nurse hovering over her to be some sort of angel, assessing her and deciding whether she should be allocated heaven or hell. *Definitely hell, love*, she wanted to say. But the worst thing was that she wasn't even sad about it; she was relieved. The disappointment had only come when she realised that she was still alive after all and that the nurse was telling her that she'd been dumped anonymously outside the hospital and that she'd had to have her stomach pumped.

It came back to her then; going to the pub, finding Shane, getting wasted at his place. Drink, drugs, then nothing. She must have passed out or something. Who had taken her to the hospital? Was it Shane? She didn't even know if anything had happened between them.

She had thought her only saving grace was that she was anonymous. But then she discovered that the nurses had rifled through her belongings and found a card in her purse with Mike's name, address and number on it. He must have hidden it in there after the police had brought her home in a state, fearing that it might happen again. She was both touched and disgusted by the gesture. The busybody nurses had clearly called him up because now he was here, waiting to see her, but there was no way that she could see him, to face him after what she'd done.

'Eve? It's me.'

Anger surged through her. How dare the nurse let Mike in when she expressly told her she didn't want to see him? Surely that was in breach of her rights? She was going to make a complaint, insist the self-righteous cow had some sort of disciplinary. But her indignance quickly ebbed away because she had no fight left in her anymore, and she sank once again into bleakness.

He was pacing around the room, finding a chair and dragging it over towards the bed. She refused to look at him, even as he sat down beside her and put his hand on her back. She moved away from his touch, curling up into a ball on the very edge of the bed.

'Eve, what on earth happened? The doctor said you were dumped outside, unconscious.'

She didn't respond.

'Anything could have happened to you. It doesn't even bear thinking about.'

She focused on the crack in the wall, willing him to leave.

'I thought you were going to a bloody AA meeting. Where did you go?'

Still nothing.

'Eve, we need to talk. Can you turn around, please?'

But she couldn't even look at him, let alone talk to him. What was left to say? She had lied to him, stolen from him, chosen getting drunk with strangers over looking after her child. And she hadn't even felt guilty about it. She had tried to blame him, and Annie, for her troubles, telling herself that if it wasn't for them then none of this would have happened to her. But the truth was that the only person to blame was her. She knew that if she turned around he would shower her with reassurances, tell her that everything was going to be okay, that he would fix her, because for some absurd reason he still seemed to believe in her. But there was nothing left to fix and pretending otherwise was a waste of everybody's time.

'Eve, I haven't got much time, I have to pick up Annie soon.'

Eve twitched slightly at the mention of their daughter's name. Slowly and reluctantly, she turned around to face him, curiosity getting the better of her. 'Where is she?' she asked.

'She's with a friend from school. I couldn't bring her here, I didn't want them to know about her because of what happened to you. I can't risk social services...'

She turned away again, unable to meet his eye. She knew exactly what he was going to say. He couldn't risk social services taking Annie away because she was an unfit mother.

'You need to leave, Mike. I don't want to talk to you.'

'Please, Eve!' He was desperate, pleading with her. She almost broke, knowing what she was putting him through. But then she remembered the pram in the pond, the moment when she thought that she'd killed Annie, and she steeled herself.

'I don't know what to do,' he said next.

Silence.

Finally, he stood up. 'I'll be back tomorrow. And we're driving straight to a rehab clinic. I'm not giving up on you, Eve. I'll never give up on you. Don't give up on yourself.' And then he left.

It was done, she thought with relief. The worst bit was over because by tomorrow she'd be gone. Some other soul would be in this bed, the next victim in the precarious and brutal circle of life, while she vanished without a trace, and she would never have to face him again.

She would never have to face Annie either.

'Eve, the doctor has said you can go home now.'

Eve nodded and got out of bed, looking around for her things. Already she could feel a tingle of excitement at the prospect of getting out and having a drink. The doctor had warned her not to, of course. But he'd assumed that she was some silly young girl who'd gone too far on a night out, along with all the other Friday night stragglers who turned up in A & E every weekend.

As she buttoned up her coat, she considered her options one last time. There was still time to call Mike and tell him that she was being discharged. She could let him drive her to rehab and she could make a conscious effort to be a better person. Annie would never have to know about it and Mike would forgive her. But he'd never forget. Neither of them would, and he would never trust her with Annie, not completely. No matter how hard he tried, he couldn't hide the pain and disappointment in his eyes, which betrayed how he really saw her now; as a waster, just like everyone else before him had seen her. Was it this that had cemented her decision not to go back to him? Was it her shame at realising what a bad mother she was, even worse than her own mum? Or was it simply the desire for another drink? Eve didn't know anymore.

She gathered her things and slipped out before anyone could ask her who was picking her up. Out on the street, she took a few deep breaths of fresh air, and then began walking, wiping a stray tear from her cheek. It was the last time she was going to cry, she decided.

There was only one place left to go. She tried to remember where he lived, reliving the route they'd taken from the pub the previous night. She could picture the house, with its boarded-up windows and overgrown front garden. The sun was making her sweat and her feet were beginning to blister but she kept walking until she found it. She stood outside, staring up at it, trying to remember what had happened the previous evening. It was hard to believe that it was less than twenty-four hours since she'd last been there. Nothing had changed. Everything had changed.

She knocked on the door and a man opened it, looking her up and down.

'I'm here to see Shane,' she told him.

The man moved aside to let her in. She made her way from room to room, peering in at the inhabitants who huddled around, talking, smoking, drinking. Then she went up the stairs, peering through doors until she eventually found Shane, lying on a mattress on the floor. He looked up when he saw her and smiled.

'Hello, Eve,' he said, sitting up.

'Hello.'

'Want to come and join me?'

He didn't ask her if she was okay and she didn't ask him what had happened to her. She just made her way over to him and sat down on the mattress beside him. He passed her a bottle of vodka and she took it greedily. As the liquid hit her body she fought back the nausea, forcing herself to keep drinking. Shane put his arm around her and she didn't move away. Slowly he lay back on the mattress, pulling her down with him. She let herself fall.

Mike found her, a few weeks later. God knows how. The poor man must have been into every pub in Northampton until someone recognised her photo and told him where to look. She was lying on Shane's mattress when he walked in and he stopped in the doorway and stared at her.

'My God, Eve.'

She knew she looked terrible, but she didn't care. Shane looked up and stared at Mike lazily. 'Who's this then?' he asked.

'Go away, Shane,' she said. He shrugged and stood up, brushing past Mike on his way out.

Mike remained rigid, refusing to enter the room, as if he was afraid of what lay inside.

'What happened to you, Eve?'

She looked down at the stained mattress, refusing to meet his eye.

'I'm getting you out of here,' he began but she cut him off.

'No, you're not.'

'You can't stay here in this dump. Come home, we'll get you some help, anything you need, we'll make it happen.'

'I'm not coming home.'

'Eve please, I need you. Annie needs you.'

Eve tried not to react to the mention of their daughter's name.

'I've seen a job advertised at a school in the south-east,' he continued. 'If I get it, we can move away from here, start afresh. I can make you better, I promise. Please, just come home.'

She shook her head. 'I'm not coming home. You need to forget about me.'

'How can I do that? You're my fiancée. You're the mother of our child!'

'Not anymore I'm not. I'm no one.'

He rushed towards her then, but she turned her body away from him.

'Don't say that. You're not no one. You're ill, that's all. You just need some help.'

'Leave, Mike, there's nothing for you here anymore.'

'Just come with me now, Eve, and we'll make it all okay. I promise.'

She shook her head.

'This is your last chance, Eve, you do know that, right? Your last chance to have a family.'

It was a low blow but he was hurting and so she let him say it, not bothering to fight back. She didn't want any more kids anyway. The idea of it was laughable.

He hesitated, as though he was trying to think of another

way to convince her. Begging, guilt and tough love hadn't worked. What was left for him to try?

'I'll come back,' he said. 'I'll come back every day until you agree to go home with me.'

'You're wasting your time. I'm never coming home. You should go, you and Annie. You should move away from here and start again without me.'

'Please don't say that!' He was crying now.

Finally, she looked up at him. 'Get this into your head, Mike. I'm done with us. I don't want anything to do with you anymore. Or Annie. Forget me. Forget I ever existed.'

He sank down on to the floor. 'I can't do that.'

'You have to.'

He sat with his head in his hands, looking as out of place in the squat as it was possible to look. He didn't belong here any more than she belonged in his pristine flat.

'What do I tell Annie?'

'Tell her I'm dead.'

The words came tumbling out of her mouth and he gasped. But she had no intention of taking them back. After all, it was half true anyway, she might as well be dead. His sobs became louder, more anguished, but she didn't comfort him and then, eventually they subsided.

'I'll be back tomorrow,' he told her.

She didn't respond. She watched him as he stood up, brushed off his trousers, took one last look at her and left. A few minutes later, Shane came back into the room.

'What was that about?'

'We need to leave,' she told him. 'It's time to move on.'

Shane nodded, no questions asked. 'I know a place,' he said.

'Good. Then it's done.'

They packed up what few belongings they had and left without a word of goodbye to anyone.

She paused on the pavement outside. She was at the very edge of the cliff but there was still time to turn back before she plummeted forever. Then she thought of Annie. She was safe now, Eve couldn't hurt her anymore. She and Mike could move on with their lives and they would be happy, far happier than they could ever be with her. Some people just weren't born to be wives and mothers. She was thirsty now, her need for a drink superseding any other thoughts. She took a quick swig of vodka and then she followed Shane down the street.

They passed by a primary school and the children were outside on their lunch break. She watched them through the fence as they laughed and ran, chasing each other around the playground. One little girl was standing with her hands on her hips, her long brown hair tied up in pigtails and her once knee-high socks saggy around her ankles. Eve imagined Annie growing up and going to school. She pictured her smiling shyly for the camera, with ribbons in her hair, while Mike took photographs. Eve tried to imagine herself in the photo, standing next to Annie, a proud mother with her daughter. She looked at the girl in the playground again. The girl had noticed Eve and was staring at her, her face contorted with fear at the sight of her. Because Eve didn't look like a mother, she looked like the drunk, wretched waster that she was.

'Are you coming or what?'

She turned to Shane and nodded. And then she continued walking, away from the school and the beautiful children who had their whole futures ahead of them. Away from Mike and Annie and the only real chance of love that she had ever had in her life.

She walked away from it all.

CHAPTER TWENTY-TWO

Eve breathed deeply, in and out, in and out. She fiddled nervously with her bracelet. Her heart was pounding, her palms clammy. No matter how many times she did this, it never got any easier. As soon as she began to speak the devil inside her would be exposed, her sins revealed, and the urge to run away was overpowering. She put her hand on her chest to steady her heart and then she looked up, her gaze fixed straight ahead, her stance determined. She braced herself.

'My name is Eve and I'm an alcoholic.'

Eve waited for the habitual applause. She scanned the circle of faces around her. Some were new to the group and wore expressions that she recognised from her own past – cynicism, denial, anger, fear, curiosity. Then there were others who she'd known for years and who, over time, had become friends. They looked at her encouragingly, nodding at her to continue.

'I've lost a lot of things to alcohol; my fiancé, my self-respect, my dignity. But they all pale in comparison to the biggest one of all, which still hurts to talk about now.

'When I was twenty years old, I abandoned my baby, Annie. I convinced myself that she was better off without me.

She was six months old. Before I left, Annie's father, Mike, asked what he should tell her about me and I said, "Tell her I'm dead". Can you believe it? I can't. It horrifies me. But that's what alcohol does to you. It devours you bit by bit, destroying not just your body but your mind too. I can make excuses for my behaviour: my own parents gave up on me; I felt worthless; I nearly died giving birth; I was robbed of the chance of ever having any more children; I had what I now know was postnatal depression and post-traumatic stress disorder. But the truth is that it was just easier to drown in a bottle of vodka than it was to ask for help.

'Of course at first, I didn't realise any of this. I thought I was drinking for fun, just letting off a bit of steam like any young person did. Before I met Mike, I drank every night to feel confident and beautiful. After Annie was born, I drank for some relief from looking after a baby. I wouldn't hear any talk of me being an alcoholic; the idea was ludicrous to me. Even when I was drinking just to get through the day, I refused to accept what was staring me in the face.

'After I left Mike and Annie, that changed. I didn't bother trying to deny it anymore. There was no point, because no one cared. I had what I'd craved for months; no responsibility, no crying babies, no fiancé watching my every move. I was accountable to no one. But I didn't feel good about it, not one bit, and the guilt and shame didn't fade. They became worse. I ran away from it every time, seeking solace in the bottom of a bottle or the arms of a different man.

'From the moment I woke up to the moment I went to bed, the only thing on my mind was when I could have a drink. I drank to have a good time. I drank to numb the pain of life and of my betrayal. I drank because I had to. And that was my life for longer than I care to remember. Years went by, each day blurring into the next, with nothing to separate them. I lived in chaos, moving from place to place, man to man; alcohol my only constant.

'I've wondered many times how I survived that period of my life. I had no real friends, I lived hand to mouth, and I dossed wherever I could find a bed. I picked up lonely men with promises of a fun time, but in the harsh light of day they soon got bored of me, or vice versa. No matter how many times I ran, I couldn't hide from what I'd done any more than I could hide from who I had become. It haunted me, day and night.

'Eventually, I'd had enough. There was no light at the end of the tunnel for me, I was trapped in the darkness, unable to see a way out. Death was a better option than the half-life I was living. My daughter thought I was dead anyway, so what did I have to live for? Once I'd decided to end my life, a kind of peace came over me for the first time in a long time. I didn't have any affairs to get in order, I could simply disappear without a trace and nobody would miss me. It was both liberating and excruciatingly depressing. I washed down a bunch of pills with some vodka and the last thing I saw in my mind before I passed out was Annie, kicking her legs and smiling at me. She would have been a little girl by then of course, but the only memories I had of her were as a baby. Then I felt sleep pulling me down and I was relieved that it was all over.

'But it turned out that, like everything else in my life, I was even a failure at committing suicide.

'When I was in hospital recovering from having my stomach pumped for the second time in my life, a social worker came to see me. She was my only visitor and she took my hand, looked me straight in the eye, without any hint of judgement, and said, "There's always another path. You just have to want to take it". I remember those words like it was yesterday.

'Something changed in me that day. Maybe I'd had enough of my pathetic existence, or the simple act of a stranger's kindness finally got through to me. Or perhaps I just had to sink to the bottom to realise I wanted to swim. I had skirted close to death for the second time in my life, yet here I was, still in the land of the living, so there was no point acting like a ghost anymore.

'I sobbed, feeling tears on my cheeks for the first time in years, and told the social worker that I was ready for a new path. She was amazing, that woman. She found me some accommodation and put me in touch with organisations that could help me. She went above and beyond for me, and I remembered how good it was to have someone looking out for me. I asked her once why she was helping me so much, more than her job required, and she said I reminded her of her daughter. When I asked how old her daughter was, she told me that she had died ten years ago. She never told me what happened, and I never asked, but it made me even more determined to grasp the second chance I'd been given; not just for myself but for this woman who had already lost so much and yet had chosen not to lose faith.

'I started seeing a counsellor and going to AA meetings. As I listened to other people's stories, I realised two important things. One was that I wasn't the only one who had made monumental mistakes. The other was that there was a way to accept them and to move on in life, never to forget but to find a way to live with them, without having to drink them away.

'At first, every day was an uphill struggle but there was something inside me, a long-forgotten determination, and I knew there was no going back. I was doing it for myself, yes, but I was also doing it for other people too; the social worker who kept in touch and Annie, who I wanted to prove myself to, even though she would never know.

'Slowly, chinks of light started to appear; small things at first, like the simple pleasure of crunching through autumn leaves or talking to a passer-by and realising that they had treated me as an equal, not something they'd trodden on. These moments spurred me on and made the struggle worthwhile. I began to believe for the first time that I would find my way out of the darkness. I began to believe in myself.

'I got a job as a cleaner for some offices in the city. Every day I got up at 4am and went to work, cleaning, dusting and vacuuming to make everything perfect before the workers came in. I was so proud of my job and even prouder of my weekly pay packet. It wasn't a lot but it was money I had earned honestly, through hard work.

'One morning, I was dusting the desks when a woman walked in. I went to leave but she started chatting to me and we got into a conversation. She was one of the most confident and glamorous women I had ever met, and she was nice with it too. She was a director at the firm, in her forties with three children and seemed like she had it all. I began to look forward to seeing her in the mornings, feeling disappointed if she didn't appear before I finished my shift. Even a five-minute conversation with her was the highlight of my day.

'One day she told me that the company was hiring a new receptionist and that I should apply. "You've got a good way with people", she said. "You should take advantage of it".

'The prospect terrified me. Not only would I have to go through the ordeal of being interviewed, but if by some crazy miracle I got the job, I'd be expected to talk to strangers, all day, every day. I'd be the face of the company and it was too much responsibility for me to handle. Even though I was slowly building my life back together, piece by piece, part of me still believed I didn't deserve to be around normal, good people. But this woman, she badgered me every day, urging me to go for it, until eventually I agreed.

'On the day of the interview, I thought I was going to be sick

I was so nervous. My hands were shaking and I had to use every ounce of strength I had to make eye contact, but somehow I pulled it off because they called me the next day and offered me the job. That night, I celebrated on my own with pizza and a cup of tea, and I told myself that this was the beginning of a new chapter, one that I wasn't going to mess up.

'The first few days on the job were some of the scariest of my life. I'm not going to lie, I craved a drink more than once. But I kept my head down, worked hard, and gradually I found my feet. The biggest challenge turned out not to be the actual job but the social aspect of working in an office. I was constantly turning down offers to go out for a drink because I knew that I wouldn't cope with being surrounded by alcohol, I wasn't strong enough yet. I was in my twenties and single, so my colleagues assumed I'd be up for going along to their Friday night blow-outs, and when I said no week after week, they gossiped about me, whispering to each other that I was a snob. It hurt but I had to brush it off. Better for them to think I was stand-offish than to know the truth.

'I threw myself into work because it was better than being alone in my room every night, watching TV. I lived for Monday to Friday, nine to five, and I quickly earned a reputation for being a grafter. The bosses complimented me, saying I was a natural with clients and the best receptionist they'd ever had. At first, I blushed and looked away but gradually I grew in confidence and started to hold my head high. After a year, they offered me a promotion and just like that, I was climbing up the ladder. Soon I had enough money to move out of the bedsit I was staying in and rent my own flat. I got a lovely little place with its own garden, somewhere I was no longer embarrassed to invite people back to.

'I started making new friends; a couple of colleagues from work, a woman who lived in the same building as me. I felt strong enough to socialise without worrying about falling off the wagon. At first, I made excuses for why I wasn't drinking; I was on antibiotics, I was driving and so on. I think they all thought I was secretly pregnant. Eventually, though, I got bored of the lies, so I came clean. I told them, "I don't drink and it's a long story, but I'll tell you one day". They accepted it without question and that's when I realised that I finally had proper friends.

'Years went by. I worked hard. I went to AA meetings every week. I started jogging. I socialised. Then I was offered a senior management role at a branch in another city. It was a great opportunity but I was scared to leave the safety net I had built for myself in Northampton. I fretted for days. *What if I can't find an AA group I like? What if I start drinking again?* But there was another voice inside me now, a louder one, clamouring for attention. *You can do this,* it said.

'I accepted the job and moved away from Northampton for good. It was a bittersweet farewell to a city that had seen me at my worst and at my best, but I never went back. I found a flat, joined a new AA group, this one in fact, and started my new life. Time went by and I did well for myself. I saved up enough money to buy my own place, found a good group of friends and even started dating. None of them stuck – a recovering alcoholic who can't have children isn't exactly a catch for most men – but it was still empowering to be putting myself out there again, on my terms, embracing life and being brave. I built a life for myself, a good one, until I no longer recognised the person I was before. I shed my old skin and grew a new, stronger one.

'A few years ago, I decided to start my own business, something I had dreamed of doing since I was a teenager but never believed I'd achieve. I applied for a loan, expecting to be rejected, and I couldn't believe it when they actually gave it to me. I now run a successful company and have even won a few awards. The rest, they say, is history.

'I haven't had a drink in decades. I'm a successful businesswoman with a beautiful house and two delightful cats. I have lovely friends. I can run five miles without breaking a sweat. I'm a trustee of a charity which supports young people with addiction.

'But I'm still haunted. I think about my daughter every day, wondering how she is and what she's doing, pushing myself to be better so that I can prove I'm good enough for her, even though she doesn't know. I've thought about finding her a thousand times but then I've talked myself out of it again, telling myself that it's impossible, too much time has passed. We talk a lot in recovery about making amends, but I haven't been able to do that and it hurts like hell. I thought the urge to see her would weaken over time, but it hasn't, it's become stronger and more overpowering. It consumes me, an addiction as strong as the one I had for alcohol.

'I've stayed away. I've persuaded myself that she's better off without me. But now I'm starting to wonder if that's true. I'm not the same person she knew for the first, brief few months of her life. I have a heart full of love ready to give to her. I want to look after her, to look out for her, to celebrate with her, to comfort her, to be there for her through the highs and the lows. More than anything, I want to say I'm sorry for the lies and the pain that I caused.

'Do I have the right to do this or am I being selfish? I don't know. Either way, there's one thing that I know for sure; I made the biggest mistake of my life when I walked away from her and I will never be at peace until I make amends.

'But how can you come back from the dead?'

CHAPTER TWENTY-THREE

Eve emerged from the dim church hall, into the sunlight. She reached for her sunglasses and slipped them over her eyes before pausing for a few moments on the pavement outside. She stood in the same spot every week. It was where her transformation took place. Inside the four walls of the hall, she laid herself bare, stripping away her new skin and exposing the old one. But once she was back outside, she covered herself back up again.

During tea and biscuits, her AA buddies had flocked around her, like an informal intervention, and urged her to be careful. They had known her, and her secret, for a long time. Long enough to know that there was something different about her this time. She was plotting.

'Think really carefully before you do anything rash,' one of them said.

'Maybe it's better to let sleeping dogs lie,' said another.

And the worst one. 'It will destroy her. Don't do it.'

But this was no impulsive, spur-of-the-moment decision. She'd spent years mulling it over, agonising, going back and forth. It had taken a long time to get here. And it came down to this: wouldn't a daughter want to know that her mother was still alive? Once she got over the initial shock and hurt, wouldn't she be curious to explore if there was something between them, a bond that couldn't be broken, even by years of separation? Even if it took years to get to that point, Eve was willing to wait. She was under no illusion that this was a Hollywood movie, her life so far had been anything but. There would be anger, recriminations, heartbreak, and heaven only knew what Mike would say when he found out about it. But if she could just explain it all to them, to make them understand that she had left to keep them safe, to protect them before she self-destructed and took them down with her, maybe there could be a future for them.

The wheels had been set in motion months ago. At first, she had told herself she just wanted to know that Annie was okay, that was all. A quick internet search and then she'd be satisfied. It hadn't been hard to track her down; after a few clicks and a couple of wrong turns she was on Annie's Facebook and Instagram pages, scrolling through a multitude of photos of her. She had known instantly that she had the right Annie Branning because she was the spitting image of her father. It had taken Eve's breath away, the total absence of any part of her from her daughter's life, as though she had even been scrubbed out of her physical appearance. Annie was no longer a baby; she was a woman and a beautiful one at that. She looked like she had a good life, family and friends who loved her, that much was clear.

Eve had devoured the photos, thirsty for more, but afraid for Annie too. She had almost wanted to get in touch just so she could warn her not to share her life so publicly, to tell her that any old person could see it, even a psycho like her supposedly dead mother could find out intimate details about her.

Does she really think I'm dead? It was a question she had

asked herself many times. Sometimes she used it as an excuse to justify why she should get back in contact with Annie. *What if Mike told her that I was still alive all along and she's been looking for me all this time?*

It was bull, though, she knew the truth. She had known it when she walked past a letting agents in town, a few months after she ran away, and saw their flat listed as to let. Mike had done exactly what she had asked him to do. He had gone off to start a new life and taken Annie with him. She had made a deal with the devil, but the devil wasn't him, it was her.

Like all addictions, though, soon scrolling through photos wasn't enough anymore. She knew what Annie looked like, where she lived, even where she worked, but she was thirsty for more. She didn't want to be a voyeur, she wanted to be a mother. She wanted to own up to her mistakes, not to hide in the shadows like she had done for so many years.

Today was the day. She had waited for long enough, biding her time, and now was the moment for action. She had been planning it for weeks. She started to walk away from the church hall, without looking back, towards her car. Once she was inside, she programmed the satnav and set off. She turned the radio on to distract herself, but her hands trembled as she drove. *It's the right thing to do*, she told herself. And then a few seconds later, *it's the wrong thing to do*. As always, the angel and the devil inside her were fighting it out, but she no longer knew which one was which.

When she arrived at her destination, she sat in the car for a few minutes, gathering the courage. Her mouth was dry and she wanted a drink. Instead, she checked her reflection in the rear-view mirror, dabbing some face powder on and reapplying her lipstick, like she was going to meet a date not a daughter. She climbed out of the car and started walking towards the high street, past the shops and the banks and the restaurants, until she reached the place she had been looking for: Annie's work. She paused outside, catching her breath. People walked past her, going about their daily business, oblivious to her inner turmoil. She felt like she was in an alternative world, hardly daring to believe what was about to happen. She had dreamed of this moment for so long and now it was finally here, and it was too momentous to grasp.

She looked over the ads on display in the window and peered tentatively in, spotting her immediately. Her beautiful, darling Annie. So much time had passed, yet somehow she still looked the same. Annie was talking to a customer and she was smiling, tucking a strand of hair behind her ear. She looked so much like Mike that for a moment Eve was transported back to the past, reliving events that she hadn't thought of in years. Chips by the sea. The engagement party on the beach. Moving into their flat in Northampton. But then the customer got up to leave and as he walked out of the door and on to the street, Eve had to move aside to let him pass, which brought her back to reality. She looked through the window again. Annie was checking her phone now, smiling at something on the screen. She was so delightful that it took Eve's breath away. She could stand there and watch her forever. She would never get bored of it.

A woman inside was looking out of the window at her curiously. She was starting to become conspicuous and it wouldn't be long before Annie noticed her too. It was now or never. But seeing her daughter in person had given her doubts again. She looked so happy and carefree; what if Eve ruined it all? Annie didn't deserve that. She was the innocent victim in this horrific web of lies, betrayal and abandonment. Eve was panicking now, her earlier resolve evaporating. This had been a terrible idea. What had she been thinking? But Annie was so tantalisingly close now and she couldn't bear the thought of walking away from her, of going home and returning to her normal life. She had run away once; she didn't want to do it again.

What the hell should she do? Should she stick to Plan A, go inside right now and introduce herself to Annie? Or should she deploy Plan B and scarper? Both options were tempting.

She had seconds to decide.

Then she had a thought. *What about a Plan C?* She could pop inside and pretend to be a customer. She could watch Annie work, talk to her a bit, and then leave again. Perhaps that would be enough to satisfy the aching in her gut and Annie never had to know who she was, saving her from any distress. There was a chance Annie would recognise her but it was unlikely. The girl had been six months old when she left. And anyway, Eve looked completely different; not only was she significantly older and several stone heavier, her once long, dark hair was now styled into a neat, blonde bob. She wore expensive clothes, jewellery and make-up. She could easily pass herself off as any other middle-aged woman looking to buy.

But if she pretended to be a stranger, did that mean she was closing the window of opportunity to tell Annie who she really was? And wasn't that the reason why she had come in the first place, to make amends? Was she simply heading down another rabbit hole of lies and deceit? Oh, this was agony. The woman inside was still looking at her and now she was standing up, like she wanted to come outside and talk to her. Then Annie looked up and saw her. Their eyes met and for a second the world stood still. But there was no flash of recognition, no gasp of surprise or horror on Annie's face. She simply smiled politely and then looked away again.

It was decision time. Fight or flight? Or neither?

Eve decided.

She opened the door and walked inside. Annie smiled at her

in a friendly way that, in any other circumstance, would have made Eve feel at ease. She had the sort of open, warm face that made you feel comfortable in her presence immediately. *I bet she has a good way with people*, Eve thought, *just like me*. The idea of Annie having inherited something from her after all cheered her.

'How can I help you?' Annie asked.

Eve's mouth was dry. She just about managed to get some words out.

Annie smiled and nodded as she listened. Then she started chatting away, but Eve was barely listening. She was too busy soaking up her daughter, every wonderful inch of her. She was bright, that much was clear. And kind, Eve thought. She definitely had a kind aura about her. Eve had to pin her arms to her side to stop herself from reaching out to touch her. All too soon it was over and Eve knew she couldn't stall anymore, she had run out of things to say. It was time to leave. But she didn't want to. She had walked away from Annie once and there was no damn way that she was going to do it again. It would kill her. Screw Plan C.

It came to her then, like the flash of a light bulb. Perhaps there was another way; a way to be part of her daughter's life without destroying it. A way to look out for her without her ever knowing who she was. It was risky and absurd. There were a million and one things that could go wrong at any moment. But she knew, in the very pit of her stomach, that it was what she had to do...

She looked at her daughter and smiled.

And then she said, 'Ever thought about being an estate agent?'

CHAPTER TWENTY-FOUR

PRESENT DAY

Lil walked her customer to the door, shook his hand and waved him off. She sighed with satisfaction. Another property on their books. She turned to look at Brian who gave her a thumbs up. On the other desk the new sales negotiator, Andy, was on the phone, his ear glued to his headset, still desperate to impress. He was a good kid. If things carried on like this, she'd be able to keep him on permanently, even after Annie returned from maternity leave.

Annie. Even the thought of her made Lil smile. She'd had the pleasure of being part of her daughter's life for a decade and they had been the very best years. It had taken a long time for Lil to accept that Annie would never know who she really was but in the end, she was reconciled with it. After all, Eve was long gone, dead and buried, just like she deserved to be.

Lil had changed her name years ago, soon after she got sober. She had wanted to start all over again, to reinvent herself and that meant saying goodbye to Eve. She didn't miss her one bit. The only time that she had continued to use her old name was at AA meetings because it was the one place where she could be brutally honest about who she was, no bullshit and no sugar coating. What had begun as a way to help her compartmentalise her life, to have a clear divide between her old one and her new one, had become a ritual. She took off her mask before each meeting and then at the end, she put it back on. She still loved the rush of relief she felt when she was no longer Eve again. No, she was Lillian Gold, successful business owner, collector of cats and waifs and strays, and slightly over-attentive employer. Particularly when it came to Annie.

That's not to say it had been easy. At first, she had lived in a constant state of fear that she would be found out. She had spent countless nights lying awake, having heart palpitations, asking herself what in God's name she had done. Then there had been the hurt. Once she'd managed to come to terms with the guilt that she was still lying to Annie, even after all these years, she had then had to cope with the disappointment of knowing that they would never have the relationship that she had dreamed of. Lil had made her bed and now she had to lie in it, and that meant keeping her distance because it was the only way to protect her secret. She couldn't risk embedding herself too deeply into Annie's life so that it started to look suspicious or increased her chances of meeting Mike. She was certain that he would recognise her, and she was petrified that the precarious but wonderful life she had built would come tumbling down around her.

But sometimes she just couldn't resist going a little too far. What mother wouldn't step in to help their own daughter? The only difference was that Annie would never know about it. Like when she and Gabe had fallen in love with that old house, but the seller was driving a hard bargain and refused their offer. Lil had waived all fees and given him fifteen thousand pounds in cash, off the books, to secure the deal. She had put her own business at risk to help Annie but it had been worth it, to hear the joy in her voice when Lil told her that the offer had been accepted. After that, Annie had talked endlessly about how grateful she was to Gabe's parents for their financial support, and Lil had smiled and nodded, firmly swallowing down any jealousy. She didn't need public acknowledgement or appreciation; it was enough just to see Annie happy.

Over time the hurt had begun to fade. She had been given a second chance with her daughter and for that she would always be grateful. *When you do a terrible thing, you must accept your punishment.* For Lil, her punishment was not being able to tell Annie who she really was, how much she loved her, and how sorry she was. But, still, she had more than she could ever have hoped for. She'd been able to build a relationship with Annie, to experience the joy of seeing her almost every day. She had mentored her, watched her grow in confidence and blossom into a talented and intelligent woman. She had witnessed her fall in love and buy her first home.

And then, of course, there was the baby. When Lil had found out that Annie was pregnant, she became so overwhelmed that she'd had to make up some excuse about buying a cake so that she could leave the office and sort herself out. Once she was out of sight, she had stood on the pavement, doubled over, tears falling down her face.

Annie was going to be a wonderful mum, of that Lil had no doubt. Nothing like she had been. But she wouldn't have her mother around to help her, to share her joy with. And Lil would never get to be a grandmother. The baby would never call her nana or granny. She would have to stay at arm's length, even if it killed her. Still, she was going to love that baby so very much. She promised herself, there and then, that she would find a way to be there for Annie and the baby. Then she had wiped away her tears, gone to the supermarket and returned to the office with a cake and a smile, ready to celebrate the happy news.

Unlike her own pregnancy, Lil had expected Annie's to be a

joyful time. This was a much longed-for baby, conceived by two people who loved it, and each other, very much. Annie was a strong, capable and determined woman who was surrounded by friends and family who loved her and wanted to support her. Lil hadn't been prepared for what happened next; Annie's growing anxiety during her pregnancy. Lil had blamed herself for everything. She knew Annie's belief that her mother had died during childbirth was to blame for her distress. It was all her fault and she had nearly screamed the truth out a dozen times, anything to protect her daughter from what she was going through.

In the end she'd forced herself to stand back, even though it had been agony. She had done what she thought was best; telling Annie to start maternity leave early, covering the financial burden, calling Gabe for updates and quietly suggesting that Annie talk to someone about how she was feeling. Even now, she wasn't sure if she had done the right thing.

The last time she had spoken to Annie she had sounded so lost and distant. Lil had texted her that morning to ask how she was doing but she hadn't replied. She'd texted Gabe too, but had heard nothing back and now she was beginning to worry.

She turned to Brian, eager to distract herself. 'Cup of tea?'

He nodded and stood up to follow her to the kitchen.

'Have you heard from Annie?' she asked him casually, as she boiled the kettle.

'Not a sausage,' he said. 'I hope it's because she's out getting a mani-pedi, but knowing Annie she's up a stepladder sanding a wall in that damn house they bought.' He paused and then added, 'Actually, when I spoke to her a few days ago she mentioned that she was going back to Northampton.'

Lil's heart started pounding. 'Northampton? Why?'

'She said she was going to see her mum's grave. Something

about needing closure. It all sounded a bit morbid but who's going to argue with a pregnant woman?'

The kettle boiled and Lil picked it up with shaking hands.

'You okay, Lil?' Brian asked.

'I'm fine,' she said, trying to keep her voice steady. This was it. She was about to be exposed. Her world was crashing down around her, the sound ringing in her ears.

'It's just that there are no teabags in those mugs, honey.'

Lil looked down at the two mugs of hot water. 'Shit.'

'No worries, not the menopause is it?' Brian said, as he reached for two teabags and popped them into the mugs. She nearly laughed. The poor man had absolutely no idea.

'When was she going, do you know?'

Brian frowned. 'Today, I think.'

From her desk her phone beeped, and Lil thought she might be sick. Was it Annie? Had she somehow made the connection already? Or was it Mike, telling her that she was a disgrace, that he couldn't believe she would stoop so low? Or was it simply a spam text and she was spiralling out of control for no reason? *Calm down, deep breaths.* But she couldn't calm down, she was in bits, frozen to the spot.

A few seconds later, Brian's phone beeped too. They looked at each other and dashed to their desks, opening the messages simultaneously. Lil stared at her phone. It was a photo of a baby that looked so much like Annie when she was born that it took her breath away.

'Christ,' Brian exclaimed, his face lighting up with pleasure. 'Annie's bun's out of the oven already? Isn't that a bit early? I thought she wasn't due for a few weeks. He's cute, right?'

Lil's eyes were glued to the photo of her grandson. Then she read the message that came with it, written by Annie.

Baby Adams, born at 3.35pm, weighing 7lb. Am so in love already.

Have never felt this happy. Baby can't wait to meet his Aunty Lil and Uncle Bri xxx

'Sounds like she never made it to Northampton after all,' Brian said.

Maybe Lil's secret would live to see another day. At that moment, though, she didn't even care because whatever happened next, Annie and the baby were safe and that was all she had ever wanted. She wished fervently that she could be with Annie, by her daughter's side in this momentous, joyful moment, but she knew that it was impossible. She was still her mum though, nobody could take that away from her. She could still love her from a distance. She could look out for her from far away. She could watch over her, always.

She allowed the tears to come, until she was sobbing with guilt, regret, joy and relief. *I love you, Annie. I'm so proud of you, my darling girl. Congratulations.*

'You okay, Lil?' Brian asked and she nodded, still crying, not trusting herself to speak.

Brian rolled his eyes. 'Definitely the menopause,' he said.

CHAPTER TWENTY-FIVE

Annie and Gabe arrived home from hospital the following afternoon to find their front door festooned with new baby balloons and banners.

'Looks like Lil and Bri have been at it again,' Annie said, gripping tightly on to the baby car seat where their son was strapped in, fast asleep.

'Yeah. I spoke to Lil this morning. She said she'd pop round tomorrow to meet the baby. She wanted to give you some space today.'

'Oh that's a shame, I was hoping she'd come over today so that she could finally meet Dad.'

'I know, but she said that too many visitors can be overwhelming, and I think she's right. Maybe we should limit it to one or two a day. When did the midwife say she was coming?'

'Tomorrow at some point. And don't worry, I'm going to talk to her about everything.'

'Good.'

They looked at each other and grinned. It was such a relief to be in sync with Gabe again, like someone had flicked a switch and reminded them that they were in the same team. Another rush of emotion engulfed Annie, a heady cocktail of hormones and happiness. Everyone had told her that she would be bruised and battered after giving birth, but she didn't feel any of that. All she felt was joy and hope for the future. For her, Gabe, and now the baby.

She barely remembered the beginning of her son's life. She had started to feel dizzy minutes after he was born and when she came round again, she was confused and disorientated. She had looked around her, trying to work out where she was. Then a figure, blurry at first, had come into focus and she realised it was Gabe, holding their baby in his arms.

'Gabe?' she asked, incredulous.

He turned to her, his face breaking out into a huge smile. 'Hey An, welcome back!'

'What happened?' Her grogginess was starting to wear off and she tried to sit up.

'You lost some blood, which made you feel a bit woozy. They had you all fixed up in no time.'

'How long have I been out of it?'

'Not long, babe, twenty minutes or so. When I arrived, you were as white as a sheet, and I totally freaked out but the doctor assured me that everything was under control. So, me and this little man have just been hanging out, waiting for you to perk up again.'

Annie looked at their baby, reaching out for him, and Gabe moved towards her, passing him gently to her, and supporting her arms until he was confident that she had the strength to hold him. She gazed at their little boy, studying every inch of his tiny, perfect face. He was alert and his eyes watched her intently, as though he was sizing her up.

'Hi, little man, I'm your mummy,' she said, liking how it sounded. He had a shock of messy, dark hair, just like his daddy. But his eyes were definitely hers.

'Annie, I'm so proud of you,' Gabe said, stroking her hair. 'You did so well.'

'I can't believe you missed it, Gabe. I'm so sorry.'

'It doesn't matter, all that matters is that you're both safe.'

'It was such a stupid idea to come to Northampton. I don't know what I was thinking.'

'Annie, it's okay. I understand. And you weren't to know that he'd decided to come early.'

Annie tore her eyes away from the baby and looked at Gabe. They had been pulled apart these past few months, so bogged down by their own problems that they'd pushed each other away when they needed one another the most. But that was about to change, starting from now. She could see him clearly again now; the man she loved, her partner, the father of her child. He was still the same Gabe after all, she realised. Grumpy and stressed right now, yes, but still the person who she could tell anything to, who would always have her back.

'When I realised I was in labour and that I was going to have to give birth in Northampton I couldn't believe it,' she admitted. 'I thought my nightmares were coming true.'

'I can imagine,' he said, taking her hand.

'But I'm okay. And so's he. Right?'

'You're both perfect. They said they'll be moving you to the postnatal ward soon and you'll probably be discharged tomorrow.'

So that was it. All the fear that had been building up for months like a pressure cooker had been for nothing. Her labour may have not been easy, but it hadn't been anything like her nightmares. The dark, terrifying images were disappearing from her memory already, just like the pain of labour.

'Where's Caz?' she asked.

'She's outside on the phone to your dad. I need to call my

parents too, but I wanted to wait until you were feeling better. Can I take some photos?'

'Of course.'

Gabe whipped out his phone and started snapping away. He took photos of the baby, then of Annie and the baby, and finally a few selfies of the three of them. He must have taken at least fifty, and as Annie said cheese yet again, she thought about how different their son's entrance into the world had been already. This child wouldn't grow up wishing for more photos of when he was first born. There would be bloody hundreds of them.

'Annie,' Gabe said tentatively, as he put his phone back in his pocket. 'I want to apologise.'

'For what?'

'You've been going through hell these past few months, and I haven't been there for you. I feel so awful that I let you down.'

'Gabe...' Annie began but he stopped her.

'Let me finish, An. I've been dwelling on my own misery, feeling sorry for myself because I felt like such a failure. And I dismissed all your worries about your mum when I should have listened because I just couldn't get my head around it all. But I should have tried. I'm so sorry.'

'It's okay.'

'It's not okay. I messed up and I hold my hands up to that. It will never happen again.'

'I'm sorry too,' she said. 'I know I haven't been myself either. To be honest, I don't know what's been happening to me. I've been so anxious and paranoid without even knowing exactly why.'

'I'm here for you, whatever you need, but I also think you should speak to someone about how you've been feeling. There's some stuff you're going through, understandably, and you won't feel at peace until you've confronted it. Please don't be ashamed to ask for help, okay?'

'I will.' And this time she meant it. 'So, what are we going to call this little dude then anyway?'

'Remind me of the top five shortlist?'

'Ethan, Jacob, Ben, Cole and Dexter.'

'I thought I vetoed Dexter?'

'Oh yes, maybe you did.'

'So don't go sneaking it back on to the list, you cheeky mare.'

They stared at their son for a while.

'I think he's a Cole,' Annie said.

'I think he's a Cole too,' Gabe replied. They nodded in agreement.

'Welcome to the world, Cole Adams,' Annie said. 'It's one heck of a pleasure to meet you.'

It had been such a relief to return home. Annie's life may have started in Northampton, but that chapter had ended before it even began and there was nothing left for her there. She realised that now. Standing outside their house, she sighed with contentment and turned to Gabe.

'Not carrying me across the threshold this time then, mister?'

Gabe grinned. 'Nah, it's this little man's turn.' He carefully lifted Cole out of his car seat, cradling him gently.

Annie followed him inside and closed the door, breathing in the scent of home. She eyed the half-full coffee cup and plate on the table, which had been hastily abandoned by Gabe when he got the call telling him that she might be in labour. She'd only been a mum for twenty-four hours but already everything had changed. The love she felt for her son was incomparable, but it was more than that. She had survived the moment she feared the most; overcome the obstacle she had been dreading for so long. She already knew that the nightmares, once so vivid, wouldn't be returning.

She still had an ache in her heart that she wasn't sure how to heal, or even if she wanted to. She wished her mum was there, with her. She had no idea how to be a mother herself and she was slightly terrified. She knew that she needed to get this off her chest, to talk to someone rather than let it eat away at her, making her dwell on the past rather than embracing her future. She knew that the next few months were going to be some of the most challenging of her life. But she had an army of people around her who would help her get through it if she just let them.

Mike and Val arrived an hour later, as she was feeding Cole. She still hadn't got to grips with breastfeeding and it hurt like hell, but she was trying her best and so was he. Her dad lingered in the hallway, embarrassed to come in, but Val had no such qualms. She marched into the room and placed herself squarely on the sofa next to Annie, legs crossed at the ankles.

'He's beautiful,' she said, flashing one of her rare smiles.

'Thank you.'

'You did so well, Annie. We're very proud.' Val patted Annie's arm. They sat in silence for a few minutes and then Val stood up as abruptly as she'd sat down. 'Right, I'll go and put some washing on. I've brought some food for lunch and some meals for the freezer.'

'Thanks, Val.'

Val nodded and marched back out of the room. She wasn't the type to coo over a baby or even ask to hold him, but she wanted to help and this was her way of doing it.

Annie looked down at Cole. He had nodded off in her arms,

so she quickly pulled her top down and called for her dad. He peered around the door to check the coast was clear.

'It's fine, Dad, I'm decent. Although you might have to get used to it, I'm afraid. I think it's going to be a fairly regular occurrence.'

He came into the room, took one look at Cole and burst into tears. 'Oh Annie, he's amazing.'

'Wanna hold?'

'I don't want to disturb him.'

'It's fine, Dad.'

She passed Cole over to her dad, who sat down and stared at his grandson, awestruck.

'He's perfect,' he said. 'Oh Annie, I'm so proud of you. Caz told me everything, about what happened, why you were in Northampton. You must have been so scared.'

'I was,' she admitted. 'Especially when I realised that I'd be giving birth in the same hospital as Mum. I'm sorry if that freaked you out. It was unfair of me to put you through that.'

'That doesn't matter. I was just so worried about you.'

'I know, but I was fine, Dad. Really. Once I was in established labour, I didn't have much time to think about where I was to be honest and then, when it was over, I was just so relieved we were both okay that nothing else mattered.'

'You're so brave, Annie, I'm tremendously proud of you.' His face darkened. 'I've let you down, I'll never forgive myself.'

'What are you talking about?'

'All this stuff with Mum, I handled it so badly. I'm sorry. We need to talk Annie, really talk.'

'It's okay, Dad. I understand. You wanted to protect me, to make sure that I only had good memories of Mum. I get it now.'

He looked like he wanted to say something else but then changed his mind. When he finally spoke, his voice was thick with emotion. 'Everything I've ever done was to protect you.'

'I know.'

'Will you be going back to Northampton?'

'No. I'm done with Northampton.'

He took her hand and she clasped it tightly. They watched Cole sleeping for a while.

'I have something for you,' Mike said, reaching into his jacket pocket and pulling out some photos.

'Are these...?'

'The photos of Mum. Val found them down the back of the radiator. They must have fallen down there. They've been gathering dust for weeks.'

He tried to give them to Annie, but she shook her head.

'Thanks Dad, but you know what? These photos aren't how I want to remember Mum. Your stories about her are what I want to carry with me.'

'Are you sure?'

'Very sure.'

'Okay, love.'

'Speaking of which, let's get a photo of you and your new grandson.' Annie reached for her phone and started clicking. These were the photos that belonged in the family album.

Mike and Val stayed for a couple of hours, until Annie's eyelids started to droop and her head nodded forwards. They quickly got up to leave, with promises to visit again soon. Annie fed Cole again and then passed him gratefully over to Gabe.

'I'll take him for a walk in the pram,' he said. 'You rest for a while.'

She nodded, falling asleep the second her head hit the sofa. She woke up an hour later to the sound of the doorbell. She stood up groggily and made her way to the door, expecting to see Gabe on the doorstep, complaining that he had forgotten his keys.

'How's mumma?' Caz asked, as she threw her arms around

Annie and then proffered a bag at her. 'I bring gifts. Hey, where is the man of the moment anyway?'

'Gabe's taken him for a walk. I've just woken up.'

'Good for you. Glad to see you're getting some shut-eye.'

Annie sat back down on the sofa and rummaged through the gift bag. There were three large bars of chocolate, a bottle of wine and some ready meals.

'Well, Cole will love these,' she said.

'Everyone will buy stuff for Cole. These are for you and Gabe. How are you getting on?'

'Really good,' Annie said. 'I mean, I have no idea what the hell I'm doing of course.'

'Oh, don't worry about that, none of us do. You scared the shit out of me yesterday, by the way, Annie. Remind me never to drive you anywhere, ever again.'

'I'm so sorry. And thank you, Caz, I couldn't have done it without you. You were amazing.'

'I might never regain the feeling in my hand. You squeezed so tightly you almost broke it, but I was honoured to be there. It was a very special moment to witness. Well, it was until you started pulling a whitey after the delivery and I thought you were going to die and all that.'

'What actually happened?'

'One minute you were holding Cole, grinning like the cat that got the cream, and the next you looked like you'd been on a bender with the cast of *The Only Way Is Essex*. The doctor said it was a post-partum haemorrhage and I nearly lost it, but he didn't break a sweat and they had it under control in minutes. Then Gabe arrived and I decided to give you some space.'

'Well thanks for having my back, Caz. And sorry I scared you.'

'Don't mention it, even with all the drama it was still far more enjoyable than giving birth to my own children. Hey, you're never going to believe this. Sally and Marcus the Sharkus are madly in love again and are renewing their wedding vows! And we're all invited!'

'Christ,' Annie said. It seemed she'd missed a lot in the short while that she'd been in hospital. 'I thought they'd only just started talking to each other again. That was quick.'

'I know, it's amazing what a bit of Botox will do.'

'Do you think Marcus will actually be there?'

'Apparently so. Sally says he's making a huge effort, I've never heard her so happy. Maybe he's finally realised that he has a damn good thing going on after all.'

'I really hope so, for Sally's sake.'

'Either that or his bit on the side's dumped him.'

'Caz,' Annie said crossly. 'Don't say that.'

She shrugged. 'That's life, Annie.'

'How depressing.'

'Yeah, you could look at it that way or you could instead be grateful for all the amazing things that *you* have in your life. And you, my darling, have many.'

'I know. I'm so excited to be a mum, Caz. I just can't wait!'

Caz laughed and gave her a hug. 'Oh love. You've got no frickin' idea what's about to hit you. But you know what? I think you're going to be just fine.'

EPILOGUE

Annie stood in the doorway, swallowing back the tears that were threatening to spill out of her. She tried to smile but it froze somewhere between a grin and a grimace.

'He's fine, duck. Go on, off you pop,' Linda, her neighbour, said.

Annie nodded but she didn't move.

'Go on, Annie, it's time,' Linda said, kindly but firmly.

Annie took one last, lingering look at her son. He was sitting on the floor, his chubby little legs stretched out in front of him, a breadstick in one hand and a doll in the other, oblivious to his mother's inner turmoil. In front of him another, older child, started banging some cups and he watched curiously, momentarily alarmed by the noise. Then he giggled. Annie nodded, to herself more than anything. Linda was right, it was time. She left, closing the front door quietly behind her and listening intently in case Cole started crying and calling for her, but there was no sound except the happy noises of toddlers playing.

She hurried down the garden path and on to the street, passing her house and walking towards the high street. She brushed a tear aside and crossed her arms over her new trench coat, which she had bought to mark the end of her maternity leave, along with the animal-print dress she wore underneath.

An odd thought entered her head. *If a tree falls in a forest and no one is around to hear it, does it make a sound? If I am not with my child, am I still a mother?*

She couldn't bear it. The separation hurt as though she had been physically severed from Cole. It didn't matter that they would be back together again by the end of the day; it was still a raw, guttural pain. It was mother's guilt, she knew, everyone had warned her about it.

'The first couple of days will be brutal,' Caz had said knowingly. 'You'll cry more than your baby. But it gets easier. Before you know it, it will be the new normal. Just enjoy it. A hot cup of coffee. Lunch with colleagues. Adult conversation. It's okay to enjoy it.'

Right now, she couldn't imagine ever enjoying it. How could she be away from Cole for a whole day? For days on end? She wanted to cling on to him forever, possibly letting go of him when he turned eighteen, or then again, possibly not. But she had delayed her return to the office twice already and now Cole was thirteen months old, and it was time for her to go back to work.

Gabe had kissed them both before he left, promising that he'd be back in plenty of time to pick Cole up later that afternoon. Annie wanted him to do shorter days with Linda at first, until he got used to the new routine. Gabe had been working at a start-up for the past year and although he lived in a semi-state of fear of them going bust at any second, he had a much better work-life balance, with a boss who didn't care where or when he worked, as long as it got done. The flexibility suited him, and so did fatherhood. He may have less hair than he did a year ago, and he could probably do with shaving the whole lot off and being done with it, but he was more content than she had seen him in a long time. They both were.

Annie couldn't believe that it had been more than a year since Cole was born. The days, which passed so slowly at the beginning as they got to grips with the challenges of being new parents, had started to speed up at some point and now it felt like her maternity leave had gone in a flash. Caz was right, of course, she'd had no idea what was about to hit her, but she'd found out soon enough. Sleep deprivation, sore boobs, leaky nappies, teething, fevers, she'd experienced it all tenfold. At any given moment she could have fallen apart with the sheer relentlessness of it all but fortunately for her, she'd had plenty of people around her who had kept her standing.

There was Gabe of course, who had been a total legend. Mike and Val had helped in their own ways – Val had confronted her fear of London to make weekly visits in the early weeks so that she could clean, cook and do the laundry while Mike looked after Cole and Annie went off to have a bath, or a nap, or meet a friend for coffee. Although she hadn't taken up residence in the end, Diana came up one weekend a month and was surprisingly good with Cole. He adored his nana and Annie had to admit, grudgingly, that the woman was a natural with babies. She'd shown an increasingly desperate Annie a trick for how to hold him when he was colicky and unsettled which had stopped him fretting almost immediately. Annie was so grateful that she had even managed to bite her tongue when Diana started harping on about baby number two. Still, though, in the midst of baby one and with no intention of ever going through it all again, Annie had wanted to bash her over the head with a rattle.

There was her counsellor too. Annie had kept her promise to Gabe and told the midwife about the anxiety and paranoia she had experienced throughout her pregnancy, and she had referred her to a local counselling service. It had been good to talk to someone, to be able to grieve the absence of her mum again, not as a child as she had done many times before, but as an adult and now a mother herself. But the depression that had gripped her when she was pregnant had not returned. The nightmares were a distant memory now. It was as though Cole's birth had pressed a reset button in her and she no longer felt a compelling need to fixate on what she didn't have or what she had lost. Instead, she wanted to celebrate what she did have.

Because she had so much. Not only her family that she was linked to by blood but her other family too. Caz had been the listening ear she needed when she wanted to cry, or laugh, or do both at the same time. Linda, who had popped round regularly for a cup of tea, had been a constant source of practical advice and support. She had been the obvious choice when Annie and Gabe started thinking about childcare, and Cole was so familiar with her that his settling-in sessions had gone seamlessly so far.

Brian had been terrified of holding Cole at first, in case he broke him, and even now he still looked at him with a mixture of suspicion and affection. Ian thought it was hilarious and it had become a running joke. It was safe to say that Brian wasn't a baby person. But he loved Cole, just as he loved Annie, and she knew that as Cole got older, their relationship would develop. Until then, he was fun Uncle Bri, the giver of the best birthday and Christmas presents.

And then there was Lil. The bond between Lil and Cole was almost visible in the air between them. They worshipped each other. There was a likeness between them that was almost physical, although Annie had never been able to put her finger on what it was. Whenever she entered the room, Cole's face lit up like she was Father Christmas personified. She was the first person he giggled at, the first one he crawled towards. Annie had already threatened that if his first word was 'Lil' and not

'Mama' she was going to be furious. But secretly she enjoyed watching them together and she knew how much it meant to Lil too. She didn't have children, or grandchildren, of her own but Cole was the closest thing to it.

Lil was sensitive to their relationship though and Annie suspected that she was worried about overstepping the mark and treading on the real grandparents' toes. She'd even turned down an invitation to attend Cole's first birthday party because she said it should be a family affair, and when Annie insisted that she was family, Lil had welled up but remained resolute. Annie didn't understand it, but she had accepted it.

After nearly a decade of speculation, she'd finally found out how Lil and Brian met. Annie had gone out for a drink with Bri one evening, her first since becoming a mother, and they'd drank too many Aperol spritzes and got tipsy.

'So, go on then Bri, tell me the story of you and Lil,' Annie had urged, leaning forward intently.

Brian chuckled. 'All right then, since you asked so nicely.' He took a deep breath. 'I was in a really bad place, Annie. I'd left home, I had nowhere to go. It was Christmas Eve and I'd spent my last twenty quid on a wrap of speed and two cheap bottles of wine so I could get blotto.'

He paused and Annie nodded at him to continue.

'For some reason I decided to go to church. I have no idea why because I've never been into religion in my life, but I was off my face and I wanted to go and sing some carols. By the time I got there, the carol service had finished and so I sat on one of the pews, alone, singing jingle bloody bells at the top of my voice.'

'Oh Brian.'

'Anyway, in she walked, and she sat down next to me. We sat there for a while, in silence. I remember feeling comforted by her presence, even though I had no idea who she was.

There was something about her whole demeanour that soothed me.'

'So, what happened?'

'Eventually she asked me if I wanted to talk, and I said no. But then I don't know what happened, it all came flooding out, like I'd been holding it all inside for so long and the gates had finally burst. I told her everything that had happened to me – but that's a story for another day. Once I had started talking, I couldn't stop. I must have kept going for half an hour at least, just a steady stream of verbal diarrhoea. And she just sat and listened.'

Annie took Brian's hand as he continued. 'She asked me where I was staying and I said probably the local squat, and then she invited me to spend Christmas Day with her. I agreed but I had no intention of going. The following morning, she came to pick me up.'

'Wow,' Annie said, imagining glamorous Lil at a squat. She couldn't see it at all.

'I never went back to that place. Lil invited me to stay with her. She cleaned me up and offered me a job. I'd never experienced such generosity in my life and there was no way I was going to fuck it up. Lil saved my life, and I wouldn't be where I am without her.'

Annie understood. Her story wasn't as dramatic as Brian's, but Lil had changed her life too, when she walked into the café all those years ago. She had offered Annie a new path, one that had led her to a rewarding career, Gabe and, finally, Cole. The best life Annie could have asked for. Maybe Cole was right after all, maybe Lil really was Father Christmas.

On her way into the office Annie went into the coffee shop and ordered a cappuccino to go.

'Annie! Lovely to see you,' the owner said. 'Where's that little one of yours?'

'Childminder,' Annie said, trying not to cry again. 'It's my first day back at work.'

'Good for you. I've missed seeing your smiling face every morning. Welcome back, this one's on the house.'

Annie took the coffee gratefully and left, continuing down the road until she reached Lillian Gold Estate Agents. She paused outside the window and looked at all the properties for sale, none of which she knew anything about. She'd have a lot of work to do to get up to speed again. For a moment she was overwhelmed, and she almost turned around and ran all the way back to Cole, but then she spotted Lil, Bri and the new guy, who was not really the new guy anymore, chatting together with mugs of tea in their hands.

Bri saw her and waved. He mouthed 'Annie' and then Lil and the new guy, who she would definitely have to stop calling the new guy, looked up too. Lil smiled warmly, her face lighting up at the sight of Annie. Annie waved back, tentatively at first and then with more enthusiasm. Her phone beeped and she glanced down to see a message from her dad.

Good luck on your first day back, Annie. I'm so proud of you. xxx

She smiled. The guilt of leaving Cole was natural but it would lessen in time. Because wherever she went, they would be together again. She was a parent now, for better or for worse, through the good times and the bad, and nothing could change that. There would be times when she was with him and times when they were apart. But she would never stop thinking about him, loving him, from near or from far. She would be with him in spirit, forever.

If I am not with my child, am I still a mother? Yes. Always.

THE END

ACKNOWLEDGEMENTS

If you had told me a few years ago that I'd be writing acknowledgements for my third novel, I would have suggested that you go and have a little lie down. To have achieved my dream of writing one book is still unbelievable, so to have produced a hat-trick literally blows my mind. And I have many people to thank for helping me to get to this point.

To all the team at Bloodhound Books, who have supported me on my journey. Your enthusiasm, professionalism, expertise and belief in me is so appreciated. Special thanks to my editor Clare Law, who spent many hours making my manuscript as shiny as it could be.

To everyone who has read, reviewed, shared or supported my books. You give me the courage and inspiration to keep on writing and I hope that you continue to enjoy my work.

And to my sister, Zoe, who reads all my manuscripts – your encouragement, feedback and suggestions make such a massive different to both my books and my confidence.

Thank you to my biggest cheerleaders, my family, for always being there. In particular, my two daughters, Rose and Alice. Being your mother is my greatest achievement. I'm still learning on the job and I'm sorry that I don't always get it right, but your unreserved love, positivity and patience makes the world a better place and me a better person.

To Sam, who gave me some invaluable insight into midwifery for this book and to the amazing midwives and doctors at The Whittington Hospital and Barnet General Hospital, who safely delivered my two babies into the world, keeping me calm when things got scary.

To all the mothers out there, the new ones, the old ones, the ones we have loved and lost. The ones who think they are getting it wrong when everyone else is getting it right. I promise you that we are all thinking the same. And to the dads, who we sometimes forget to thank, but who are just as important, special and amazing.

And finally, to my mum, Robin. You always believed in me and taught me that anything is possible, and I wouldn't be where I am without you. There's not a day that goes by when I don't wish that you were still here, to watch me grow, have children of my own and realise the dream I had as a girl. I know how proud you would have been. But I've always imagined that you're out there somewhere, watching over me from afar, so perhaps, in some way, you know already. You may no longer walk beside me, Mum, but you are always with me, and this book is for you.

A NOTE FROM THE PUBLISHER

Thank you for reading this book. If you enjoyed it please do consider leaving a review on Amazon to help others find it too.

We hate typos. All of our books have been rigorously edited and proofread, but sometimes mistakes do slip through. If you have spotted a typo, please do let us know and we can get it amended within hours.

info@bloodhoundbooks.com

Printed in Great Britain
by Amazon